ECHO LAKE

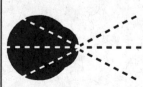

This Large Print Book carries the
Seal of Approval of N.A.V.H.

ECHO LAKE

CARLA NEGGERS

THORNDIKE PRESS
A part of Gale, Cengage Learning

GALE
CENGAGE Learning·

Farmington Hills, Mich • San Francisco • New York • Waterville, Maine
Meriden, Conn • Mason, Ohio • Chicago

GALE
CENGAGE Learning®

LIBRARY OF CONGRESS CATALOGING-IN-PUBLICATION DATA

Neggers, Carla.
    Echo Lake / Carla Neggers.
        pages cm. — (Thorndike Press large print basic.)
        ISBN 978-1-4104-7666-1 (hardcover) — ISBN 1-4104-7666-9 (hardcover)
        1. Large type books. I. Title.
    PS3564.E2628E27 2015
    813'.54—dc23   2014047349

Published in 2015 by arrangement with Harlequin Books S.A.

Printed in the United States of America
1 2 3 4 5 6 7 19 18 17 16 15

For my friend
Sally Fairchild Schoeneweiss

ONE

As much as Heather Sloan loved a bright New England winter day, chasing a puppy through knee-deep snow in seventeen degrees wasn't her idea of fun. Rohan — the runaway puppy, a twelve-week-old golden retriever — wasn't quickly tiring of his romp or sticking to the plowed driveway and shoveled walks, either. Not a chance. She spotted his tracks, leading through the woods straight for quiet, frozen Echo Lake.

She wasn't following a rabbit or deer by mistake. They definitely were puppy tracks. She paused, noting that the trail veered to the right, parallel to the lake. Something must have caught Rohan's attention. A bird, a breeze, a noise.

Great.

Heather followed the tracks through a deeper drift, but they disappeared under the low-hanging, snow-laden branches of two gnarly hemlocks. Rohan could easily fit

7

under them. She couldn't. The trees grew so close together that trying to squeeze between them meant getting snow down her back. Going around them would risk a delay in finding the tracks again.

She was already cold. She wasn't dressed for a puppy rescue. Ankle boots, leather gloves, a wool scarf and her three-quarter-length chocolate-brown wool coat. *Why?* Of all days, why hadn't she worn her Carhartt jacket and L.L. Bean boots? It wasn't as if her attire would impress Vic Scarlatti, the newly retired diplomat whose renovations she was overseeing. His 1912 lake house was out of sight now, up through the trees past a small guesthouse. He was searching the garage, shed and porches. Adrienne Portale, the wine-expert daughter of one of Vic's Foreign Service friends, was searching the house, in case Rohan hadn't slipped outside, after all.

But he had, and he would be in serious trouble in this cold if Heather didn't get to him soon. What was a little snow down her back? With five older brothers, it wasn't anything she wasn't used to. They'd had an epic snowball fight on New Year's Day.

She plunged between the hemlocks, moving as fast as she could, but there was no way to avoid disturbing the snow clinging

8

to the evergreen branches. She got a spray in her face and a clump down her back and almost lost a boot, but when she emerged on the other side of the hemlocks, she was practically standing in Rohan's tracks.

She went still, quieting her breathing as she listened. Her cheeks were numb, and her fingertips and toes ached with the cold. She'd pulled her scarf over her head as best she could in lieu of a hat, but it was loose now, one end dangling down her front. The late-January afternoon sky was cloudless, the air as crisp and clear and cold as it had been since the latest storm earlier in the week. She glanced to her left toward the snow-covered lake. Echo Lake wasn't big, but it was one of the largest lakes in out-of-the-way Knights Bridge, Massachusetts.

There.

Heather spun around at a sound up ahead and forced herself not to move. She listened, positive she heard something besides her own breathing.

Yips.

A high-pitched, mournful cry.

It had to be Rohan.

With a mix of worry and relief, she surged in the direction of the distressed yips and cries, following the tracks through bare-limbed maples and oaks and past white

pines. The ground was uneven, the snow sometimes drifting up past her knees. Snowshoes or back-country skis would have helped, but she had left hers in her truck and Vic wasn't much on winter sports. "I like looking at the snow," he'd told her. "I don't necessarily like going out in it for fun."

She came to a shallow, rocky brook that emptied into the lake but now was mostly frozen. Water trickled and swirled in a few spots among the snow and ice where the current was stronger.

"Rohan," Heather called softly, not wanting to startle him by yelling. "Where are you, buddy?"

She heard panting then a whimper. She eased closer to the edge of the brook and peered upstream. Her heart jumped when she saw a golden ball of fur — little Rohan, struggling to climb out from the midst of the water, snow, ice and rocks.

"Oh, Rohan. You are in a mess, aren't you?"

Trees crowded the bank, and it was steeper up where Rohan was stuck. Getting to him wasn't going to be easy. Staying close to the brook, she grabbed hold of saplings and branches, using them to help her keep her balance in the difficult conditions.

Once she was parallel to Rohan, he let out

an eager, full-fledged bark.

He must have frolicked his way out here, got stuck in the ice and snow and had run out of steam. He was, after all, only a puppy. Heather could see there was no way he could get out of his predicament with just a bit of encouragement from her. She would have to grab him — preferably without ending up trapped in the cold brook herself.

"Easy, Rohan," she said, holding on to a thin tree and reaching with her free hand to the shivering puppy. "Let's get you warm and safe, okay?"

She stretched, her fingertips within inches of him, but she slipped in the snow. She couldn't regain her footing and went down on one knee, planting her free hand in the snow to keep herself from falling in the brook. She felt cold water flowing into her left boot and up her lower leg but bit back a yell lest she panic Rohan. She finally righted herself, losing her glove in the process.

She didn't hesitate. She scooped up the puppy and moved quickly, launching past the tree she was using for balance then sinking against another one. She anchored her feet in the snow to prevent her and Rohan from skidding back into the brook.

She cuddled the furry dog against her. She could feel his little heart racing. "I've got you," she whispered, her own heart thumping madly. "I've got you."

She wanted to sit in the snow and catch her breath, but she knew that wasn't wise. Her shivering was a warning she was in danger of hypothermia. It would be a cold, wet trek back to Vic's house, so she had to get on with it and keep moving.

As she stood straight, she thought she smelled wood smoke — from a fireplace or a woodstove, perhaps. How was that possible? She was too far from the main house. It had to be her imagination or her natural optimism at work.

She heard the snap of a twig and looked up through the trees behind her, away from the brook. A man she didn't recognize stepped comfortably down to her and Rohan. He wore a black suede jacket and solid boots but no hat or gloves.

He scanned her from head to toe before he spoke. "Nice job with the puppy rescue."

"You watched?"

"Yes, ma'am. I didn't want to startle you."

Heather felt Rohan stir in her arms, but he didn't bark. Probably too tired. "Ready to come to my rescue if I fell in, were you?"

"You did fall in," he said, pointing to her wet lower left leg.

"Not all the way in."

12

"You'd be a popsicle if you fell all the way in. I was on my way to rescue the little guy myself. I'm staying at Vic's guesthouse. I got in late last night. My name's Brody, by the way."

"Heather Sloan," she said. "Good to meet you."

Except she felt as if she should know him. *Did* know him.

He narrowed his eyes — dark, flecked with gold — on her. He had short-cropped dark hair, a square jaw, a cleft chin. She shook off the idea that he was familiar somehow. She didn't know anyone who would be a guest of Vic Scarlatti.

He stepped past her and picked up her fallen glove out of the snow. She took in his broad shoulders and his dark canvas pants covering muscular thighs. He looked strong and incredibly fit. Another diplomat? Somehow Heather didn't think so.

He stood straight and tucked her glove into her jacket pocket. "It's filled with snow. It's not going to keep you warm. I can take the pup if you'd like. Give you a chance to pull yourself together."

"I'm fine, thanks, and I can handle Rohan."

"Rohan?" Brody stroked the soft fur behind the puppy's ear. "He doesn't look

13

much like a rider of Rohan at the moment, does he?"

Heather agreed the Tolkien-inspired name was incongruently regal for such a rambunctious, cute-as-the-devil puppy. He was getting heavy in her arms, but she noticed his heart rate had settled down.

"He's not my puppy," she said. "I just helped look for him."

"Vic Scarlatti has a puppy?" Brody grinned as if the prospect both amused and surprised him. "I guess retirement will do that even to a guy like Vic."

"He's a stray. Rohan, I mean. Vic found him wandering around alone out here a few days ago and took him in."

"Well, good for Vic."

"Another guest named him Rohan. Adrienne Portale. Are you two friends?"

"Nope. Don't know her."

Rohan snuggled deeper into Heather's arms. "I should get back. It's cold even for January."

"I'll walk with you."

She sucked in a breath. When it came right down to it, she had no idea who this man was. "Thanks, but I can manage."

"Mind if I walk with you as far as the guesthouse?"

"How do you know Vic?"

"We go back a ways."

A vague answer. "You're a lot younger than he is."

"Yes, I am."

Heather hesitated. "I should let Vic know that Rohan is safe."

"I already texted him that a dark-haired woman in a brown coat had just rescued a puppy from the brook."

"That was efficient."

"He hasn't responded. I also told him you could use some dry clothes." Brody nodded up through the woods toward the main house. "Shall we?"

Heather could feel Rohan settling into her arms. He wasn't a light puppy. She needed to get moving if she was going to carry him all the way back to the house.

She took a step up the hill. "I guess if you're one of Vic's friends, it's safe to go off with you. You're not going to bonk me on the head and dump me in the guesthouse cellar. It doesn't have a cellar, for one thing."

"That's a dramatic imagination you have there."

"It's not drama. It's being practical. I'm very practical."

"Do you say everything you think?"

"No. Do you?"

His gaze slid over her. He smiled. "No."

Despite the frigid temperature, she felt heat in her cheeks. Maybe she *should* think before she spoke. She adjusted Rohan in her arms again as she took another step up the hill. "I'm also good at taking care of myself."

"Come on. You pushed hard through the snow, and you're frozen. Let me take Rohan."

Heather didn't protest when Brody scooped up the half-asleep puppy. She tried not to shiver or let her teeth chatter, but with the cold weather and her partial dip in the icy brook, she had to admit she was frozen. "I didn't expect Rohan to end up down here by the lake."

"He bolted past the guesthouse. I saw him out the window but couldn't get out fast enough to grab him before he hit the brook. You're okay to walk, aren't you?"

"Yep. No problem."

"Didn't think it would be. Tough as nails, right?"

"Just used to New England winters."

"Sure thing."

There was something in his tone Heather couldn't quite place. Familiarity? Sarcasm? Amusement? A mix of all three? She couldn't deny she was madly curious about him, but maybe he just had funny ideas

16

about Knights Bridge and the people who lived there.

She resisted asking him the four thousand questions she had. She needed to get Rohan back to Vic's. With her wet pants and case of the shivers, she ought to get dry and warm herself

She was happy to let Brody lead the way back to Vic's house, thus allowing her to step in his footprints instead of in virgin snow. It was much less tiring, and the snow didn't seem to faze him.

"How do you like Knights Bridge so far?"

He glanced back at her. "Do you really want to ask me that right now?"

"Seventeen degrees, snow, ice, a golden retriever puppy on the loose?" Heather grinned at him. "What's not to like?"

"Oh, yeah, Heather Sloan." Just the faintest of smiles. "What's not to like?"

Vic Scarlatti bought his house on Echo Lake twenty years ago, when he was a rising star in the US diplomatic corps, and had done virtually nothing to it since. That suited Heather. The previous owner, the granddaughter of the Boston financier who'd built the house, had updated the plumbing, wiring and heat about ten years before the property went on the market upon her

17

death. It was classic Arts and Crafts, oriented to take in the best views of its long-neglected garden and the lake.

Brody showed no sign of appreciating the house's charms and potential as he set Rohan on his puppy bed in the small, cluttered mudroom off the kitchen. The little golden retriever immediately gave a deep sigh and rolled onto his side, dozing.

"The bed looks new," Brody said.

"It is," Heather said, walking past him through the open doorway into the kitchen. "I bought it at the country store in town. I figured Rohan needed a bed."

"Does Vic plan to keep him?"

"He says absolutely not."

She sank onto a chair at the kitchen table. She was stiffer than she wanted to admit after her adventure, but at least she was warming up fast. She pulled off her ankle boots. Both socks were wet, but her left one was sopping. Another of her out-into-the-cold sins was her choice of thin cotton socks. She peeled them off and stuffed them in her boots. She'd figure out what to do about them later, when she didn't have Brody for an audience.

He grabbed Rohan's water bowl and filled it at the deep porcelain kitchen sink, one of the granddaughter's additions. He brought

18

the bowl to Rohan and set it close to his bed. The puppy stirred. At first he was too lethargic to care about anything except yawning, but he managed to get onto all fours and lap at the water.

"You should have some water, too," Brody said as he rejoined Heather in the kitchen. "It's easy to get dehydrated in this dry cold and not realize it."

"Water would be nice."

Before she could stand, he had a cupboard open and a glass in hand. He filled it with water and set it on the table in front of her. "Drink up."

"You remind me of my brothers. They never look cold, either. You don't even have a red nose. I do, don't I?"

"You were out in the cold longer than I was."

"A diplomatic answer. My brothers won't go easy on me for almost freezing to death while chasing a puppy."

"What would they have had you do?"

"Not take chances. Wear wool socks, at least." She smiled suddenly. "But all's well that ends well, right?"

"And you don't have to tell your brothers."

"True, but it's too good a story not to tell. I wish I'd spotted your footprints instead of

19

Rohan's, though. I'd have let you do the rescuing."

Brody unbuttoned his jacket but didn't take it off. He had on a dark sweater over his taut abdomen. Heather was accustomed to fit guys, and he was obviously and decidedly fit. She averted her gaze and drank her water. She was noticing too much about this man. Maybe dehydration and adrenaline had put her senses on overdrive.

"Do you have dry clothes here?" he asked.

"Why would I?" She snapped up straight, almost knocking her water glass off the table. "Wait. You don't think —" She gulped in a breath. "I'm almost forty years younger than Vic. No. Absolutely not."

Brody grinned, his dark eyes sparking with humor. "That's not what I was thinking. I was just wondering if you kept a change of clothes here given your work. You and Vic Scarlatti? Damn, that's funny. Seriously funny."

"What do you mean, *seriously funny*? You say that as if I'm not . . ." She stopped herself, abandoning that train of thought in the nick of time. "Never mind."

"As if you're not attractive, you mean? That's not what I'm saying." He paused, warmth replacing the humor in his eyes now. "Trust me."

Heather jumped to her feet, baffled by why she was blurting out things she had no business blurting out. She'd never been good at policing what she said, but she didn't know this man — never mind that he seemed familiar. A trick of her imagination, no doubt.

"Right. Well." She took a quick breath. "Main point is, I'll be fine in these clothes. Obviously, I didn't show up here dressed for a puppy rescue. I'm from Knights Bridge — I live in the village a few miles from here."

"Have you always lived in town?"

"Except for college, but I went to UMass Amherst. That's not far."

"No wanderlust?"

"Lots of wanderlust. I have all sorts of places I want to go and things I want to do, but Knights Bridge is home." Heather didn't understand why he was asking her such questions. Brody didn't seem the type to make idle conversation. "Where's home for you?"

"Wherever I take a shower in the morning." He looked out the window above the sink at the snowy driveway and backyard. "Vic always said he planned to retire in cute little Knights Bridge."

"Have you known him for a long time?"

21

"As you pointed out, Vic's a lot older than I am."

It wasn't a direct answer. Few of his answers were, Heather realized. "Vic's owned this place for twenty years, but I don't know him that well. I don't think anyone in town does. He's spent most of his career abroad. I guess you already know that, though."

Brody turned from the window but made no comment. She noticed he wasn't winded from their hike up from the brook. Definitely a man in great shape. Vic would have been gasping for air if he'd traipsed through the snow.

"Any plans while you're in town?" she asked, finally shrugging off her coat and draping it over the back of a chair.

"Like what?"

"I don't know. Snowshoeing, cross-country skiing, bonfires, hot cocoa."

"Sleeping late."

Not a picture she needed in her head right now. "I hope you enjoy your stay. There's also ice-skating on the town common, if you're interested. Do you skate?"

"Badly," he said.

"Me, too. I was out skating with a couple of my brothers last weekend. I'm hopeless. I have the bruises on my butt to prove it."

22

Brody's expression was unreadable. "No proof required."

"I can't believe I just said that. It's having five brothers. I never think . . ." *Just stop right there,* she told herself, then smiled. "I'll start today. Thinking. I have a few things to do before I head home. Thank you for your help with Rohan."

"Anytime."

"Brody!" Vic Scarlatti clapped his hands together as he entered the kitchen from the hall. "Good to see you, my friend. Sorry I didn't stay up to greet you last night, but I'm to bed with the chickens these days. Everything was in order in the guesthouse?"

"Perfect order. Good to see you."

Vic was sixty-two, his hair thick and gray, his angular face tanned and lined. He was wiry and quick-witted, his mix of hardheadedness and can-do optimism no doubt suited to his decades as a career diplomat. "Did you rescue Rohan?"

"Heather did."

Vic turned to her. "Good for you. Thank you. I'm glad you and Brody met. I didn't think to tell you about him. Can you believe he's a DSS agent?"

Heather drew a blank. "I don't know what that is."

"Diplomatic Security Service. Short answer, he protects idiots like me." Vic smiled. "Our Brody. Can you believe it?"

She tried not to look dumbfounded. *Our Brody?*

Brody said nothing, but she thought she saw a distinct hardening of his jaw, as if he were steeling himself against some inevitable revelation.

Vic was still smiling, obviously unaware of his guest's tension. "I've been trying to get Brody back here for years. His feud with the Sloan boys didn't help."

"There's no feud." Brody's tone was even, without any hint of emotion. "There was a fight, but it was a long time ago."

A fight? A long time ago? Heather's head was spinning. She could feel her brow furrowing with her confusion, and her heartbeat quickened with what could only be called dread. What were Vic and Brody talking about? What was she missing?

"The fight involved pumpkins, as I recall," Vic said lightly, addressing Heather. "Brody wasn't arrested. He got out of town before the situation escalated further."

"Always a good thing," Brody said, still with that even, unemotional tone.

Vic sighed. "Honestly, though. Pumpkins. I swear, only in Knights Bridge. But look at our Brody now. He's one hell of a kick-ass

24

federal agent."

"Vic," Brody said, a note of exasperation creeping into his voice.

"What? It's the truth."

"Wait. *Our* Brody? A fight with my brothers?" Heather turned to Brody, feeling some of the warmth drain out of her. "Exactly who are you?"

"There you go, Brody," Vic said, clearly amused. "Heather doesn't remember you. Maybe her brothers won't remember you, either."

"I'm not that lucky." He took a half step toward her, the faintest glint of humor in his dark eyes. "It's okay, Heather. I remember you. Wild hair, braces, cute little dimples and a serious crush on me." He winked. "Guess the crush didn't last, huh?"

"Wait." Heather realized she wasn't breathing. "You're *that* Brody? Brody Hancock?"

"The same."

He grinned as he nodded a farewell to Vic and left through the back door.

Vic let out a long breath. "Brody is one intense man. He always has been. You really don't remember him?"

Heather grimaced. "I do now."

Vic eyed her a moment then peered into the mudroom at Rohan, sound asleep in his

25

bed. "He looks as if he's had his adventure for the day. I searched high and low for him in the garage and on the porches. I hate to think what could have happened to the little miscreant if you hadn't found him. Not that it's his fault he scooted off."

"Do you have any idea how he got out?"

He didn't answer at once, his gaze still on the sleeping puppy. Finally, he shook his head. "No idea. I turned my back and off he went. Not used to puppies, I guess." He smiled at Heather, his infectious warmth again in place. "Thank you, Heather. Rescuing puppies is above and beyond the call of duty."

"Glad to do it, Vic."

"And Brody?"

She wondered if Vic could tell being around his house guest — finding out he was Brody Hancock from Knights Bridge — was doing things to her insides. "I managed without him, but I'm sure he'd have been helpful if he'd been needed."

"He's a good man to have on your side."

"No doubt."

"Heather . . ." Vic inhaled, clearly ill at ease. He picked a stray thread off his sweater and flicked it into the sink. "Brody hasn't stepped foot in Knights Bridge since the summer after he graduated high school.

He was an angry, troubled teenager then."

Sexy, too, Heather thought. But she'd been in middle school, and if anything, he was even sexier now.

She noticed that her scarf had fallen onto the floor and scooped it up. It, too, was wet. She slung it over her coat. "How long has Brody been a DSS agent?"

"At least ten years. He was recruited his senior year in college."

"You had something to do with that?"

"Only to answer his questions. He got in on his own merits. He's good, too. Damn good. It's a tough job."

"I'm sure," Heather said, no doubt in her mind.

"Did you fall in the brook before or after he came to your rescue?"

"I didn't fall in the brook, and he didn't rescue me."

Vic laughed. "That's what I figured you'd say." He motioned toward the front of the house. "Why don't you go and warm up by the fire? You're done in, Heather. Relax before you head home. Get your bearings."

"Thank you," she said, realizing she still was barefoot, with wet boots, wet socks and wet pants. She smiled at Vic. "Warming up by the fire sounds nice."

Two

Heather splayed her fingers, still a bit red from her Rohan rescue, in front of the orange flames roaring behind a black screen in the massive stone fireplace, one of the many distinct original features of the century-old house. She wriggled her toes as she stood on the hearth. Her brother Adam, a stonemason, would be taking a look at the chimneys and fireplaces, as well as the outside stonework, all part of the renovations.

That was where her mind should be, she told herself. Not on a DSS agent who'd left Knights Bridge under a cloud more than a decade ago.

"You should dry your socks in front of the fire," Adrienne Portale said as she entered the living room, carrying two bottles of wine. She set them on a side table. "Vic wouldn't mind. He'd think he was roughing it out here. It would appeal to his romantic

28

idea of being a gentleman farmer."

Heather laughed. "There's nothing romantic about my wet socks."

Adrienne sank onto an overstuffed chair. She had thick, dark curls that hung past her shoulders and a pretty, heart-shaped face that complemented her hour-glass figure and preference for dressing in black. She wore faded black jeans and a black-beaded tunic she'd found, to her delight, in a wardrobe in the first-floor guest suite where she was staying.

She tucked her feet up under her. "I invested in wool socks my first week here. They have a decent selection at the country store in town. I grew up in San Francisco. It can get chilly there but not like this. I never knew there were so many different kinds of wool socks. Why don't I grab a pair for you before you go? In fact, you can have them. I was terrified I'd run out and bought far more than I need." She grinned, settling back in the big chair. "That's a better idea than drying your socks by the fire, don't you think?"

"I do, yes, thank you." Not, Heather thought, that she had any plans of drying her socks by the fire.

Adrienne fingered the label on one of the wine bottles. "Wine, wool and a hot fire.

29

The perfect Knights Bridge winter evening. Add a wandering puppy and a rugged federal agent, and I have no complaints." She sat forward. "He is rugged, isn't he? Vic's DSS agent guest? I haven't met him yet."

Heather balled up her hands, warmer now, but kept them in front of the fire. "I was focused on rescuing Rohan."

"Mmm, and it would take a whole lot of ruggedness for you to notice with those brothers of yours. I can't imagine life with one brother, never mind *five* brothers." Adrienne gave an exaggerated shudder. "And to be the youngest. Yikes."

"It's normal to me."

"Of course it is. Thank heaven that little devil Rohan survived his ordeal. I hoped I'd find him asleep under a bed. It was decent of Vic to take him in, but he doesn't know much about puppies. Neither do I. They say crate training is the way to go, but maybe Rohan's past that."

"No one's put up notices in town about a missing puppy that I know of," Heather said, sitting on a chair on the other side of the hearth from Adrienne. "My guess is someone from out of town drove out here and dumped him like a bag of garbage."

"It's disgusting." Adrienne waved a hand.

"But we won't think about that now. He's safe here, even if we're having a bit of a learning curve on how to take care of him. Three days, though, and he's already got Vic rolled."

"How long will you be staying this time?"

"I don't know. I guess it depends on Vic. He won't need me to house-sit if he's going to be here full-time. He says I can stay whether or not he's here, but I don't want to get in his way." She stood, grabbing a poker from a rack and pulling back the screen. "I thought I'd get nervous being out here by myself, but it's been great. I'm getting a lot of work done."

Heather smiled, warm again, less achy. "And now you've got Vic interested in installing a wine cellar."

Adrienne stirred the fire. "He'll love it."

"I'm sure I will," Vic said, joining them. "I can picture myself up here at ninety, opening a good Bordeaux and watching the snow."

"Will you be alone?" Adrienne asked.

"More important, will I be alive?"

He chuckled, taking a log from a small stack on the hearth. Adrienne pulled back the screen a bit farther, allowing him to place the log on the fire. She adjusted its position with her poker. "That's not funny,

Vic," she said.

"Gallows humor. When you're my age, you'll understand."

"You won't be ninety for another thirty years," Heather said.

"Gad, that long?" He stepped back from the fire. "What kind of wine are we having tonight?"

Adrienne returned the poker to the rack. "I thought we could try something from Noah Kendrick's winery."

"Kendrick," Vic said. "Rich guy. High-tech entertainment company in Southern California. He's engaged to the Knights Bridge librarian."

"Former librarian," Heather amended. "She resigned a couple of months ago."

"Phoebe O'Dunn. Her mother lives up the road. Elly. Raises goats. I asked her if she knows who Rohan belongs to, but she said she doesn't. She was on her way to San Diego to visit Phoebe and Noah." Vic settled onto a sofa facing the fire. "See? I'm not that out of touch with the locals."

"I've met Elly," Adrienne said. "She's a widow. Did you buy this place before her husband died?"

Vic nodded. "Patrick. He was a great guy. Sad he left behind a wife and four daughters. Life isn't fair sometimes. I've survived a number of close calls during my time in the Foreign Service, and here I am, alone and unscathed."

"I'll fetch wineglasses." Adrienne started for the adjoining dining room. "I don't think I've met any of Elly's daughters. I suppose I could have run into them in the village and not realized it. Elly says they all have red hair."

"They do," Heather said with a laugh. "Maggie O'Dunn is my sister-in-law. She's married to my brother Brandon. She's the second eldest of the four O'Dunn sisters, after Phoebe. She's a caterer, and she's making artisan soaps using milk from her mother's goats. She and Brandon have two little boys."

"I thought they lived in Boston," Vic said.

"They did for a while." Heather didn't want to get into the details of Maggie and Brandon's near-divorce last year. Not that she knew many of the details. "Now they're back in town."

"Brandon's a skilled carpenter as I recall."

"He'll be working on your renovations."

Heather watched through the double open doorway as Adrienne got wineglasses from a built-in cabinet with stained-glass panels, original to the house. She brought the glasses into the living room and set them on

33

the coffee table. "You're a mysterious character around here, I think, Vic. Elly told me you've always seemed exotic and fascinating, kind of a diplomatic James Bond."

"A diplomatic James Bond," Vic said. "I like that."

What did that make Brody? The real deal? Heather stood, her hands and feet warm and her pant leg almost dry but her mood suddenly off. She felt restless, confused — faintly irritated. Why hadn't Brody told her who he was right from the start? She obviously hadn't recognized him while she'd been in the midst of rescuing Rohan and keeping herself from falling in the icy brook.

Adrienne opened one of the wine bottles. Heather noticed the elegant, distinctive Kendrick Winery label. She'd met Noah a few times but didn't know him well. His best friend and business partner, Dylan McCaffrey, had beat him to Knights Bridge, arriving last spring to check on property he had discovered he owned there. Dylan, too, had fallen in love with a woman from Knights Bridge.

The short version of *that* story, Heather thought with a smile.

"What's on your mind, Heather?" Vic asked quietly.

"Nothing. Just warming up."

He studied her a moment then got to his feet. "You two chat and start on the first bottle. I'll check on Rohan and invite Brody to join us. Last night I waited too long, and he peed on the floor. Rohan, I mean. Not our Agent Hancock."

After Vic left, Adrienne poured two glasses of wine and handed one to Heather. "I think we're going to enjoy this," she said, raising her glass. "Cheers."

Heather smiled. "Cheers." She sipped the wine, enjoying the smooth flavor. "It is good, but you're the expert."

"I think of myself as a wine enthusiast more than a wine expert."

"But you enjoy what you do," Heather said.

Adrienne nodded, returning to her chair. "I love it, even when it doesn't pay the bills. I've always had a keen sense of taste, and it felt natural to put it to use with wine. I know what I like, I know what's good and I know how to describe wine in a way that's entertaining and makes sense to other people."

"You're also not a wine snob."

"I couldn't be a wine snob and do what I do, or love it as much as I do."

"When you think about it, snobbery doesn't get anyone very far," Heather said.

"It wouldn't in Knights Bridge, that's for sure. You all would run me out of town if I had my nose up in the air about wine — or anything else."

Heather laughed. "Now, now. Live and let live, right? We have a soft spot for our snobs."

"Every place has them, I guess. Vic's more down-to-earth than I expected. I only met him a few times before I worked out this house-sitting arrangement. It's been good getting to know him."

"Any closer to deciding where you want to be after this?" Heather asked.

Adrienne shook her head. "I've been on the road constantly for more than a year. Maintaining an apartment made no sense, but now I feel rootless. Well, more rootless than usual. I haven't lived anywhere for more than six months since I got out of college." She smiled. "That must be hard for you to imagine."

"I'm definitely not rootless, but I do want to travel."

"Would you ever consider living somewhere besides Knights Bridge?"

"I have considered it."

"But it's home." A touch of melancholy had crept into Adrienne's voice. She raised her wineglass and seemed to make an effort to cheer up. "I'm enjoying hanging out here and teaching Vic about wine. No one thinks I'm taking advantage of him, I hope."

"Who do you mean by *no one*?" Heather asked.

"People in town."

"Ah. You're not the subject of local gossip that I know of, but I wouldn't necessarily know since I don't pay attention to local gossip unless forced. Elly O'Dunn knows everything that goes on in town. She'd be the one to ask when she's back from San Diego. Anyway, what difference does it make if people gossip about you?"

"Good point. No one takes advantage of Vic Scarlatti, that's for sure. He's good-natured and mild-mannered, but he also has a spine of steel." Adrienne drew herself up straight. "My parents say he almost got to the altar a couple of times. I wonder if there's a woman out there he regrets letting get away."

"Any candidates?"

"None that I'm aware of. Maybe there's a woman out there who gave him up for her career, or couldn't take the rigors of his life as a career diplomat."

"Or who gave him up for his career," Heather added.

"Oh, now that's a fun one to think about.

Vic Scarlatti besotted with the wrong woman. The woman recognizing it and walking away from their relationship so he could go save the world." Adrienne drank more of her wine. "I doubt it ever happened, but I don't doubt our Vic has secrets. I, however, will concentrate on designing him a proper wine cellar and stocking it with proper wine."

"Do you think you'd ever relocate out here?"

Adrienne's eyes opened wide in obvious surprise. "Here? In Knights Bridge? What would I do?"

"What you're doing now, I guess. You don't go into an office."

"True, but I need more asphalt and concrete around me than you have here. Total city girl. I can't see myself enjoying an expensive red wine while watching a bald eagle sail above Echo Lake. *Are* there bald eagles here?"

"A few, thanks to the reservoir and its protected watershed."

"Quabbin. What a beautiful place. I can't help but think about the towns that were wiped off the map to create it. Can you imagine Knights Bridge under thirty feet of water, everything you know gone? The Swift River Valley was a very different place in

38

1912 when this house was built."

"There was talk even then about damming the valley to provide drinking water for metropolitan Boston." Heather set her wineglass on the coffee table. She didn't want to drink too much before she got on the road, especially on an empty stomach. "I love to snowshoe on some of the old Quabbin roads. Why don't you join me one day, if it's something that appeals to you?"

"That would be great." Adrienne seemed genuinely interested. "I don't know how to cross-country ski, but I can manage snowshoes."

"I wish I'd had mine while I was chasing Rohan. I should head home. Thanks for the wine."

"I'll fetch your dry socks while you pack up."

Heather thanked her and headed through the dining room and a small hall into the kitchen. Rohan was asleep on his bed in the mudroom. The back door was shut tight, preventing any further mischief on his part.

Vic was at the counter with a cutting board and paring knife. "I'm about to start hors d'oeuvres," he said. "Adrienne made a list of ingredients, and I found everything on it at the country store in town. They won't take long to prepare. Brody's on his way back up. Why don't you join us?"

Wine and hors d'oeuvres with Vic Scarlatti, Adrienne Portale and Brody Hancock. The idea was at once tempting and impossible. "Thanks, but I have to get back." Heather grabbed her laptop and measuring tape off the table. "Enjoy."

"Another time, maybe."

Adrienne arrived with the fresh wool socks and echoed Vic's invitation, but Heather didn't budge. It wasn't them, she knew. It wasn't even Brody Hancock as a Diplomatic Security Service agent, back in Knights Bridge. It was herself. She couldn't pin down what she was feeling, just that she was off — and such uncertainty wasn't her norm and made her decidedly uncomfortable.

"I'll see you tomorrow," she said, slipping on the dry socks and her boots.

Vic had the refrigerator door open and was pulling out vegetables and different varieties of local cheese. Adrienne grabbed a knife and a cutting board and smiled. "We'll save you some for lunch tomorrow."

"Thanks. Your hors d'oeuvres will be better than anything I bring."

"What was that you had today?" Vic asked her.

"Leftover lasagna."

He raised his eyebrows. "That was lasagna?"

Heather laughed. "Now you sound like my brothers. I've never been much of a cook."

"But you'll build me a great new kitchen," Vic said.

"In the meantime, we will definitely save you leftovers," Adrienne added.

Heather thanked them again and headed out, careful not to disturb Rohan as she shut the door softly behind her. With any luck, she'd be on her way before Agent Hancock arrived for wine and hors d'oeuvres.

Naturally, her truck wouldn't start.

Heather banged the steering wheel with one hand. Frustration wouldn't get her anywhere, and she wasn't wearing gloves. It was dark and her truck — which she'd bought at a deep discount from Eric, her eldest brother — wasn't in the mood for the late-January cold.

That kind of day was turning into that kind of night.

She climbed out as she debated her options. Before she could decide what to do, she heard the crunch of footsteps on the sanded driveway behind her.

"Of course you drive a truck," Brody said

41

as he approached her from the guesthouse.

Heather realized right away that her intense reaction to him at the brook hadn't been a fluke. It wasn't going anywhere, not tonight, at least. She tried to ignore it.

"I'm in the construction business," she said. "A truck is practical."

"And you're a practical sort."

"Do I hear skepticism in your voice, Agent Hancock?"

"You went after Rohan with no hat, lousy gloves, lousy boots —"

"Not *lousy.* They're actually quite nice gloves and boots. I admit they weren't the best choice for what I ended up having to do."

"You'd have been in a mess if you'd fallen out there."

"I left a trail. Vic or Adrienne would have found me, and, as it turns out, you were on the case, anyway."

"As tough as any Sloan, aren't you? Are you ever a girly-girl?"

"I met you three hours ago, and you're asking me a question like that?"

He grinned. "I didn't say I expected an answer, and we didn't meet three hours ago. We met when you were a wild-haired kid in braces."

"*Everyone* remembers me as a wild-haired

kid in braces. It doesn't faze me that you're another one. Now I'm all grown up, and my truck won't start. I could get one of my brothers out here to help jump-start it."

"I was hoping to avoid your brothers."

"A tough guy like you afraid of a few local guys? I don't believe it."

"I didn't say I was afraid."

His quiet, self-assured tone sent another surge of heat through her. She had to get a grip. *Truck,* she told herself. *Work the problem.* She peered down the driveway toward the back road that led into the village. "I could walk," she said. "It's not that far, but it's very cold tonight."

Brody shook his head. "You've already had one go at freezing today. What are the odds Vic has jumper cables?"

"Slim to none."

"That's what I think, too. Come on. I have a car. I'll give you a ride home. You can leave your truck here tonight and figure out what to do in the morning."

"You haven't had too much wine?"

He seemed amused. "No, ma'am. I haven't had a drop of wine yet."

"Sorry. It was rude of me to ask." *Why* couldn't she control her mouth around him? "I only had a few sips because I knew I had to drive. If you're a federal agent on duty

43

day and night, you have to watch yourself, right? You can't be getting drunk."

"Again this habit of saying whatever is on your mind. You can walk with me to get my car or wait here."

"I'll go with you. I don't want to stand still in this cold." She shut her truck door. "Thank you."

"Not a problem."

He set off down the driveway toward the guesthouse, setting a brisk pace as Heather caught up with him.

"I wouldn't have guessed you'd be working for Sloan & Sons," he said. "It got its name before you were born, didn't it?"

Heather nodded. "My parents had given up on having a girl and figured one or more of the boys would end up working in the family business. No harm done if they didn't."

"Do all your brothers work there?"

"Three of them. Justin, Brandon and Adam. Eric's a police officer, and Christopher's a firefighter. Justin's a volunteer firefighter, too." Heather shoved her hands into her coat pockets. She was already cold from her failed attempts to start her truck. "Do you remember the order? Eric, Justin, Brandon, Adam, Christopher, me."

"Big family," Brody said, his tone neutral.

"No guy in your life?"

"You know, you have no room to talk when it comes to saying whatever's on one's mind."

"So that means no guy. Having five older brothers — particularly *your* five older brothers — must make having a relationship a challenge."

"You mean do my brothers vet potential guys in my life? It doesn't work like that, but I can hold my own with them. I'm good at taking care of myself — as you saw earlier today, I might remind you."

"Here we go again. You did great except for falling in the brook and getting hypothermia."

"I accomplished my mission while minimizing the risks. I did fine without you."

"You did better with me."

Heather rolled her eyes. "Not funny, Agent Hancock."

He shrugged. "True, though."

They came to his car, which she hadn't noticed earlier. It wasn't a rental. It was an old BMW two-door with New York plates. "You're from New York?"

"It's where the car's registered."

"That's not what I asked, is it?"

He didn't respond. He wasn't pretending he hadn't heard her, she decided. He was flat-out ignoring her. She wondered if it was a polite way of getting across that he was a federal agent who had no intention of telling her much about himself. Maybe he couldn't. Maybe his background was secret.

It wasn't a thought she liked having running around in her mind as she got into the BMW next to him.

"Are you armed?"

"Armed?"

"You know. With a gun."

He started the car. "Heather, I'm just a guy visiting an old friend. Where in town do you live?"

"Thistle Lane. Do you remember it?"

He shook his head. "No."

"It's in the village, off the common. The town library is on the corner."

"Quaint little Knights Bridge."

"Phoebe O'Dunn owns the house. You remember her, don't you?"

"The eldest of the O'Dunn sisters. They were our closest neighbors when we lived out on the lake."

"Everyone in town expects Phoebe will be announcing her engagement soon. I think she'll keep the house even after she's married. It's in good shape. I'm drawing up plans for a new kitchen and bathroom." Heather wasn't sure why she was telling

Brody all this, but he didn't seem uninterested. "It's fun. I've discovered I have a passion for interior design."

"Often helps to know your passions," he said.

She wasn't sure what he meant but decided not to pursue the subject since it involved the word *passion.* She'd blundered on that score enough for one day.

As they reached the end of Vic's driveway and turned onto the winding road into the village, she noticed that the winter conditions and the absence of streetlights didn't seem to bother Brody in the least. He drove with a confidence that Heather realized she should have expected.

"Phoebe's house is the last one on the right," she said when she pointed out Thistle Lane. "It was also built in 1912. It must have been a good year in Knights Bridge, don't you think?"

"I didn't know Knights Bridge had any good years."

"That, Agent Hancock, is a negative attitude."

He smiled at her. "Practical." He pulled in front of the little house. "If you need a ride up to Vic's in the morning, give me a buzz, and I'll come fetch you."

"I don't have your number."

47

"Yes, you do. I got yours from Vic and texted you."

"Efficient."

He sat back. "Don't forget to bring jumper cables."

"I won't." She started to open her door but angled him a look. "What did you do to annoy my brothers?"

"There's what I did and there's what they thought I did."

"Bet the two overlap."

"It's all in the past."

"Bigger fish to fry now, huh? Nothing's wrong, is there?"

"Wrong as in what? An abandoned golden retriever running off into the woods?"

"Wrong as in a federal agent turning up in Knights Bridge."

"Good night, Heather."

"Wrong as in Brody Hancock turning up in Knights Bridge after all this time."

"Do you ever quit?"

"Can you arrest me for asking questions?"

"Thinking about that."

"You'd tell me if I was in any danger, wouldn't you?"

"I told you today, and you told me to go to hell." He leaned closer to her. "Go, Heather. Have a nice dinner and relax."

"You didn't answer my question, you know."

"Good night, Heather."

That was two good-nights. Time to be on her way. She got out of the car and made her way up the walk, which she'd shoveled herself after the last storm. Her brother Adam had plowed the driveway. She'd thrown fresh sand on the walk and the driveway before leaving that morning, never imagining she would rescue a puppy, slip into a brook and run into Brody Hancock, formerly of Knights Bridge, Massachusetts.

He waited until she was on the small porch and had the front door open before he turned around and headed back down Thistle Lane. Heather didn't know why the prospect of him watching her made her feel so self-conscious, but it did.

Probably shouldn't have mentioned the ice-skating bruises on her butt.

She ran inside and turned up the thermostat in the short hall between the front room and kitchen. No point keeping the place toasty warm when she wasn't there. Not that she kept it toasty warm when she *was* there. Most evenings she watched television under a quilt and then went to bed.

Alone.

She'd hoped moving into town from the

49

apartment above the Sloan & Sons offices in her parents' converted barn would help her social life. Specifically, her romantic life. It wasn't just being on top of her parents and her brothers all the time that discouraged "suitors," as her grandmother called them. It was also that with such a big family, she had a built-in social network. They all lived in Knights Bridge. One of them was bound to be available to hang out. She had friends, too, but she decided to stay in for the evening.

She heated up a can of black bean soup and took it into the front room with her. It was a quiet, dark night, and very cold. Even indoors, she was aware of the dropping temperature. She glanced around the attractive room, feeling oddly out of place. Phoebe and Noah had met at a costume ball in Boston, a charity fund-raiser. Phoebe had been dressed as an Edwardian princess, Noah as a swashbuckler. He'd had no idea she was a small-town librarian. She'd had no idea he was a billionaire.

So romantic.

Heather wasn't sure she'd know a swashbuckler if she saw one. Sometimes she wondered if she had a romantic bone in her body.

She reached for her laptop. What would

happen if she did an internet search for Diplomatic Security Service agent Brody Hancock?

Would she learn anything interesting?

Would he find out?

She smiled but felt a quiver of uneasiness, too. She put aside her laptop and investigated the shelves of books. She chose a worn copy of *The Scarlet Pimpernel* and took it to bed with her, but abandoned it after seven pages and went back downstairs for her laptop. She brought it upstairs with her and, with a deep breath, did an internet search to see what she could find out about the Diplomatic Security Service.

She eyed the list of results, suspecting it would be best if she returned to her swashbuckler tale and put aside her questions about Brody Hancock and his return to their little hometown.

THREE

Brody opened a beer and sat at Vic's kitchen table. Rohan was racing back and forth between the refrigerator and the back door with a chew toy that Heather had brought for him, at least according to Vic. Brody wasn't confident his old friend was paying close attention to the puppy goings-on in his Knights Bridge home.

He had helped himself to a plate of hors d'oeuvres, but he'd never been a big wine drinker. He'd only taken a few sips of Adrienne Portale's selections for the evening. She hadn't seemed to mind. Brody couldn't remember Vic ever mentioning Adrienne or her parents, Sophia Portale, a marketing whiz with her own firm based in San Francisco, and her ex-husband, Richard Portale, a corporate lawyer also in San Francisco. Adrienne's house-sitting arrangement with Vic didn't strike Brody as anything out of the ordinary.

Just as well nothing was jumping out at him to cause alarm since he doubted Heather Sloan would give up on trying to find out why he was in her little town. She was a Sloan. Every last one of them was stubborn. He doubted that had changed in his absence.

Heather wasn't what he'd expected. Pretty, sexy, curvy . . .

He didn't need that kind of distraction right now. An attractive woman — one from the hometown he'd sworn he would never step foot in again.

Also one with five older brothers. Bad enough if he stopped right there, but he couldn't. He'd left Knights Bridge while Heather's brothers were heating up the tar and gathering the feathers.

His negative history with the Sloans aside, Brody didn't need them or anyone else in town meddling in whatever was going on with Vic. If Vic was being paranoid, no one else needed to know. Knights Bridge was his home now. That kind of gossip wouldn't help him.

"What a day," Vic said, yawning as he entered the kitchen. He put his full wineglass on the table, pulled out a chair and flopped down. "Adrienne's reading by the fire. I think she's disappointed we didn't

53

drink all the wine, but one more sip and I'll pass out on the floor."

"The leftover wine will keep. She's got some gadget that helps." Brody took a swallow of his beer. "You weren't close to passing out, though."

"I was. I don't hold my alcohol like I used to."

"Another of the myths you live by these days."

Vic quirked an eyebrow. "Another?"

"You're an optimist and a romantic at heart, Vic. Maybe that's why you lasted as a career diplomat for as long as you did."

"Forty years. Damn, that makes me feel old."

Brody grinned. "You *are* old."

"Hell, no. Sixty is the new forty." Vic watched Rohan tear across the kitchen. "The little fella's no worse for the wear, anyway. Heather didn't recognize you right away. That surprise you?"

"Not really. She wasn't pretending. She's not one to hold back what's on her mind. I didn't ring a bell at all." Brody set his bottle on the table. He'd spent far too much time thinking about Heather Sloan ice-skating. "Why didn't you tell me a Sloan was working on this place?"

Vic shrugged. "I didn't think of it. Nobody

remembers your fallout with the Sloans. You haven't been back here since then, so it's on your mind. That's understandable. Anyway, they didn't run you out. You left of your own accord. You're a federal law-enforcement officer now. A respected agent with the Diplomatic Security Service. You're as big a hard-ass as any Sloan."

"Not Heather. She could kick my butt."

"Ha. I have no doubt." Vic lowered a hand at his side and snapped his fingers to get Rohan's attention. The puppy bounded to him. "His fur's so soft. He wore himself out on his romp in the woods, but he's got his energy back now. What would have happened if Heather hadn't found him when she did?"

"I'd have found him," Brody said.

"You're just saying that so I don't feel like an incompetent fool for having lost him in the first place. I'd have had to sell the house if I'd let the poor little fellow freeze to death in that brook. More to the point," he said, sitting up straight as Rohan ran off again, "I'd have felt terrible."

"You're new to puppy care."

"Trial by fire."

The puppy careened into the mudroom and climbed into his bed with his chew toy. Watching him helped Brody anchor his thinking. Too many memories in this town. There were some good ones, but the bad ones were clawing at him now. Heather Sloan wasn't a kid anymore. That didn't help. He hadn't considered her — that she would be overseeing Vic's house renovations — when he'd agreed to return. He'd expected to have a chat with Vic, talk some sense into him and leave after a couple of nights.

Brody took his beer bottle, still half-full, to the sink. It was pitch-dark outside, and dead quiet. Vic's was the only house on this part of the lake. "You're not used to the quiet and isolation out here, Vic. It's worse now with the cold weather."

Vic pushed his wineglass aside. "It's been a while since either of us has been in a cold climate during winter."

"Yes, it has." Brody hadn't expected to appreciate the bracing temperature and stark-white landscape — the quiet. Only the puppy's playful growling disturbed the silence. He turned to Vic. "How are the renovations? Are you decisive, or do you dither?"

"We're still pulling everything together and making decisions, but I wouldn't say *dither*. I deliberate."

Brody grinned. "Sounds like dithering to me."

"I haven't driven Heather crazy yet. I think the architect is about to bail on the project. Heather says not to worry, that's just how he is. Mark Flanagan. You know him?"

"I did. I never thought he'd stay in Knights Bridge. Now he's an architect here?"

"A damn good one, too. He left town and came back again. He married a local woman in September. Jessica Frost."

"I remember her. She's younger — more like Heather's age, as I recall. I didn't have much to do with either one of them."

Vic stretched, looking stiff and tired. "The Frosts still have their sawmill. They're doing the custom woodwork on this place. Jessica's sister, Olivia, married Noah Kendrick's business partner on Christmas Eve."

"Dylan McCaffrey."

"I see you're up to speed on the newcomers." Vic didn't sound surprised. "Dylan and Noah are exceptionally wealthy. What if their presence in Knights Bridge has attracted whoever is harassing me?"

"*Harassing* is a strong word, Vic."

"Yeah, okay. Maybe the goings-on haven't escalated to that level. Not yet, anyway."

Brody leaned back against the sink. He had no concrete reason to suspect Vic was in real trouble. He was only weeks into retirement, but there were no lingering threats against him. "Sure you're not just having trouble transitioning to retirement? Turning a draft into a suspicious incident."

"I've never been a worrywart."

"You worked nonstop in a high-pressure, high-profile environment, and now you're chasing puppies and renovating your country house and stocking a wine cellar."

"I was thinking about taking up bird-watching, too," Vic added dryly.

"It's not the life you're used to."

"It's one I've been dreaming about for years." He watched Rohan wander back into the kitchen. "Elly O'Dunn told me not to let him run wild."

"Puppies need structure and a steady, firm hand. You need to be the alpha dog, Vic."

"This is why I never was a father. I'd have had nothing but spoiled brats. I need to find him a good home. Winter's a deterrent. People tend to get puppies in warmer weather. It's no fun to train a puppy in January, but I can't imagine someone abandoning the little guy out here."

"Think that's related to what's been going on with you?"

"I hope not. We're dealing with a real sick SOB, then. It's been long enough that you'd think if he were lost an owner would have come forward by now." Vic pulled his gaze from the puppy. "Why don't you adopt Rohan, Brody? You can have a dog in the Diplomatic Security Service."

"Not the places I've worked the past few years." Brody stood straight. "Rohan seems to be at home here. Why not adopt him yourself? You could use the company now that you're retired. You could take a puppy-training class so you know what you're doing. It's not too late. It would give you something to do."

"Besides fretting about odd occurrences that don't sound odd to you, you mean?" Vic put up a hand. "Don't answer. Did you ever have a dog when you were growing up? I don't remember."

"Two before we moved to the lake and one after. No golden retrievers, though. Whatever's up with you, Vic, doesn't have to do with puppies."

"No. Rohan's a handful, but he's not our culprit." Vic grabbed his wineglass but didn't take a sip. "Things not in the same place I left them. Anonymous hang ups. They aren't a puppy's doing."

"Were the hang ups on your landline or

cell phone?" Brody asked.

"Both. I think someone's been pawing through my files, too. My physical files in the library. I haven't given up my apartment in New York yet, but I've been moving things here bit by bit. It's like . . ." He paused, his eyes distant then focused again on Brody. "I don't know. It's like I'm being watched. Studied."

"Only here? Nothing in New York?"

"Only here."

"When you're here alone, or when Adrienne and Heather are here?"

Vic shrugged. "Mostly when I'm here on my own. I had a hang up at least once when Adrienne was here. It was shortly after she started house-sitting for me in early December. She's not here all the time. She went out to San Francisco for a week after New Year's, and she pops down to New York every now and then." He shook his head, as if he were reading Brody's mind. "It's not Adrienne."

"What about Heather Sloan?"

"Heather? Why would she want to spook me?"

"I'm not concerned with whys right now," Brody said. "How often is she here?"

"As necessary. She's in charge of renovations. There's a hell of a lot to do. We're down to it now, so she's been here every day since I arrived last week. There will be people in and out of the house once renovations start, but there aren't now. I'm telling you, Brody, something weird is going on around here."

As Vic spoke, Rohan yawned and headed for his bed in the mudroom. Brody was ready to do the same with his spot in the guesthouse. He didn't want to delve deep into Vic's mind, but he knew he had to, at least to a degree. "Could you have moved things and not remember?" he asked.

He half expected Vic to spring up out of the chair, offended, but instead he tapped a finger on the rim of his wineglass, thoughtful. Finally, he shook his head. "I don't think so, no. I admit that I've wondered if I'm losing it. I asked myself that repeatedly before I contacted you. I decided no. If I had decided yes, I would have called a doctor instead of you. I'm retired, but I'm in good mental and physical health."

"I had to ask," Brody said.

"I know you did." Vic sucked in a breath and smacked a hand down on the table, an unusual display of frustration for the career diplomat. He exhaled. "I've nothing concrete to give you, Brody. No evidence. It's possible someone toyed with me for a while and figured out I'm not that interesting, and that's that."

"Do you have any reason to suspect you're in danger, Vic?"

"I have enemies. There's no question about that."

There wasn't, but it wasn't Brody's point. "Is one of them in Knights Bridge?"

"That's why I asked you to come here, Brody." Vic's voice was quiet but intense, his frustration with his situation unabated if under control. "I need your objectivity and professionalism to help me figure out what's going on."

Brody crossed his arms on his chest. How many times had he stood in this same spot as a kid, getting Vic's advice? How many times through college, training and his years with the DSS had he counted on Vic Scarlatti to be a phone call or an email away?

"All right," Brody said. "We'll figure this out. Anything else you can think of?"

"I was followed," Vic said. "I didn't mention that. The other day this black car followed me from Amherst right to my driveway, then kept on going out toward the upper lake. You tell me that was a coincidence, Brody. You tell me."

"Did you get the plate number?"

"Did I —" He stared at Brody, looking

baffled. "No, I didn't get the plate number. I had my hand on my cell phone in case I had to call the cops."

Brody lowered his arms to his sides. Vic wasn't paranoid by nature, and even now Brody didn't sense that his mentor and friend was afraid. Curious, annoyed, uncertain. Not fearful.

At this point, Brody couldn't tell his old friend anything except that he was here now, and he'd have a look around.

He felt a cold draft coming through the kitchen window. The place needed work. It had for a long time, and Sloan & Sons was the outfit to do the job.

He didn't need to go there right now.

He shifted back to Vic. "You could have called the police and asked them to look into these incidents instead of calling me."

"I don't want to sound like a crazy old man. I call the cops, it's a thing."

"It's a *thing* when you call me, Vic."

"I asked you here as a friend with experience in these matters. I know you're a law-enforcement officer. That's not what I mean. I'm talking about the local cops. Heather's brother is a police officer. Knights Bridge is a small town. I'm an unknown. People are curious. They gossip."

"I'll need to bring in the police if it looks

as if there's more going on here than a bored retired diplomat with an overactive imagination."

"Yeah, yeah, I know. Once I decided to contact you, I knew there was no good outcome. Either I'm overreacting, or something's going on." Vic pushed back his chair, the legs scraping on the worn floor. "You're not here just because of me, anyway, are you, Brody?"

He glanced at the window above the sink but could only see the darkness and the reflection of the lights in the kitchen. "I dreamed about Echo Lake right before you got in touch with me."

"A sign, you think?"

"A sign it's time I saw about the land I own here."

"Think you'll put it on the market?"

He shrugged without answering Vic's question.

A gust of wind rattled the kitchen windows. The age and condition of the house could be responsible for some of what had Vic unnerved, or at least for triggering him into ratcheting up normal occurrences.

"I'll need to ask Adrienne and Heather if they've noticed anything," Brody said.

Vic clearly didn't like that idea. "Be tactful."

"Sure, Vic. No problem. Tact is my middle name."

"Tact is an unknown concept to you," Vic muttered.

Brody grinned and started for the mudroom. "I've got some work to do."

"I thought you were on home leave."

"I am. You relax and let me know if you remember anything else. Write every incident down. You can email it to me or hand me a sheet of paper."

Vic shook his head. "I'm not writing a damn thing. I don't want you or anyone else using it against me if this turns out to be nothing." He raised his wineglass. "It's called plausible deniability. If I'm losing it, we'll all know soon enough."

"I doubt you're losing it, Vic."

"But you also doubt I'm in danger."

"Correct."

Vic didn't seem offended. "How was it seeing a Sloan again?"

"I told you I never had much to do with Heather."

"But she *is* a Sloan. She didn't stir up old wounds?"

"No."

"Then your feud with the Sloans is in the past. No hard feelings."

It wasn't a feud, and it had never been a

feud, but Brody wasn't indulging Vic, especially if he was in a mood to stir up trouble as an outlet for his own problems. "Call if you need me. Otherwise, I'll see you in the morning."

Brody headed into the mudroom where Rohan reigned. It was immediately evident that the fur ball had relieved himself in the corner. Brody grabbed some newspaper to clean up the mess but felt his phone vibrate in his jacket.

He saw he had a text from Greg Rawlings, a DSS colleague and friend recovering from a bullet to the shoulder incurred two months ago during a difficult mission.

How's Knights Bridge?

Brody decided to answer.

I'm cleaning up puppy poop.

Auto-correct problem?

No.

Oh man. At least it's not Vic's poop. Later.

Brody didn't know whether to laugh or grit his teeth, but tackling the mess on the

floor wasn't optional. It had to be done, and he might as well be the one to do it.

He noticed Vic standing in the doorway. "Thank you," Vic said, his relief palpable. "Cleaning up after Rohan isn't my favorite activity, and I hate to ask Adrienne to do it. I never had a dog. A cat, either. I had a goldfish once, but it disappeared. My parents told me it died and they got rid of the body before I could see it. Suspiciously, we were about to leave for a month in France."

"Think they flushed it?"

"It wasn't well . . ." Vic sighed. "I suppose I should take them at their word. Think our pup here misses his siblings and that's why he's been tearing up the place?"

"Alpha dog, Vic."

Vic scowled and headed back into the kitchen. Rohan sat on Brody's foot, looking irresistible. Brody pointed the newspaper at him. "No more messing on the floor, you hear?"

Whether Rohan was worn-out or heard something authoritative in Brody's voice, the puppy sat politely, as if he were the best-minding golden retriever in the world.

"Good dog," Brody said.

Rohan responded by diving face-first into his water bowl and then licking Brody's hand as he squatted down to clean up the mess. When he finished, Rohan had curled up in his bed, all innocence.

Brody took a picture and sent it to Greg.

Meet Rohan.

Greg texted him back immediately.

All hope is lost.

Brody was surprised to find Adrienne standing in the driveway, looking at the stars. She must have gone out through the front. "I can't resist the night sky here," she said, crossing her arms on her chest. She had on a coat and hat but no gloves. "There isn't much ambient light to spoil the stars. It's freezing, though. I think this is the coldest it's been since I've been here."

"It's supposed to drop below zero tonight."

"I can't remember the last time I was in below-zero temperatures."

"You sound excited."

She laughed. "I guess I am. Vic's never stayed here through an entire winter. He says he likes winter, but I wonder if he'll end up buying a condo in Florida."

"How well do you know him?"

"Not well at all. He goes way back with

my parents. I looked him up one day when we were both in New York, and we hit it off. Next thing, I'm house-sitting."

"When was this meeting in New York?"

"November." She shot him a quick look. "Easy, there. It was just lunch. Vic didn't pass me any state secrets."

Brody smiled. "That's good."

"We got to talking about wine, and he mentioned he'd like to know more about wine now that he was retiring to his country house in Knights Bridge. I'd never heard of Knights Bridge." She stuffed her bare hands under her arms, presumably to keep them warm. "Vic says you're like a son to him. He's relaxed since you got here, even with Rohan's escape this afternoon. He's been keyed up. He won't tell me why."

Brody buttoned his jacket, trying to appear casual. He wanted to get a read on Adrienne without alarming her. "Vic's had an intense job for a lot of years."

"You'd know more about that than I would. He doesn't talk about his past with me, or with Heather, that I've been able to see." There was no trace of criticism in her tone. "He's been great to me, though. I'm not broke or desperate or anything, but I'm between apartments."

"Your work doesn't tie you to an office,"

Brody said.

"Exactly. I have a freedom of lifestyle that I'm taking advantage of in a variety of ways. Fortunately, I have friends all over the place who let me stay with them. I help with things like wine tastings and stocking wine cellars." She gave an easy smile. "I always bring a few bottles of my favorite wines."

Brody looked up at the spray of stars in the black sky. "It's quiet here. Do you like the quiet?"

"Right now I do. Vic's excited about renovations, but I think retirement has taken him by surprise. It's one thing to have it figured out intellectually. It's another to experience it. He's used to a fair amount of drama. There's not much drama around here."

"Small towns often seem sleepier than they are."

"Well, there might be local dramas. People are people, after all. I doubt international diplomacy is ever at stake."

Brody shrugged without answering. He pointed to the dark sky. "Nightfall comes early this time of year. Plans for the evening?"

"Vic and I were going to make dinner together, but the hors d'oeuvres filled us up. An early night with a book sounds good to me. The comforter on my bed is to die for. Fluffy goose down. I snuggle under it and read until my eyes can't stay open. It's a luxury, that kind of night." She shivered. "It's almost always colder than I expect when I come outside. You're welcome to help yourself to any food you want, of course. I stocked the pantry."

"Thanks. I'm not hungry, either."

"Do you cook?"

"Not well, but I can chop, slice and clean."

Adrienne turned to him, the light from the back door catching her dark eyes. "I will keep that in mind."

"I can set a table, too. I even know my wineglasses."

"Vic makes it easy. He only has one kind."

"You'll be correcting that?"

She laughed. "Absolutely." She hunched her shoulders. "I'll say good-night. I'm freezing."

Brody waited as she dashed up the back steps and went inside. It was damn cold, but it felt good to him. He didn't have a good sense of Adrienne Portale and her reasons for house-sitting in Knights Bridge, but he hadn't found anything suspicious, never mind alarming, in their conversation about Vic, wine and dinner.

He took the shoveled walk to the guesthouse but didn't go inside, instead heading through the snow down to the lake. The stars were out in full force now, penetrating the darkness and creating shadows in the woods and on the lake. He could see Heather's footprints from her Rohan rescue. He pictured her climbing up from the brook with the puppy in her arms, her pant leg soaked, her scarf dangling, one glove. She'd been focused and determined, and she hadn't needed his help.

He ducked past white pines to the lakeshore. A breeze whistled in the clear night air. He remembered standing in this spot as a boy, waiting for the stars to come out, imagining being on a different planet — in a different place. He hadn't hated Knights Bridge then. He'd wanted to go places, see things, do things, get out in the world.

He'd done that in spades, and now here he was again, on the shore of Echo Lake. He hadn't lied. He had dreamed about Echo Lake in the days before Vic's call. He'd just returned to the US to begin an extended home leave, and it had struck him that he had no real home, except for his land in Knights Bridge — and it wasn't home. He'd picked up his car and considered dividing his time between visits with his mother in Orlando and his father in Key West.

He felt the cold sting his face and ears. He gritted his teeth. *Damn.* He was a tough federal agent. He'd endured all sorts of extreme conditions. He could handle a southern New England January evening.

He turned away from the lake and walked up to the guesthouse. He'd had a rough few months on the job, and being back in Knights Bridge — running into Heather, even if she wasn't one of the Sloan brothers — was messing with his head. He didn't like digging into his emotions. Didn't want to go there. Thinking about the past wouldn't help him size up what was going on with Vic. So far, it seemed as though he was in the throes of adjusting to retirement and making mountains out of molehills. Brody wasn't even sure there were any molehills, never mind mountains.

He went into the guesthouse through the side door. The two-bedroom cottage was solid and only about forty years old, a late addition to the original 1912 estate. It needed work, but not as desperately as the main house. He didn't care one way or the other. It suited his purposes. He liked keeping some distance between him and Vic, and time alone, even here, with the past so near,

73

worked for him right now. He hadn't been back in the US in months, and his mind was still thousands of miles away in North Africa and his unfinished business there.

He filled the wood box and started a fire in the woodstove. Its crackling was the only sound in the place. He stood at the windows and looked out at the night sky. His mother loved stars and had pointed out various constellations to him when he was a kid. It wasn't until he was in middle school that he'd realized her names were all of her own creation and not the actual names. Eric Sloan had told him. "Dude, that's not Camel Head. That's Orion. There is no Camel Head constellation."

Brody had felt like a dumbass. At first he'd blamed his mother for lying to him, but she hadn't lied. She'd made up her own names because she didn't know the real ones — couldn't sort herself out enough to go to the library and find out — and needed something to grab on to for herself, and maybe for her only son, too. She'd been restless and depressed, hating her life, hating Knights Bridge, and by his fourteenth birthday, Mary Hancock had left him and his father.

Brody hadn't told Eric he'd gotten Camel

Head from his mother. He'd covered for her.

That was what he was good at — watching people's backs.

She'd loved Echo Lake itself, though. "It's the most beautiful place I've ever lived, Brody. I can't imagine any place prettier than right here, even if it's not for me."

She was happy as a clam these days in Orlando, where she'd moved his senior year in high school. His father had been right behind her, beelining to South Florida twenty-four hours after Brody had turned eighteen, two weeks after his graduation.

He smiled, thinking of his parents. A couple of flakes. He wondered if they'd have stayed together if they'd moved to Florida instead of to Knights Bridge. He needed to go see them while he was on home leave.

He felt the heat of the woodstove. He was surprised at how tight his throat was, but he knew it wasn't just being here. Being back "home." That was an aggravating factor, but it was also the weight of the past few months, the tension and the uncertainties of what came next for him.

The fire popped and hissed, the sounds launching him back to a mission in November to secure a small consulate that had been shut down the year before. He remembered the heat, the dust, the eerie stillness. He and Greg Rawlings had looked at each other, sensing — *knowing* — something was off. They hadn't exchanged a word. They'd had a split second to react before gunfire erupted, but it was that split second that had saved their lives.

Brody had emerged uninjured. Greg hadn't been so lucky. He had taken a bullet to his shoulder that he and Brody both had believed would end Greg's seventeen-year career as a DSS agent. Blood seeping through his fingers as he applied pressure to his own wound, Greg had looked at Brody with pain-racked eyes. "Now what, Brody? Hell. I don't have a life to go back to."

"You do, Greg," Brody had said. "Think of those kids of yours."

"I've never been there for them. What, start now?"

Before Brody could respond, Greg had drifted into semiconsciousness. Two months later, he was making a full recovery. He could go back to work if he wanted to. His call. He didn't have to take on another dangerous assignment. He had married young and had a couple of teenagers, if also a wife who didn't want to "indulge" him anymore. Laura Rawlings didn't care if he

was good at his job, if it made him happy
— she was done. Even before he was shot,
Greg had expressed his doubts that a non-
hazardous post where she could join him
wouldn't make any difference.

But as in need of TLC as Greg's home
life was, at least he had one to come back
to. Brody didn't. He didn't have a family, a
pet or even an apartment.

The wind howled out in the dark January
night then settled down again. It had been a
long time since he'd experienced such quiet.
He turned from the stove and sat on the
sectional sofa. He'd slept here last night.
He'd grabbed a pillow and a blanket from
one of the bedrooms. The front room was
warmer with the woodstove, and it had a
view of the lake. He'd wanted to wake up to
the sunrise over Echo Lake. He didn't know
why.

Maybe he didn't *want* to know why.

He leaned back and stared up at the ceiling, listening to the crackle of the fire and
trying not to think, not to remember and
especially not to feel now that he was back
in Knights Bridge.

FOUR

Heather woke up to no truck and no food in the house — not so much as a slice of bread for toast or a drop of milk for coffee. Fortunately, Smith's, the only restaurant in the village center, was open and within easy walking distance, one of the perks of living on Thistle Lane. Smith's was popular with loads of people she knew, including her brothers. Someone would be willing to loan her a set of jumper cables and give her a ride up to Vic's.

Phoebe's sole bathroom had its original claw-foot tub, with a brand-new shower curtain she'd added when Heather moved in. She'd found a kids' one decorated with little hammers, saws and wrenches. "I thought that would be fun for you," she'd told Heather. "Make you smile when you jump in the shower. I was tempted by the one with puppies, but I went with the tools."

It probably hadn't occurred to Phoebe

that Heather could have a guy over and the shower curtain might not convey the sexiest image of her.

Then again, it was just a shower curtain, and it was clean and did the job. Heather was nothing if not practical.

And it did make her smile.

She took the time — for a change — to blow-dry her hair since she didn't want to go out into the cold morning with it partially wet. It'd turn into icicles. She dressed in warm layers and added a hat, proper gloves and her L.L. Bean boots. If Rohan escaped today, she'd be ready to chase him across Echo Lake if need be.

The sting of the early-morning cold chased away any lingering fuzziness from her late-night delving into the United States Foreign Service and its elite corps of security personnel, the Diplomatic Security Service. She hadn't been overstating yesterday when she'd concluded Brody was extremely fit. He had to be, given the work he did. Ten to one he took on the most dangerous posts.

He wasn't the Brody Hancock she had known as a teenager.

Heather walked the short distance up Thistle Lane to South Main Street. The town library was on the east corner, a quirky nineteenth-century brick-and-stone building that occupied a large lot dotted with old shade trees and evergreens.

Had Brody ever so much as stepped foot in his town library?

Heather shook off the question. Why even think about such things?

She crossed South Main to the town common. The air was still and very cold as the gray early morning gave way to a lavender sunrise, glowing on the snow and the classic houses that surrounded the large, oval-shaped common. The seasonal skating rink on the eastern end of the common was quiet now, but it was a favorite gathering place during these short winter days.

Staying on a shoveled, sanded walk, Heather walked past the Civil War and World War monuments, bare-limbed oaks and sugar maples and empty benches. She scooted across Main Street and ducked down the side street where Smith's was located in a converted house with white clapboards and black shutters. In warm-weather months, the porch would be decorated with hanging flower baskets and white-painted wicker furniture. Now the furniture was in storage, replaced by a stack of wood, a bucket of sand and a shovel. A grapevine wreath decorated for Valentine's

Day — still a couple weeks off — was hung on the glossy green-painted door.

When she went inside, Heather wasn't surprised to see her brothers Eric and Justin at a square table near the front. Both were dressed for work, Eric in his police uniform, Justin in canvas pants and a dark, heavy sweatshirt and down vest similar to hers. They had fresh coffee, their breakfast orders obviously on the way.

Justin tapped the table next to him. "Have a seat," he said.

He was a skilled carpenter who specialized in older buildings, and, more and more, he was taking over the day-to-day operations of Sloan & Sons. He'd been reluctant to let Heather oversee the renovations on Vic Scarlatti's house, but he'd acquiesced in the end — with reservations. "Just do your job," he'd told her. "Stay out of Vic's dramas."

Good advice, Heather thought as she unzipped her vest and sat down, aware of her brothers eyeing her. It was as if they knew all wasn't normal in her world. She wondered if they'd heard about her puppy rescue yesterday and if it that qualified as one of Vic's dramas. What about Brody Hancock's return to Knights Bridge? Vic had invited him. He was a DSS agent.

Would that raise her brothers' eyebrows?

Heather ordered coffee, eggs, sausage and toast and decided not to speculate — or at least try not to. On his sporadic visits to Knights Bridge, Vic had managed to gain a reputation, at least with her brothers, for things happening when he was in town. He managed his property himself but was clueless about minor issues that could wait versus major ones that couldn't wait. Every leak was about to cause catastrophic damage. Every branch lost in a storm meant the tree was about to fall on his house. In working with him, Heather had discovered it wasn't that he was dramatic, and certainly not that he was demanding, so much as he simply didn't know. He lacked experience and erred on the side of caution.

When the waitress, one of Heather's classmates from high school, withdrew, Justin picked up his coffee mug and leaned back in his chair. "How's work at Vic's place going?"

"Great." An honest answer, she thought, grateful when her own coffee arrived. "He wants to see loads of lumber and guys with saws and hammers, but we're not there yet. He's decided to add a wine cellar. I've been working on that. Adrienne Portale is advising me. She's toured some of the best wine cellars in the world. Have you met her?"

"Not yet," Justin said.

Eric shook his head. "Me, either. You've been spending a lot of time up there, haven't you?"

Heather shrugged. "I guess. It's a complicated job."

"We have nothing against Vic, but I wouldn't describe us as fans, either," Justin said. "He might have been a stellar diplomat, but he's also an old womanizer with no family to speak of."

"What's that got to do with me?" She dumped cream into her coffee. "Trust me, Vic has no designs on me. He's lived in a different world from us but not *that* different."

"I was thinking more on the lines he could have regrets," Eric said.

Her brothers' breakfasts arrived. Justin picked up a triangle of buttered whole-grain toast. "Vic won't take to retirement easily. He's not the type. He's used to a lot of adventure, adrenaline and attention. When he was working, Knights Bridge was a break from that."

"Maybe it's all he wants now," Heather said.

"Peace and quiet and a nice house in the country?" Eric shook his head. "I doubt it."

Justin added fresh-ground pepper to his eggs. "People often take some time when they retire to look back at their lives. Vic's never married. He's never had kids. He's never cultivated friendships in Knights Bridge, which he now wants to call home after living all over the world. Is he keeping his apartment in New York?"

"I don't think he's decided yet," Heather said.

"He's in transition." Justin handed her the pepper grinder, but there was nothing casual about him this morning. "Your work up there puts you in the middle of that transition."

"He says he's committed to the renovations. I've no reason to doubt him." Heather's own breakfast arrived, and she grabbed her fork and stabbed a bit of onion in the home fries. "Vic doesn't strike me as a man with many regrets."

"You never know," Eric said. "You get older and start thinking about what you missed, what you gave up for reasons good and bad — what you screwed up. He's had an all-consuming career, and he's calling it quits on the young side for a diplomat. What's he going to do with himself?"

"I don't know. Read books and drink wine. He'll figure it out." Heather drank some of her coffee, aware of her brothers' scrutiny. Nothing new, but best to resist any hint of defensiveness. "Anyway, I'm overseeing renovations. I'm not his retirement consultant."

Eric studied her in that big-brother way she sometimes found reassuring and other times found annoying. He wasn't a police officer for no reason. "Heather," he said. "What's on your mind?"

"I'm hungry. I woke up forgetting I don't have any food in the house."

Eric shook his head. "That's not it."

"Come on," Justin said. "Out with it."

She reached for the little dish of homemade strawberry jam. "I had to walk over here. My truck wouldn't start last night, and I ended up leaving it at Vic's. Dead battery."

"How did you get home?" Justin asked.

"I got a ride."

"Vic? This house sitter, Adrienne Portale?"

"No." Heather set the dish in front of her. "Not Vic or Adrienne."

Justin sighed. "Then who?"

She spread jam on a triangle of her toast.

Eric snatched up his coffee. "Hell, Heather, why are you stonewalling? If you've got some secret boyfriend, just tell us to mind our own damn business —"

"Brody Hancock gave me a ride home."

"Brody Hancock? Are you serious?" Justin groaned, looking as if he were about to jump up out of his chair. "Damn, Heather. You could have called me for a ride. You didn't have to rely on Brody. What's he doing here?"

"I don't know. He says Vic invited him. I had no idea until I ran into him yesterday. He got in late the night before. He's a Diplomatic Security Service agent now."

She deliberately left out finding Rohan in the brook and her reaction to Brody. She didn't need to get into those particular details. There were some things her brothers didn't need to know, and she had a good feel for what they were. In any case, she'd chalked up her intense, immediate physical attraction to him to the adrenaline of her puppy rescue. It wasn't as if she wasn't used to being around buff guys.

Eric held on to his coffee mug without picking it up. "Brody's a DSS agent now? You're sure nothing is going on out there?"

"Vic took in a golden retriever puppy who's causing him fits. Other than that, no, nothing." Heather ignored both brothers' scrutiny and tried her toast. "Strawberry jam reminds me of summer. Look, if you guys have any questions about what's going on, ask Vic. Ask Brody."

"You're just minding your own business," Justin said.

"Do I hear a trace of sarcasm, Justin? Yes, as a matter of fact, I am minding my own business. I didn't even recognize Brody at first."

Eric pushed his mug away from him. "He drove you home last night."

"Why wouldn't he?" She didn't wait for an answer. "He didn't interrogate me about anything, if that's what you're wondering. It's not like there are any secrets in Knights Bridge, anyway."

"There are a million secrets in Knights Bridge," Eric said.

"And not one of them is mine. My life is under constant scrutiny."

Justin rolled his eyes. "Relax. We haven't searched Phoebe's house yet now that you're staying there."

"I know. I can tell. I leave a thread in a door to detect intruders."

It wasn't true, and she was only half-serious, but bringing up her position in their family had become her refrain whenever she was feeling the heat. Sometimes it even worked. But she didn't know why Eric and

Justin's questions about Brody were getting to her.

Eric rubbed the back of his neck. He'd always been more patient than Justin, if only marginally so. "Look, Heather, we know you can handle yourself. That's not the issue. Brody didn't leave town on good terms and vowed never to return."

"Things change," she said.

"So they do. I'm surprised he's a federal agent now. Good for him."

Heather picked up her coffee mug. "But?"

Eric's gaze leveled on her. He had the Sloan deep blue eyes. "But my one piece of unsolicited advice is to spend as little extra time at Vic's as possible."

"I agree," Justin said. "Do what you need to do. Go home. Stay out of any dramas out there."

"The puppy is the biggest drama I've noticed. Do you know of anyone who's missing a twelve-week-old golden retriever? He doesn't have any tags. We figure he was abandoned out at the lake."

Justin made a face. "We?"

"I did have an opinion, yes. Come on. Ease up." When neither brother responded, Heather stared at them. "You two are worried about me? Seriously?"

Eric held up a hand. "Hold on. Don't get

wound up. Vic's never let anyone from town into his life. He's kept his distance because that's who he is and what he wants."

"You don't want me getting ahead of myself, thinking he's — what? A friend?"

"Let's just say Vic isn't looking for us to invite him over for potluck night," Justin said.

"Maybe he will now that he's retired, but that's up to him."

Heather tackled her eggs, wishing now she'd waited for the country store to open and grabbed something there. She was bound to have run into someone she knew who would have driven her up to Vic's. Justin smiled suddenly — not, she realized, because of her or her situation. Samantha Bennett, his fiancée, had just entered the restaurant. She wasn't wearing a hat over her short golden-brown curls, but she had her winter coat buttoned up to her chin.

Heather grinned at her second-born brother. "You just got giddy."

"Giddy, Heather?"

"Happy? Excited? Pleased? I admit I didn't think you and Samantha would last past Thanksgiving, but here you are, a couple of lovebirds."

Justin looked past her to Eric. "Can I throw our little sister off the front porch?

Would you arrest me?"

"No point arresting you," Eric said. "There isn't a jury that would convict you."

"Funny, you two," Heather said. "Very funny."

Justin grinned. "Eric and I need to mark the calendar. You just admitted you were wrong."

Heather grinned back at him. "I'm seldom wrong only because I have the guidance of my five wise older brothers."

Eric and Justin laughed in disbelief as Samantha breezed over to their table. She sat across from Justin and rubbed her hands together. She was very fit, energetic and new to Knights Bridge. She'd arrived in October looking for eighteenth-century pirate treasure and instead had found Justin, a carpenter and volunteer firefighter.

"Cold, Sam?" he asked.

"It's single digits out there. I don't know how you people can be laughing."

"Laughter warms you up," Eric said with a wink.

"So does coffee." Samantha unbuttoned her coat but left it on as she reached for Justin's mug. "I could be in South Florida with my parents. They're working on salvage plans for their sunken World War II submarines. They'll go back to Scotland in

April. The forecast high today in Key West is eighty. The forecast high here is twenty."

"And it'll last for five minutes at two o'clock," Heather added.

The widespread skepticism in town about Justin Sloan and Samantha Bennett as a couple was giving way to optimism. They were just so different. Justin was the second of six siblings and had lived in Knights Bridge his entire life. Samantha was an only child, an adventurer from a family of prominent adventurers, and a woman who'd never lived in one place for long. She was staying at the Sloan family cabin, supposedly doing research on Captain Benjamin Farraday, her mysterious eighteenth-century pirate. Heather suspected Samantha was at least as interested in being close to Justin.

Samantha put her hands around the mug with a sigh. "Warmth. It feels so good. I keep forgetting to wear gloves. Does the cold ever get to you, Heather?"

"Sometimes, especially when I'm not prepared."

As was the case yesterday, she thought. She didn't so much as glance at her two brothers at the table in case her expression gave her away and they realized she hadn't told them everything about her first encounter with Brody.

"We want Vic's renovations to go well for you," Justin said. "Leave whatever Vic Scarlatti and Brody Hancock have going on to them."

"Who's Brody Hancock?" Samantha asked.

Heather waited a half beat but she already knew Eric and Justin weren't going to respond. They would let her explain Brody and watch her reaction. She decided to keep it simple. "He's a Diplomatic Security Service agent who used to live in town."

Samantha set the mug on the table. She already looked warmer. "There's a lot of fine print in that answer, isn't there? You all knew him growing up?"

"We did." Justin handed her a triangle of his toast. "The Brody Hancock we knew didn't like to be bored. I doubt that's changed."

"Not if he's a DSS agent," Eric said, pushing back his chair. "That can be a hellishly dangerous job. I don't know where he's been posted, but I would bet real money that he's taken on the toughest assignments."

"An adrenaline junkie?" Samantha asked.

The Bennetts could be described as adrenaline junkies, Heather thought, but she said nothing as her eldest brother shrugged. "Maybe. I haven't seen Brody since he was eighteen." He got to his feet. "If you're ready, Heather, I can give you a ride out there."

Heather would have liked to stay and chat with Samantha, who was endlessly interesting but also interested in others. "If you and Justin are thinking about getting a dog, Rohan is cute as anything and has a great personality. He just needs some training."

Samantha smiled. "A way of saying he's rambunctious, isn't it?"

"He'll learn well once he's settled into a permanent home," Heather said.

"You mean once he's away from Vic," Eric said with a grunt. "Let's go, Heather. I've got jumper cables in the car."

Samantha looked confused. "Jumper cables?"

Heather let Justin explain about her truck. She grabbed her gloves and hat, said goodbye to him and Samantha and headed out with Eric. It was entirely possible that Brody had decided not to stick around in Knights Bridge and had gone off to wherever DSS agents went off to when they were on home leave.

Just as well, maybe, if he wasn't at Vic's when she got there with Eric.

FIVE

Not only was Brody still at Vic's when Heather arrived with Eric, he was also standing at the end of the driveway. She wasn't sure what he was up to. Checking for icy spots? Looking out at the lake? Then Rohan burst over a snowbank and leaped down to Brody in a ball of golden, snow-encrusted fur.

Her brother glanced at Heather without a word. She shrugged. "Meet Rohan. And that's Brody. Do you recognize him? I didn't."

"I recognize him," Eric said, tight-lipped.

Heather pointed back toward the trunk. "I can grab the jumper cables and return them to you later."

Eric shook his head. "I've got a few minutes. I'll help get your truck started and make sure that's what's wrong with it. I did tell you it needed a new battery when I sold it to you."

No argument from her. "Yes, you did."

She got out of the car. She was grateful for his help, but at the same time was uncertain about having him and Brody meet in front of her — uncertain of her own reaction to Brody.

Not like her.

Rohan was rolling on his back in the snow. Heather grinned casually at Brody, who had on his suede jacket, unbuttoned over a dark sweater. "A playful puppy isn't what you're used to, is it?"

"Not lately."

"Puppies need protecting, I suppose."

"Don't tell Rohan. He thinks he's doing the protecting."

"Maybe you two have something in common."

Eric joined them and nodded at his one-time friend. "Long time, Brody. I don't know if you remember me. Eric Sloan."

"I remember you, Eric," Brody said, his tone neutral.

"What brings you to Knights Bridge?"

"I'm visiting Vic."

Eric didn't look convinced. "I understand you own your family's old place on the lake."

"The cabin is gone but I'll check on the land while I'm here."

"It's the dead of winter," Eric said. "Not the best time for a visit."

Brody smiled. "I won't be kayaking, that's for sure."

"You're on vacation?"

"Close enough."

"Well, then. Welcome back." Before Brody could respond, Eric turned to Heather. "Let's get your truck started."

Brody scooped up Rohan and headed inside. Heather tried not to watch him mount the steps to the small porch and then go in through the back door. Her overnight conclusion chalking up her reaction to him to adrenaline wasn't holding up, and it had nothing to do with Eric's presence. If she'd come up here on her own, she would have had the same reaction to Brody. She decided she would be smart to remain calm and in control around this man. Even without the bad blood between him and her brothers, she had no business messing with Brody Hancock in any way, shape or form. They had nothing in common beyond a Knights Bridge upbringing.

"You aren't twelve anymore, Heather," Eric muttered, then headed to her truck.

The jumper cables did the trick, and her cop brother took off back down the long driveway without further comment on Vic

Scarlatti's new guest.

Heather left her truck to run for a few minutes and went inside, trying to focus on her to-do list for the day. She found Brody at the kitchen counter with a mug of coffee. "Where's Rohan?" she asked.

"Wandering."

"I can't imagine you expected to be on puppy duty when you got here. Bored yet?"

"I'm never bored in Knights Bridge."

She noticed the slightest smile as he drank some of his coffee. She pulled off her hat and gloves and set them on the table. Rohan galloped into the kitchen from the adjoining dining room, his furry softness and endless cuteness in sharp contrast to Brody's broad shoulders, muscles and general seriousness.

Heather unzipped her vest. "It's hard to believe you'd come back here in the dead of winter just to see Vic's renovations. Is Vic in some kind of trouble?"

"Maybe I'm the one in trouble, and I want to talk to Vic."

"That's not an answer." She shrugged off her vest and hung it on the back of a chair at the table. "You're the one who's supposed to prevent trouble. This *is* your first visit back home, isn't it?"

"My first visit back to Knights Bridge. It

was never home. It's where I lived until I turned eighteen." There was no trace of bitterness in his tone. "Vic's a friend."

"Your only friend in town?"

Brody didn't hesitate. "That's right. My mother and father went their separate ways when I was fourteen, but they both managed to end up in Florida. Different parts of the state." He set his mug on the counter. "We were never like the Sloans."

"And the Sloans would be — what?"

"Tight-knit, stubborn, fixtures in a little town that time forgot a hundred years ago."

Heather grinned. "That sounds about right."

She untucked stray hair from inside her sweatshirt, which she decided to leave on. She noticed Brody watching her but warned herself not to read anything into it. In his work, he probably watched people as a matter of course.

"Might as well take a look at my land while I'm here." Brody set his mug on the counter. He seemed casual, at ease with himself and his surroundings. "I figure I'll walk over there later on."

"Today? In this cold?"

"I thought a tough Sloan like you would relish the cold weather. You did look a little frozen yesterday when you rescued Rohan, but I assumed it was because you weren't in your kick-ass carpenter clothes." He nodded to her. "I see you are today."

Now she felt sexy. "The road's plowed out to your old place. That'll help. You know, Justin and Adam will be out here soon to look over some of the renovation plans."

"Warning me?" Brody seemed amused by the idea.

"What happened between you and my brothers?"

"Ask them." He started for the mudroom. "I'll shut off your truck and leave your key on the seat."

"Thank you."

He paused and smiled at her. A deliberate, sexy smile. "Anytime."

He was outside before Heather could get a decent breath.

Definitely couldn't chalk up yesterday's reaction to adrenaline. The man had her senses on overdrive. Other people, she thought, might be intimidated by him, but she wasn't. She was even more determined to find out what he was up to in Knights Bridge.

She reminded herself she was here to work and continued on to the front room, where Vic was settled into a big chair by the fire, playing a game of Scrabble on his iPad.

"The bastard cheats," he said without looking up. "I know it does."

"How badly are you losing?"

"A hundred points. Could be worse, since the SOB has access to the Scrabble Dictionary, and I only have access to my poor brain." Finally, he looked up, squinting at her. "Did you get your truck started?"

Heather nodded. "Eric gave me a jump start. Brody was outside with Rohan when we arrived."

"Ah. Brody and a Sloan brother meet again. They behaved?"

"They were civil. Vic . . ." Heather debated but decided she couldn't resist. "What happened between them?"

He waved a hand. "I told you. Some feud involving pumpkins."

"You know more than that."

He raised his gray eyes to her, studied her in a way that reminded her of his long career as a diplomat. "You don't remember?"

"I don't know. Maybe vaguely. I tried to stay out of my brothers' fights. I don't remember anything about pumpkins, but there was a vandalized job site, as I recall. Was that Brody?"

"Talk to him. Talk to your brothers. I wasn't involved."

"Were you here at the time it happened?"

Vic shook his head without hesitation. "No."

"I guess in your world a fight between a bunch of Knights Bridge teenagers wasn't a big deal."

He winked at her. "*Especially* when it involved pumpkins."

Heather smiled. Whatever had happened between Brody and her brothers, Vic's reaction suggested he wasn't troubled by it, and probably hadn't been at the time. "I should get busy. Do you know where Adrienne is? I have a few more questions about what she has in mind for your wine cellar if she's around."

"I haven't seen her yet this morning, but I'll send her to you when she surfaces."

"I'll be in the cellar. If I need to find you for anything?"

"I'll be here by the fire. I won't be playing Scrabble the entire morning, though, I assure you. I'll bring Rohan in here with me. He'll need another walk before lunch. That can be my adventure for the morning. When I decided to look after him, I wasn't thinking he needed to go out. I hope he wasn't abandoned because some idiot didn't want to walk him on a cold night."

"I can't imagine such a thing," Heather said.

"That's good, Heather. I'm glad you can't. Adrienne says she'll see what the town library has for puppy training books."

"Then you think you'll keep him?"

"I didn't say that. DSS agents can often have dogs. Maybe I can convince Brody to take him."

Heather doubted Vic was serious. He resumed his Scrabble game, and she returned to the kitchen. She ducked into the mudroom and opened the door to the cellar. Heather Sloan on the job, she thought with a smile. She tried to picture Brody in the field as a DSS agent but got nowhere, and she knew it wasn't something that would take her anywhere she needed to be.

She flipped on a light on the steep, dusty cellar stairs.

Where she needed to be, she thought, was right here, venturing into the cellar of the classic 1912 house she was renovating. She couldn't wait to dig into the nitty-gritty of Vic's wine cellar. She'd never been involved in building a wine cellar and wasn't sure her family had, either.

She started down the steep stairs. She was leading the life she wanted to lead. One day it would include the right man, but that man wouldn't be Brody Hancock. Some things in life just weren't possible, and that, she knew, was one of them.

Heather had been at work in a dark corner of the cellar for an hour when Adrienne joined her, dressed in slim black jeans, a thigh-length black sweater and black ankle boots. "I feel like the city mouse," she said with a smile.

"The cellar stairs aren't kind to heels."

"Or to black. I thought it wouldn't show the dust and cobwebs, but I'm already covered. Honestly, I need to make a trip to the country store and get some sensible shoes if I'm going to stay here much longer." She glanced up at the low beams and network of pipes. "Doesn't it give you the creeps down here?"

Heather shook her head. "Not really, no."

"You don't ever get spooked in your work?"

"What do you mean? Do I worry about ghosts and skeletons and that sort of thing?"

Adrienne laughed. "From your reaction, I guess not. You're very practical, Heather. You must have to be in your work. A rusty nail is a far more realistic concern than a ghost." She shifted her gaze to a wall where old tools, obviously long unused, hung on nails and pegs. "It doesn't look as if anyone's been down here in decades, does it?"

"That's because Vic's owned the house for decades," Heather said lightly.

"Mmm. I doubt he's ever been down here. I haven't, either, during the time I've been house-sitting. What are you up to?"

"Just looking at whatever might be relevant to the renovations."

" 'Measure twice, cut once'?"

"Something like that. We try to head off as many problems as we can with careful planning, but there are always surprises." Heather stepped out of the dark corner, into the slightly better light from a bulb screwed into a socket. "Not that I'm a great planner in my personal life."

"Ack," Adrienne said cheerfully. "Who is?"

Heather smiled. "Good point."

"Look at Vic. Do you think he meant to be alone at sixty-two?" She held up a hand. "Never mind. It's none of my business. He's been great to let me stay here in exchange for very little work." She ran her fingertips over the worn wood of a workbench, scarred from long-ago projects. "Vic's getting rid of this, isn't he? I've gathered he's not the handy type."

"He's keeping it around in case there's a need for it," Heather said. "There's plenty of room down here."

"Sure is." Adrienne stood straight, clearly reluctant to continue. She took a deep breath. "What about this Brody character, Heather? I know he grew up on the lake, but he's a federal agent now. Doesn't that freak you out a little?"

It freaked her out more that he'd grown up in Knights Bridge and had a past with her brothers, but Heather didn't know why any of it should matter. He was one sexy guy, and she'd noticed. Better if she hadn't.

"Heather?"

"Sorry. Mind wandering. I looked him up on the internet last night."

"I did, too!" Adrienne covered her mouth with one hand, as if she were afraid she'd been too loud and Brody would hear her. "I wonder if he knows, being a DSS agent and all."

That had occurred to Heather during her late-night internet wandering. "I can't imagine he would care if he did know."

"More likely he'd find out about me since I'm on Vic's Wi-Fi. Brody would tell us if there was any danger, though, wouldn't he?"

"Is there any reason to think he could be here because of a threat?" Heather asked. "Have you noticed anything suspicious?"

"Not at all. Well, just Vic's taste in wine."

Adrienne winced. "Sorry. That was a lame attempt to calm my nerves. I don't know why I'm on edge. I've stayed here by myself on and off since early December and haven't once had a problem."

"It's easy to read into why Brody is here when we don't actually know."

"That's true. There's no reason to believe he's here in any sort of security capacity. We could just be picking up on Vic's ambivalence about retiring. He's still relatively young, and he's used to a more nomadic lifestyle."

"Brody and my brothers have a history. You could be picking up on that, too. You're more intuitive than I am." Heather grinned. "Sometimes I need a rock to the head to tune in."

"A defense mechanism given your five older brothers, maybe. Vic's never said so in as many words, but I gather they're a tough lot."

"Depends on your point of view, I guess. Justin and Adam will be up to look at the place. You can meet them and see for yourself. You're staying on for a while, right?"

Adrienne nodded, looking more relaxed. "I'm trying to get ahead on my wine blog. It's always a struggle to balance planning and spontaneity. I just like to sample wines and talk about them."

"You also know what you're talking about," Heather pointed out.

"I suppose. I try to be honest and accurate. I never refer to myself as a wine expert. There are real experts out there. I'm not sure how long I'll keep up my blog. I've been doing more and more consulting, helping to create wine lists for restaurants and personal wine cellars. I can do a lot of that by email." Adrienne paused, glancing around the dusty corner. "Vic said you wanted to talk to me. Is this where you want to install his wine cellar?"

"I think so, yes. I have just a few more questions for you."

"Great. There are so many options for wine cellars these days. More fun to talk about wine than to ponder Vic and his DSS agent friend, don't you think?"

Heather smiled but didn't answer. She launched into her questions about what would constitute a proper wine cellar for Vic, given his lifestyle and budget. For once, she would heed her brothers' advice and keep her distance from Brody Hancock and whatever he was up to in Knights Bridge.

Six

Vic put his tablet aside and sprang to his feet, restless and out of sorts. It was his third time up and out of his comfy chair since breakfast. First he'd gone upstairs, convinced he should tackle a cedar-lined closet filled with boxes of junk he'd shoved in there when he first bought the house twenty years ago. Couldn't get into it. He'd gone back to his chair. Then he'd checked on Rohan, who'd wandered off — this time safely to his bed in the back room. He was such a cute little fellow. How could anyone dump him out here in the cold?

Now — the third time to his feet — Vic figured he would distract himself by filling the wood box, but it was already full. Adrienne's doing, no doubt. Maybe Brody's. Not Heather's. She hadn't emerged from the cellar since first thing that morning. It was noon now. Was she going to *eat* down there?

He went to stir the fire, but it didn't need stirring.

He raked a hand over his head in frustration. A big house like this, and he didn't know what to do with himself.

Not true. He knew. He just didn't want to do any of it.

One more solo Scrabble game on his iPad, though, and he would go out of his mind.

Adrienne had come up from the cellar and gone off to another part of the house to work, she said, on his wine list. Vic realized she was at some kind of turning point and was figuring out her life. House-sitting for him while continuing to consult and work on her blog gave her a chance to catch her breath, put things on pause before she made any major changes. He suspected there was a love affair gone bad in her recent past, but she hadn't mentioned a broken heart, and he hadn't asked.

He could see Adrienne with a man like Brody. She was restless, adventurous. She would be suited to his life as a DSS agent.

Vic wasn't sure what Brody knew about wine, though.

He gave an inward groan. He felt like a worm in hot ashes. Peas on a hot knife.

"Crazy," he muttered.

Pacing and grumbling wouldn't get him

anywhere. Brody had made a good point. Vic hadn't wanted to hear it, but the truth was, he wasn't prepared for retirement. He was prepared for not working. Two different things. Mentally and financially, he was fine. It was figuring out what to do with himself day to day that was killing him. His delight and relief at having free time and limited obligations — being out of the pressure cooker of his life as a senior Foreign Service officer — had quickly shifted to . . . *what the hell am I going to do for the next thirty years?* Both his parents had lived into their nineties. Odds were pretty good he wasn't in for an early grave.

"I should fire the housekeeper and clean the place myself," he said under his breath. "That would give me something to do."

Adrienne appeared in the double doorway between the living room and the dining room. She placed a hand on the woodwork, frowning at him with obvious concern. "Vic? You okay?"

"Yeah, yeah. Talking to myself."

"One of the perks of living out here on the lake." Adrienne shivered as she entered the living room and approached the roaring fire. "I had to run out to the car. It's colder than I thought out there. Why did you buy a place in Knights Bridge, Vic? There are so many places where you'd be more likely to find people who have more in common with you."

"Because Knights Bridge isn't any of those places. I love to visit friends, but being here . . ." He glanced around the room with its massive stone hearth and views of Echo Lake, now blanketed with snow glistening in the midday sun. His throat tightened with emotion, catching him by surprise. He wasn't used to choking up. "I don't have any connections in the area. Maybe that was part of the attraction. When I saw this place, I snapped it up. I never wanted to leave."

"But you did leave. You've lived all over the world."

"I know. That was part of it. Knowing that Echo Lake was here, waiting for me."

Adrienne flopped onto the couch. "I think I get that. I'm not sure I would have before I spent time here. You haven't done much with the house since you bought it. Were you waiting to retire and do everything at once?"

"I didn't think about it that much. Everything worked okay. When I started to think about retiring, I figured it was time to update the place."

"Make it your dream house."

He shrugged. "I guess. I still have to decide what furnishings to keep and what to toss. Some of the furniture was already here. Most of the dishes were, too. No wineglasses, though. The previous owner was a teetotaler. She was the granddaughter of the couple who built the house. She was what we used to call a spinster. I never met her. I wonder if she haunts the place."

Vic noticed Adrienne giving him a worried look and hoped he wasn't babbling. He felt off balance, uncertain of himself in a way he rarely was. The odd incidents he'd reported to Brody had unsettled him, but he knew they were probably nothing. The overactive imagination of a man with too much time on his hands.

What if he *was* losing his marbles? What if this was the start down the slippery slope of dementia? Just because his parents hadn't suffered from it didn't mean he wouldn't. He'd had an aunt who'd gone down that road, deteriorating before his eyes. A smart, sweet old gal . . .

Vic waved a hand, dismissing his own wild thinking. He wasn't suffering from early dementia. He just needed to find out what was going on with these unexplained incidents.

Adrienne got to her feet, obviously as restless as he was. "Vic, you look preoccupied.

Is there anything I can do?"

"No, no, it's nothing. Mind wandering." He didn't need her fretting about him. "Did you come in here to ask me something? What can I do for you?"

"I'm going to run into town for a few things. I thought I'd stop at the library. Do you have a library card?"

A library card. He loved to read but next someone would mention the local garden club. Bird-watching. Volunteering at the senior center. He was only sixty-two.

Maybe he'd pulled the trigger on retirement too soon.

He breathed out slowly, noticing Adrienne's increasingly concerned look. He made an effort to smile. "A library card."

"Right. I thought I might be able to use it. Vic — are you sure you're all right?"

"I am, yes. I'm just panicking about being retired. I decided to get out of the pressure cooker first and then figure out what to do with myself. Everyone tells you not to do it that way, but I didn't listen. I probably should have taken a vacation and done some soul-searching and planning before I called it quits."

"There must be all sorts of things you can do given your experience," Adrienne said. "Of course, you might want something altogether different now. For what it's worth, I think you should do what you enjoy and never mind anything else. You're lucky that you can afford to retire at your age and that you have so many options available to you."

"So I am," Vic said, chastened. "I thought retirement would come naturally, like being a kid."

"When you're a kid, you've got parents, school — structure. Now you're in charge." Adrienne smiled suddenly. "Well, you enjoy wine, right?"

"I do, but I don't drink too much — and I don't drink alone."

"Definite pluses. Learning more about wine can keep you occupied for decades. My mother loves that I know a bit about wine. It gives her bragging rights. Very important, you know."

"How is your mother, Adrienne?"

"The same."

"She's never remarried," Vic said.

"Nope. She won't, either. She and my father were divorced when I was seven, so it's been a while. She loves being on her own. My father remarried, but you know that. I don't see much of him."

"I haven't seen either of them in far too long. We used to run into each other at the occasional cocktail party when they were married."

"My father would be quite happy never to attend another cocktail party, but my mother still loves to dress up and impress people."

Vic heard a note of bitterness — even shrillness — in Adrienne's tone. "But you get along with both of them?"

"Oh, sure. I figured out by the time I was four that Sophia Portale would never be a warm, fuzzy mother. I made my peace with that inalterable fact later on. She's game for anything, though, I'll give her that. I learned to take risks because of her."

"And your father?" Vic asked, remembering a quiet, intelligent man who couldn't keep pace with his high-energy wife — who perhaps had been attracted to her because of their different natures.

"He's there but not there. I don't know how else to describe him or our relationship. It's just . . ." Adrienne paused. "Neutral."

"I suppose we all come to see our parents as flawed human beings at some point in our lives."

"I suppose. There's no animosity between us. That's good, anyway. Do you regret not having someone in your life, Vic?"

"Someone permanent, you mean." He

didn't make it a question. "I don't know. I kept telling myself there's time. Perhaps there is, but the sand's running out of the hourglass, that's for damn sure."

Adrienne put her hands palm up in front of the fire. At least she'd stopped shivering. "There's always your neighbor up the road."

"What neighbor? You mean Elly? Elly O'Dunn?" Vic laughed in disbelief. "You don't play matchmaker for your friends, do you, Adrienne?"

She scoffed at him, her cheeks red now from her proximity to the fire. "Within a few miles of where you are standing right now, Vic Scarlatti, is a pretty redheaded widow who raises goats. I can see you getting into goats. Elly produces the milk for her daughter's goat's milk soap. Another daughter is marrying a billionaire. The two youngest are twins, both getting graduate degrees in theater." Adrienne grinned at him and kissed him on the cheek. "Honestly, Vic, I can see you roping goats in the back forty and reading Shakespeare on the front porch. Elly has a big garden, too. I've only seen it covered in snow. She cans her own tomatoes."

Vic gave a mock shudder, although he rather liked the idea of canning his own tomatoes. And he loved Shakespeare, of course. Goats, though. Last count, Elly had more than a dozen. He didn't know how she managed them on her own.

"You're tempted," Adrienne said.

"Don't you have wine to taste?"

"Actually, I still need to finish choosing wines for your cellar. My wish list is amazing. I've restricted myself to the probable size of your wine cellar but not to a budget. I'm pretending there are no limits to what you can afford."

"Ha."

"I'm going to get several blog entries out of this process."

"That's great. Have fun with it."

"Thanks for giving me this opportunity. Heather feels the same way about the renovations. You enjoy helping people get a leg up, don't you, Vic?"

"Who doesn't? But it's earned, in both cases. I'm not a soft touch."

"Why Knights Bridge?"

Her question took him by surprise, but then he noticed Brody walking through the dining room toward them. He was stronger, fitter and far more controlled than he'd been as a teenager — and he wasn't aimless anymore, unaware of the opportunities and possibilities available to him outside Knights Bridge, or even within his small hometown.

His happy-go-lucky father and pie-in-the-sky mother had done the best they could with their only son, but had often scratched their heads. Brody might as well have been a throwback to one of Samantha Bennett's pirates.

Vic had heard about Samantha and her romance with Justin Sloan from Elly O'Dunn.

His *neighbor.* His *friend.* Nothing more. He'd met her husband, a kind, troubled man who'd left his wife and four daughters far too soon.

A reminder, Vic thought, that he had no complaints worth fretting about.

He pulled himself out of his thoughts — mind wandering again — and saw Brody was at the fireplace, pulling back the screen and placing a log on the crackling flames. "That's a good question," he said, replacing the screen and turning to Vic. "I don't think I've ever asked why you decided on Knights Bridge. You don't have family in the area."

"Schenectady." He grunted. "Close enough."

"Who's there?" Adrienne asked.

"A few cousins I never see. I was an only child. My folks had me in their midthirties after they figured they couldn't have kids. I was the proverbial surprise package. They

118

pulled out the stops for me, and ingrate that I was, I felt suffocated. I went to Harvard and came out here one weekend to get away from it all. I pitched a tent on the shores of Echo Lake. Twenty years later, when this place went on the market, I made an offer and now here we are."

"Did you return to Knights Bridge in the years between coming out here for the first time and buying this place?" Adrienne asked.

"Often, yes. Didn't matter the weather, I always pitched a tent."

She smiled. "I don't see you in a tent."

"You should see some of the places I've lived during my career. Compared to some of them, camping on the shores of Echo Lake is five-star living. I had a tent, a warm sleeping bag, a cooking stove, potable water, plenty of food. I'd listen to the critters in the woods and the lapping of the lake on the shore." He stared at the fire, seeing himself in his twenties and thirties, wanting nothing more than a few nights on Echo Lake. "I always came here alone. I don't know why."

Adrienne nodded thoughtfully. "Was this place unoccupied then?"

"Most of the time. The owner went into senior housing and then a nursing home.

She hung on to this property until her death. At least she never wrecked it with bad renovations."

"Now the Sloans can do their thing," Brody said without a detectable trace of sarcasm.

Vic pulled his gaze from the fire. He could feel melancholy creeping in, and that wasn't like him. "It's strange that I've been coming here for forty years, and yet I'm just getting to know Knights Bridge."

"Let's hope familiarity doesn't breed contempt."

Brody's comment, Vic suspected, was for the benefit of Heather Sloan, who came in through the main door off the entry. Brody must have spotted her. He would, since his job was to notice things. Heather gave him a look that was one or two notches under scathing and then smiled at Vic. "I need to talk to you whenever you have the time. No rush."

"But by the end of the day?"

"That would be great."

"Then there is a rush by my standards." Vic didn't know if Heather was picking up on his mood or if Brody had said something to her, but he found her unusually serious, even tense. He winked at her. "I'm trying to get into the spirit of retirement."

"It'll be easier to once the renovations are done," she said. "Even just getting past the planning stages and having the work started will make a difference. It can be hard when you're betwixt and between with such a huge project."

"New kitchen, new bathrooms, new wiring, wine cellar, sauna —"

Adrienne held up a hand. "Whoa, whoa. Who said anything about a sauna?"

Vic grinned. "I just added it to the list."

"Then we definitely need that chat," Heather said.

"Let's do it now." He realized how much better he suddenly felt. It wasn't the idea of a sauna by itself. It was *doing* something. He turned to Brody, who no doubt had followed every word of the conversation. "Is there anything you needed from me?"

Brody glanced at Heather as if he needed something from her — Vic couldn't imagine what — but then shook his head. "Nothing that can't wait."

"Excellent. Most of the time when a DSS agent shows up on my threshold, whatever he wants can't wait." Vic grabbed his tablet off his chair and pointed it toward the dining room. "Lead the way, Heather. Adrienne? Do you want to join us for our chat? I like my idea of a sauna. I like it a lot."

121

"I'd love to join you," she said.

Vic started to invite Brody, too, but his DSS agent friend was already on his way through the entry. In another moment, there was a draft as Brody went out on the front porch. The guy probably didn't notice the cold, Vic thought, as he followed the two women into the kitchen.

A sauna as well as a wine cellar.

He grinned. *What could be more perfect?*

After his chat with Heather and Adrienne, Vic slipped upstairs to his bedroom overlooking the lake. It would remain the master bedroom, but they would add a master bath and walk-in closet in the renovations. Nothing huge or extravagant, but it wasn't 1912 anymore. He wanted to retain the character of the room while modernizing. For some reason, it was a place where he could settle down and think. One of his strengths as a senior Foreign Service officer had been his ability to focus on a problem no matter what sort of chaos was reigning around him. He'd trusted his security details to keep him safe — the Brody Hancocks of his world — and then let his own training, education, experience and discipline go to work on tackling inevitably complex and often intractable problems.

His job had been all-consuming, but he'd always known who he was and what he needed to do.

He stood at double windows original to the house and looked out at the lake. He'd fallen in love with this area decades ago and had long dreamed of being here, with nothing more consequential on his mind than which wine to have with dinner.

Maybe that was his problem now. He had too much free time, too much peace and quiet. Too much solitude. They led to free-floating anxiety. He had nowhere to anchor his mind, no natural way to channel his thoughts.

He had never wanted to have anyone who depended on him. He hadn't wanted to matter to someone so much that it became a distraction. Selfish, maybe, but he'd been ambitious and restless, willing and able to go to where he could do some good at a moment's notice. With his responsibilities, the freedom of not having a wife and kids had appealed to him on a practical level. He knew himself, and he hadn't wanted a string of divorces. Kids who didn't know their father, or, worse, hated him.

Then there was always the belief — deep in the back of his mind — that there was still time. That the right woman would happen into his life and he'd have his happy-ever-after. Regardless, he'd never seen himself becoming a lonely old man, whether or not he remained single.

So why the hell had he called Brody? Why was he turning what anyone else would likely regard as normal incidents — normal life in an old house on an isolated lake — into potential threats?

No way to back out now without looking like a damn fool.

He'd long believed Brody needed to come back to Knights Bridge and make his peace, but that was an after-the-fact rationalization for having called him.

And what if he now was trying to down-play incidents that did, in fact, need an explanation?

Vic turned from the windows and got a photo album off an antique oak secretary he'd brought down from Schenectady. It was one of the few decent pieces of his own he'd added to the house. It had belonged to his mother's mother. It wasn't worth much to anyone but him, the unsentimental grandson.

He opened the album. He'd always been good if not perfect about logging photos, although he still had photos downstairs he needed to get into albums. It could be a retirement project. He didn't know who would want them once he was gone, but he enjoyed the process of placing them in albums, labeling them, reliving the moments he'd captured on his camera.

London, Moscow, Cairo, Beirut, Kabul . . .

His life in photos. He had digital albums now, too — which he also kept well organized — but he liked to have prints of the photos and put them in real albums.

This particular album went back to predigital days.

Back to Paris, thirty years ago.

He flipped to a page with photographs of him with Sophia Portale, Adrienne's mother. She'd been Sophia Cross then. She wasn't beautiful, but he'd found her utterly irresistible, with her gleaming dark hair, incisive dark eyes and seemingly inexhaustible sexual stamina. She'd had a kind of ruthless ambition and calculating approach to life that he would have expected to find repugnant but instead had found intoxicating.

At least for their five days together that April in Paris.

Later he attributed their affair to the gorgeous, romantic setting and the particular nature of Sophia's predatory self-absorption. She wasn't so much amoral as convinced her behavior was necessary to getting ahead in her world. Vic had known similarly narcissistic, driven men and women throughout his career, but he had remained steadfast in his refusal to believe their approach to life was necessary to succeed. "Cream and bastards rise," he would tell himself. "I'd rather be the cream."

Naive of him, maybe.

Before, during or after those five days in Paris, Sophia had neglected to mention the fiancé waiting for her in San Francisco.

Lovely, that, Vic thought, placing a fingertip within a breath of her face in the fading photograph. He could almost feel her smooth skin, the heat of her embrace. He had found out about the fiancé through a mutual friend a few days after Sophia had left Paris. He hadn't been hurt or surprised, just profoundly disgusted with himself. Of *course* she'd used him. That was what men and women like Sophia Cross Portale did. They used people.

Vic had put her and her bedroom gymnastics — her laughter, her dark, shining eyes, her legs wrapped around him — out of his mind and went on with his life and work as if Paris had never happened.

Sophia's marriage hadn't lasted, but he

126

wondered if she had softened with the birth of a daughter.

He shook his head. "Nah. No way."

He didn't need to tell Adrienne about Paris. He sensed in her a desire — a longing she knew would never be fulfilled — to have parents who loved her unconditionally, who focused on her and not just on themselves. It wasn't a need, really. Food, water, shelter, security — those were needs. The mother and father you wished you had?

Vic shrugged. "Luck of the draw."

You played the cards you were dealt. He'd been lucky with his parents. In many ways, so had Adrienne. Sophia and Richard Portale were interesting, successful and well-off. Maybe they could have done better by their daughter, but they hadn't. If house-sitting on Echo Lake helped Adrienne accept her parents' imperfections and move on with her own life, then it was a damn good thing she was doing.

"Oh, Sophia," Vic whispered, staring down at her smiling, heart-shaped face, feeling again the betrayal, the heartbreak, the ache of falling so hard and so fast for a woman who was incapable of loving him back. Sophia was wired to manipulate people. She would figure out what they wanted from her — who they wanted her to be — and use it to reel them in and get what *she* wanted.

Then she would dump them when they were no longer of any use to her.

A little harsh, perhaps, Vic thought, but essentially true. Richard Portale had escaped Sophia's grip early. Adrienne, their daughter, couldn't escape.

No wonder she was a wanderer, a lost soul with no real home.

Time to make peace with that.

Ah, yes, Vic thought, so much easier to figure out someone else's life, wasn't it?

He pulled his gaze from the photograph of Sophia of old. It was good Adrienne and Heather had become friends. Heather was solid and rooted, a woman who knew who she was and what she wanted and probably had since preschool. Knights Bridge was home for her in a way it would never be for him — or for Adrienne or Brody.

Maybe the two of them would hit it off.

But Vic thought of Heather's reaction to Brody earlier in the living room and hoped having him back in town wasn't throwing a grenade into her life.

Vic closed the album, aware his thoughts were pinging all over the place. He glanced at his watch. Not even two o'clock. The day stretched ahead of him like a giant yawn. What the hell was he going to do with himself?

Surely the fire had died down by now.

"More wood," he said, heading out of the bedroom.

SEVEN

By midafternoon, Heather was at Vic's kitchen table with a pot of tea as she typed up her notes from their conversation and her foray among old pipes, beams and cobwebs. Rohan was safely asleep on his bed in the mudroom. She could hear a man and woman talking in the dining room. Vic and Adrienne, no doubt. She hadn't seen Brody since she'd happened on him with Vic and Adrienne in the living room. For all she knew, being back in Knights Bridge for two nights had reconfirmed the wisdom of his original decision never to return, and he'd left town. She wondered if he had an apartment or a house somewhere in the US, or if he stayed with family and friends when he was on home leave.

She heard the back door creak open and shut. Rohan barely stirred as Brody entered the kitchen. He hadn't bothered with a jacket. He wore his dark sweater that seemed to accentuate his broad shoulders and taut abdomen.

Heather shut her laptop.

Nope. He hadn't left.

He greeted her with a curt nod. "Do you know where Vic is?"

"I think he and Adrienne are in the dining room."

Another nod and Brody went into the hall, presumably to find Vic.

Heather sprang to her feet and took her mug to the sink, not sure what was going on with her — why she felt so uneasy, so self-conscious. Why she kept noticing every little thing about Brody.

She dumped out the remains of her tea and put her mug into the dishwasher, shutting the door more firmly than was necessary.

Maybe she'd breathed in too much dust in the cellar, or she needed sunlight.

Something.

It couldn't be being in Brody's presence for all of thirty seconds.

She returned to the table and opened up her laptop again. She had to review the specs on the last of the custom millwork she needed to order. She had done a thorough check of the house and decided what could and couldn't be saved of the original trim, moldings, doors and the built-ins characteristic of an Arts and Crafts house. Vic, Mark Flanagan and she all agreed they wanted to modernize the house without sacrificing its unique character.

Heather was deep into typing when Brody returned to the kitchen. She glanced up. "One more number and I'm done with numbers for a while," she said.

He stood next to her. "A lot of what you do involves numbers?"

"Some days all I do is wade around in numbers."

"Is Vic hard to pin down, or does he know what he wants?"

"A little of both. He likes to consider every possibility."

"What about your brothers?" Brody asked, stepping back a little. "Are they involved in every decision on Vic's renovations?"

"Not every decision, at least not yet. Obviously, Eric and Christopher won't be. They help out sometimes, but they have full-time jobs."

"Cop and firefighter. When does the actual work on the renovations start?"

"Soon. Vic still has an apartment in New York. I don't think he's decided if he'll stay there or at the guesthouse here during renovations. They'll take a while."

"Would it be easier to tear down the house and start fresh?"

Heather shrugged. "In some ways, given what he wants, but it's a great house. It'll be fun to work on. I've enjoyed it so far. I'm thinking about pursuing interior design, and this project is giving me an idea of what that would entail." She sat back, not sure why she was telling him all this. "Interior design isn't the same as interior decorating. A lot of people confuse the two."

"Wouldn't want to do that," Brody said with a slight smile.

"Are you patronizing me, Brody Hancock?"

He laughed. "Never."

The amusement in his dark eyes — the almost imperceptible dimple in his left cheek — caught her by surprise. Her pulse raced. Her face felt flushed. She wished she still had her mug so she could take a gulp of tea to cover for her reaction. But would it do any good? Would an experienced federal agent see through her?

"Cobweb," he said, brushing above her eye with the tip of a finger. "Crawling around in the attic?"

His brief touch just about undid her. She cleared her throat, covering for her reaction. "The cellar. It's not my favorite place, but at least it's dry. That's a good sign."

"Do you like being in construction?"

"Sure. It's a good job. I'm fortunate I have work I enjoy. Are you surprised?"

"No, but I almost forgot the Sloan brothers had a baby sister."

Heather closed her laptop. "I made that big an impression, huh?"

"Let's just say you've changed since then."

"So have you. I didn't even recognize you at first." Now, why had she said *that*? She had a tendency to blurt things, but she had warned herself to exercise more self-control around Brody, given his history with her family and Knights Bridge and what he did for a living. "I recognize you now, of course."

"You stayed in Knights Bridge to work in the family business. Was that what you imagined at twelve?"

"I don't know at twelve. I think I imagined being swept off my feet by a swashbuckler. Do you remember Grace Webster? She was a legendary English and Latin teacher in town, before our time. Turns out she loved to read classic adventure novels. We've all been reading them lately. Well, I just started one."

"So you have swashbucklers on the mind," Brody said, his tone unreadable.

134

"Yes. Well . . . no. Not for real." She had to stop. *Stop, stop, stop.* "Anyway, I started working for my father in high school and kept up through college, and now here I am. It's a good job, and I enjoy the work. I'm very fortunate. This is the first big project I'm overseeing on my own. I do a lot of planning, ordering and bookkeeping, more so than hammering and nailing."

"But you can hammer and nail."

"Yes, I can. My father put a hammer in my Christmas stocking when I was two."

"I'll bet that's a true story. What about your mother?"

"She's supportive of whatever I want to do — within reason, of course. She's handy herself, but she says it's only because she can't get anyone to pick up a hammer or drill around the house."

"I can't imagine raising six kids."

"It was a madhouse growing up," Heather said with a laugh.

"Did you feel like you had something to prove as the youngest and only girl?"

"That's not something I ever waste time thinking about."

Brody touched a finger to the measuring tape she'd left on the table. "Meaning you do have something to prove."

"Not me. Nothing to prove." Heather eyed

him. Definitely not an easy man to read, but she doubted he was chatting with her just to get to know her better. He had another agenda. "You've known Vic since you were a teenager, but you've never turned up in Knights Bridge until now."

"That's a fact."

"Why now? Are you going to tell me?"

"I have told you."

"Because he invited you and it's time to see your land." Heather shook her head. "That's not why. Most people probably can't see past your broad shoulders and scary looks, but I have five brothers. I'm not intimidated. I know you're not telling me everything about why you're here."

"Good for you."

His comment didn't come across as either a compliment or an insult. Just another fact, maybe. She grabbed her measuring tape and laptop and got to her feet. "I read up on what you do," she said, trying to sound as if it hadn't made her break out in a cold sweat. "DSS agents are an elite group of federal agents who provide security at US embassies and consulates all over the world. You protect dignitaries visiting the US. You advise private citizens and companies on overseas security. You conduct criminal

investigations and hunt for fugitives overseas."

"All in a day's work."

"How many languages do you speak?"

"A few." He stood straight. "Are you looking to take a break?"

His non sequitur caught her off guard. "As
a matter of fact, I am."

"Good. You can hike out to my property
on the lake with me and tell me what else
you know."

"About what?"

"Life in Knights Bridge. Puppies. New
England winters. The Diplomatic Security
Service. Whatever." He nodded toward the
window over the sink. "It's cold out there. I
shouldn't go alone in these temperatures."

"You're not worried about the cold
weather or about going alone."

"But you'll come with me?"

It wasn't an order from a federal agent,
she realized. It was an invitation — or
maybe something between an invitation and
a request. A little of both, even. He could
want company on his walk out to his property but also want to seize the opportunity
to get more information out of her.

Although she had no idea what she could
know that would be of use to a federal agent.

With that unsettling thought, she grabbed

137

her vest off the back of the chair. Whatever Brody was up to, she wouldn't mind getting some air after crawling around in the cellar. Maybe she could turn the tables on him and find out for real why he was in Knights Bridge. Call it mad curiosity on her part, but being away from the house could get him to open up.

The exposure to him on the walk might also help her get control of her hyper-aware reaction to being close to him.

Now, *that* was a rationalization.

Heather zipped up her vest and followed Brody out into the cold winter afternoon. He might not intimidate her, but he wasn't one of her brothers.

Not even close.

A private, narrow dirt road, plowed but not sanded, wound past the end of Vic's driveway into the woods above the lake, then cut down to its western shore. The north shore of the lake and its adjoining woods were town conservation land. There were two small seasonal cottages on the eastern shore. The Hancock house had started its life as a summer cottage, but Brody and his parents had converted it into a year-round home, if only marginally so. Heather didn't know if they'd enlisted Sloan & Sons for help. Probably not.

Brody said nothing as the road curved down to the lake. Heather had no trouble matching his pace. He wasn't in any hurry, despite the cold temperatures. "Thinking about being back on your home turf?" she asked.

"A trip down memory lane? Not really." He glanced at her with a small smile. "Mostly I'm trying not to fall on my ass in front of you. There'd go my swashbuckler credentials."

"That'd do it," she said lightly. "I imagine it would be tough to go back to your DSS bosses and tell them you broke your wrist in a fall on the ice."

"I'd never live it down."

Heather realized he wasn't serious, nor was he worried about falling, although there were a few treacherous patches of ice where the packed snow had melted during the day and refrozen overnight. There'd be no melting today. It was too cold, even in the sun.

They continued down a steep section of the road. Brody kept his eyes pinned ahead of him. "Have you noticed anything unusual since you started coming out here?"

It wasn't what she'd expected him to say. "Unusual? Like what?"

"You tell me."

"I'd describe things as *new* rather than *unusual.* Vic's retired, Adrienne's house-sitting and now you show up."

"Have you been up here much on your own?"

"A few times."

"Then you have a key."

"I do, yes."

"Does anyone else have access to it?"

"Just me." She wasn't sure she liked his tone. "Why?"

"Making conversation."

"No, you're not. You're asking questions."

His pace slowed, and he turned to her. "You're blunt, aren't you?"

"Direct."

"When did you start coming out here on a regular basis?"

"After New Year's. On and off before that. Vic hired us last fall. I've been working directly with the architect, but the heavy lifting on that end is done."

"The architect is Mark Flanagan," Brody said.

"You remember him, then."

"He and I had a few classes together. Half the time he was asleep in the back of the room. I never saw him as a successful architect, that's for sure."

"He left town for a few years and then

came back. Same with my brother Brandon —"

"Who married Maggie O'Dunn, the next-younger sister of Phoebe the librarian, who is engaged to billionaire Noah Kendrick." Brody resumed his earlier pace as they came closer to the lake. "Maggie and Brandon were an item back in high school."

"I'm not sure I remember when they weren't together. Did you ever consider you might stay in Knights Bridge?"

"For ten minutes when I was twelve, maybe. You?"

"I never thought much about it. I went to college — I commuted, though. Knights Bridge has always been home. I imagine it always will be."

"So, why no man in your life?"

Heather almost slipped on the slick road. "Now, what kind of question is that?"

Brody shrugged. "An idle one. Old times' sake. We grew up together, right?"

"Not quite. You're older than I am. Doesn't matter. I've got no secrets. Anyone in Knights Bridge will probably give you a host of reasons as to why there's no man in my life. My brothers aren't a deterrent, if that's what you're thinking. I'm just busy right now with Vic's renovations and . . ." She abandoned her thought. "Why am I

141

explaining myself to you?"

"I don't know, Heather. Why are you?"

"No idea. I went to a movie before Christmas with a guy who told me we weren't meant for each other because he doesn't know how to fix things."

"Did you offer to give him a tutorial on running a power saw?"

"Ha-ha. No, I did not. He was being sarcastic. He knows how to fix things. He just didn't like it that I know, too."

"I know the type. He's from Knights Bridge?"

She shook her head. "Amherst. Friend of a friend."

"Not a friend of one of your brothers, then. Did he realize you have so many brothers?"

"Yeah, sure. It's not something I hide."

"You might want to hold off on saying 'I have five older brothers' until a guy gets to know you."

Heather grinned. "Eric tells me that, too." She noticed the road ended just ahead. "This guy also told me I look like my 'buff, professional firefighter brother.' His exact words."

"Meaning Christopher." Brody shook his head. "I'm not seeing it."

"He said it's my jaw. In his mind, I was

another Sloan brother."

"There's a strong family resemblance between you and your brothers, but no one would mistake you for a man, Heather."

"Well, thank you," she said.

Nineteen degrees out, and she wasn't even close to being cold. Walking within inches of Brody was keeping her quite warm. He didn't have to touch her. Not that she wanted him to, of course — not that she wanted to be thinking like that out here alone with him.

He stayed close to her as the road narrowed. "Knights Bridge is a small town," he said. "You must run into the occasional guy who has issues with your brothers and plays them out on you."

"Imagine that," Heather said half under her breath.

"I don't have issues with your brothers, Heather. Not any longer. If they have issues with me, they can take them up with me." Brody slowed his pace. "Are their problems your problems?"

"Not in the way you're thinking. We're a strong family. We care about each other and listen to each others' ideas and concerns, but I'm not under my brothers' thumbs. Now, what about you, Agent Hancock? Is there a woman in your life?"

"At the moment? No."

His tone didn't invite further comments or questions. Heather wasn't nosy by nature, but she did tend to speak her mind. "It's not easy to have a relationship given your work, is it?"

"Not lately."

"Because of where you've been posted, you mean. It's dangerous?"

Wrong question. She saw it right away. He went ahead of her. She paused, noticing how still and quiet it was, not even a chickadee chirping in the white pines and hemlocks. Just ahead, the road dead-ended at a small clearing.

Brody stepped into the untouched snow. "This is where we used to park our cars. No point keeping it plowed now." He glanced back at Heather. "You haven't answered my question about Vic."

"Have I noticed anything unusual?" She continued the short distance down to the clearing. "I'm not one to see danger at every turn."

"I didn't say there was any danger."

She shrugged. "Okay. If you could give me a hint about what you're after —"

"Anything that stood out to you as odd. Unexplained."

"The sorts of things that get your imagination running wild but aren't scary enough to get you to call the police?"

"That's a start."

"Not that I can think of, but I wouldn't necessarily notice." The man was all business. She followed him into the snow, grateful she'd worn proper boots today. "Is that why Vic asked you to come here? He's worried about something that's happened?"

"His imagination running wild is likely why he called me."

She could see the snow-covered lake through the trees, sparkling in the bright afternoon sun. "Are you on duty? You mentioned you're on home leave, but if you're concerned about Vic —"

"I'm here as Vic's friend, but I'm a DSS agent all the time. There is no 'on' and 'off' switch in the way you're thinking."

"It's like being married."

"I wouldn't say that."

His voice had lowered, and she realized her mistake. If only she would think before she spoke, at least with anything that could remotely be construed as involving sex. But if she wasn't one to agonize over every word, she also wasn't one to dwell on her screwups.

She'd just be more careful next time.

Or try, anyway.

At least he'd dropped the all-business tone, if only for a few seconds. She flicked snow off a branch on a white pine at the edge of the clearing. "Should I be worried?"

"No. Not that it would matter. You're a Sloan. You're not the worrying type. You're action oriented, and I don't need you taking action. Just tell me if you remember anything unusual or if something unusual happens. Don't you decide whether it's worth mentioning. If it's enough for you to wonder whether to tell me, it's enough to tell me."

"Got it. If Jacob Marley shows up in the attic dragging a chain, I'll definitely let you know."

Brody didn't laugh.

"Okay, okay," Heather tried not to let him see she was now ever so slightly intimidated by his role as a DSS agent. "I'll let you know if I think of anything or if anything strange happens. Right now, I can't remember ever thinking about calling Eric because of anything that's gone on up here."

"That's good."

He walked through the snow to a trail that wound through the trees. He motioned to her. "Come on. Let's walk down to the lake."

She hesitated, wondering if it'd been such

a good idea to join him on this little adventure. Finally, she followed him onto the snow-covered trail. "I can't remember exactly where your house is," she said.

"Other side of the clearing. It wasn't much of a house. My grandfather built it. My parents and I moved out here a couple years before they split up. My mother stayed in Amherst until my senior year in high school. She grew up in New England but couldn't wait to get to a warmer climate. I encouraged her. She was miserable. She loves Florida."

"Has she remarried?"

He shook his head. "My father hasn't, either. He says we're not the marrying kind."

"Maybe he and your mother aren't. That doesn't mean they get to write that script for you. You couldn't wait to leave town, either."

"I had some encouragement from a certain Sloan posse," he said with no hint of bitterness.

Heather wasn't going near that one, not now, at least. "And your father?"

"He liked it here well enough, but he needed a fresh start. I knew I wasn't sticking around. He took off for South Florida right after I graduated high school and turned eighteen. He's a fishing guide in the Florida Keys. He loves it. He says he likes to be able to fish year-round without having to drill holes in the ice."

Heather followed him past the spot where his house used to be. "You stayed in town the summer after graduation," she said.

"I lived out here on my own."

"Vic encouraged you after your parents moved to Florida?"

Brody nodded and pushed through the soft snow down to the lake, leaving no opening for further discussion. Heather joined him on the shore. A breeze stirred up the light snow out in the middle of the lake, but she couldn't feel it where they were standing.

"What happened to your house?" she asked.

"I demolished it the night I left town." He kept his gaze pinned on the lake, but it was obvious he wasn't seeing snow and ice or the winter blue sky, or feeling the cold. He was back to that summer when he'd lived out here on his own. "Call it my personal going-away party. It didn't take much effort to tear it down."

"How long after your feud with my brothers was this?"

"There was no feud."

"So what was it — a fight, a misunderstanding?"

Brody turned to her, his smile surprising her, disarming her. "A hell of a fight."

"A hell of a fight that involved pumpkins," she said.

He winked. "You have to love Knights Bridge, don't you?"

"There's more to the story, but I will let you enjoy being back here in peace. It's a beautiful spot, Brody."

"Yes, it is."

She thought she heard his voice crack slightly but couldn't be sure. For so controlled a man, it would amount to overwhelming emotion. "When you lived here as a kid, did you ever think you'd do the things you've done since then? Become a federal agent, travel the world, protect embassies, consulates, important people?"

"I doubt I knew what an embassy was, never mind a consulate."

"It's easier to talk to you than I thought it would be. Or does your job teach you how to draw people out? I'm not under suspicion, am I?"

"Under suspicion of being a good walking companion."

"So is Rohan," Heather said with a smile.

"You're at least as cute as Rohan."

"Cute?"

Brody grinned. "Thought you'd appreciate that. I didn't say cuddly, at least."

"That's good. Definitely. Cuddly would be almost as bad as saying I have Chris's jaw." She brushed snow off the top of a waist-high boulder. "Do you ever think about selling this land?"

"Sometimes. I'll have to figure that out at some point. Lakefront property is popular, but Echo Lake is out-of-the-way and largely undeveloped. Motorized boats aren't allowed on the water. There's no beach, no ice cream stand or clam shack."

"That's an attraction for some people."

"Vic, for one. He kayaks, but that's about it. He doesn't swim, a good thing, maybe, since the water's cold most of the time."

"I like swimming in colder water," Heather said. "Otherwise it feels like I'm in a bathtub. Did you notice the cold as a kid?"

"Yep. There's a cold spring right over there." He pointed to a small cove to their left. "Hit that, and you knew it. Have you ever gone swimming out here?"

"No, but I've dipped into some freezing-cold brooks."

His gaze lingered on the cove. Heather felt as if he'd gone somewhere else in his mind and wasn't with her on Echo Lake on a January afternoon. She studied him, unsure of whether he was aware of her next to him. She noted the line of his jaw, the shape of his mouth.

"I've had days when I would have loved to jump into that cove." He spoke quietly, without looking at her. "I wouldn't have complained about the cold water."

"You've worked in desert heat, haven't you?"

He pulled his gaze from the lake and shifted to her. His dark eyes were unreadable. "A hundred eighteen degrees with no shade."

"I've never been in that kind of heat. Right now it's hard enough to imagine fifty degrees."

"Are you cold?"

"Not really. I'm dressed for the weather today." She squinted out at the lake. "It's so quiet and beautiful here. When things get tough in your work, do you ever imagine yourself living here again? Building your own place? Or wouldn't that help because Echo Lake is in Knights Bridge?"

"It helps. Sometimes."

"But you have to keep your mind on your job."

"Don't we all? Letting your mind wander can lead to getting fingers chopped off in your line of work. Your brothers came out here a few times. Eric, Justin and Brandon, not Adam and Christopher."

"You've had nothing to do with them since you left town."

"That's right."

"You remember their names."

He smiled. "Burned into my brain."

"They didn't cut you any slack with that epic fight of yours, did they?"

"Not the Sloan style." He pulled off a glove. "They were right not to cut me any slack."

"They weren't nice about it, though, were they?"

He laughed. "No." With his ungloved hand, he adjusted her hat for her. "It was crooked. One side was about to cover your eye. I know you could have managed, but your gloves are covered in snow."

"That's what I get for playing in the snow. They're still warm, though."

He flicked a small clump of snow off her shoulder. "Thanks for walking out here with me, Heather."

"Anytime." She caught herself. "Well. I mean . . ." *Gad.* Desperate, she looked up toward the road. "We should get back."

Brody leaned in close to her. She didn't draw back, didn't say a word. "We should,"

152

he said softly.

Before she could respond, he kissed her on the lips, his mouth lingering on hers just long enough that she knew this wasn't an entirely impulsive act. Even so, she barely had a chance to react before he stood straight.

He smiled at her. "Might as well get that out of the way, don't you think?"

"Out of the way? Damn, that's romantic, Brody. Thanks."

His smile broadened. "You didn't object."

"I didn't say it wasn't pleasant." Because it *was* pleasant. Her heart was still racing. She took a breath, determined to remain as unaffected by the quick kiss as he seemed to be. "What are you planning to do, Agent Hancock — reel me in and break my heart so you can get back at my brothers and Knights Bridge?"

"Nothing that Machiavellian. I don't do revenge, and I don't reel in women with five older brothers." He spoke lightly, as if kissing her had given him an energy boost. He slung an arm over her shoulders. "Body heat helps prevent hypothermia."

"I'm not in danger of getting hypothermia, thank you very much. You're getting a kick out of this, aren't you?"

"Out of you, Heather. I'm getting a kick

153

out of you. Come on. Let's head back."

She found herself leaning into him as they walked up the trail to the road. He kept his arm over her shoulders. She resisted putting her arm around him. That would have been going too far. This was friendly.

Well, maybe a little more than friendly.

The wind picked up, chilling her face, but she could still feel his lips on hers. What she was in danger of, she knew, was being hopelessly attracted to this man — a federal agent who would clear out of Knights Bridge in a matter of days and likely never return.

She put the thought out of her mind when she and Brody reached the road. It was a long walk back to Vic's house, and she had work to do before she called it a day. She was an optimist, but she was also practical.

Besides, Brody showed no sign he wanted to repeat their kiss.

No sign he regretted it, either, Heather thought as she slipped out from under his arm, grabbed a fistful of snow and tossed it at him.

He batted it away and laughed. "What was that about?"

"Making sure your mind's on the road." She grinned at him. "It's good to be back home, isn't it?"

"It has its moments."

"Back there . . ." She shook excess snow off her gloves. "That was you at eighteen again."

He frowned at her. "Me at —" He smiled. "I see where you're going with this. Sorry, Heather, but no, it wasn't. I had a lot less control at eighteen than I do now."

Not again. She groaned to herself, but if nothing else, she'd just made sure she wouldn't be cold on the walk back to Vic's house.

EIGHT

Brody veered off to the guesthouse with a quick — almost curt — goodbye. When Heather arrived back in Vic's kitchen, she gathered up her stuff and got out of there. She didn't want to run into Vic and have him guess there was a bit of sexual tension crackling between her and Brody, and she needed to get her head back into her work.

She *was* working, after all.

She dismissed and suspected Brody had dismissed the kiss and the arm over the shoulders as arising from his emotions, however much he was trying to repress them, at being back at the spot where he'd grown up.

Easier to kiss her and fix her crooked hat than to acknowledge the impact of his return to his hometown.

Heather stopped at Frost Millworks, located in a modern building above a mid-nineteenth-century sawmill that had been converted into an apartment and storage. Jessica Frost had lived there until her September marriage to Mark Flanagan, and now Heather's brother Justin was renovating it. Technically, he was still living there, but he was spending most of his time with Samantha.

Randy and Louise Frost were the proprietors of Frost Millworks. Heather expected to find Louise in the small front office, but instead Randy was there, a solid man in his early fifties and a recently retired stalwart of the Knights Bridge volunteer firefighting force.

"I hear Brody Hancock's back in town," Randy said by way of greeting.

Heather wasn't surprised he knew. "Yep. He's staying up at Vic Scarlatti's place."

"How long's he in town?"

"I've no idea. He's not involved in renovations."

Randy eyed her. "Why are you so prickly?"

"I'm not. I don't want to have to explain Brody to everyone in town just because I'm working up there. I don't know anything. I don't even know why there's bad blood between him and my brothers. I don't want to know, either."

"Don't want to know?" Randy grinned. "That'd be a first for our Heather Sloan."

His infectious good nature made her smile. "Calling me nosy?"

"You like to be well-informed," he said, still grinning.

"That's true. I guess you're right, and I am prickly. Sorry. I don't know why Brody is here or how long he's staying. He and Vic Scarlatti are friends, and he still has property on the lake."

"He's also a federal agent. He's not expecting trouble here, is he?"

"I wondered the same thing, but I think he'd tell us if there was anything to worry about. I'm running behind today. I have a few questions about the rest of the order for Vic's renovations. Do you have a few minutes?"

Randy nodded. "Sure thing."

When they finished going over the order, Heather drove out to the offices of Sloan & Sons, located in the converted red-painted barn at her family homestead south of the village, instead of north where Echo Lake was located. Her father, Jack Sloan, a solid man in his early sixties, was in his worn chair with ten coffee mugs lined up on his desk.

Heather grinned at him. "That kind of day, huh, Pop?"

"Nah. I collected them from around this

place." He pointed a thick finger at the lineup. "Any of them yours?"

"Not a one."

"I'm having a meeting on leaving crap around here. Or maybe I won't, and I'll just knock some heads together. Not that it'd do any good. It was your mother's idea to get rid of disposable cups." He sighed heavily. "Look at the mold in that one. That predates the shift to real mugs. I found it in the office supply closet."

Heather sat on a chair next to his desk. "Pop, you know we're talking about coffee mugs, right?"

"I'm obsessed. It started this morning. It's like an Easter egg hunt, except all the eggs have gone bad. We need a dishpan where we can all put our mugs and then we wash them at the end of the day. What do you think?"

"Great idea."

"You don't care. My biggest problem of the day, and it doesn't move my one-and-only daughter's needle."

It wasn't Jack Sloan's biggest problem of the day, and they both knew it. Heather unzipped her vest but didn't take it off. She wasn't staying long. She hadn't bothered with her hat and gloves.

"Brody Hancock just left," her father said.

"Brody was *here*? Why didn't you say anything? Why are we talking about coffee mugs?" But when she noticed her father's eyebrows go up, she forced herself into a more neutral reaction. "What did he want?"

"To say hello."

She bet that wasn't all. "I see."

"You didn't tell us he's staying up at Vic Scarlatti's place."

"I told Eric and Justin this morning. It's not a big deal. It doesn't affect my work."

"Yeah. He said he drove you home last night."

"My truck —"

"Wouldn't start. Got that part, too." He pointed at the ceiling. "When you lived upstairs, I knew most everything that was going on with you."

Heather smiled and leaned toward him. "Why do you think I seized the moment to stay at Phoebe's house?" she asked him in a conspiratorial whisper.

"Brandon lives within spitting distance of Thistle Lane. Chris and Eric are close by, too."

"Going to put a spy detail on me, Pop?"

He grunted. "Tempting with a federal agent with a bad history in town driving you around in the dark."

"It was six o'clock, and he wasn't driving

me around. I'm not a kid anymore. I can handle myself."

"Yeah, yeah. Don't remind me."

Heather knew he wasn't serious about being overprotective. Half-serious, maybe. She sometimes joked that being the youngest of six and the only daughter came with certain privileges and responsibilities and a whole lot of scrutiny, no matter her age.

"What happened between Brody and my dear, kind, sweet brothers?" she asked.

Her father waved a hand. "Six kids — something was always going on. I couldn't hold a grudge for every scrap you all got into as teenagers or we'd never have stayed in town or in business." He got to his feet. He wore a heavy sweatshirt, faded work pants and scuffed boots, his uniform for as far back as Heather could remember. "Note my use of the past tense. Any scraps you all get into now that you're adults are your problem."

"So if Brody Hancock drives me home from work again, it's my problem?"

He ground his teeth. "Heather."

"I know. It's unsettling to have him back when he's a Diplomatic Security Service agent and Vic's a newly retired diplomat. Did Brody ask you any questions?"

"Like what?"

"About unusual goings-on, anything like that."

"No. I got the feeling he wanted to check out the place and see how we're doing, but he's a federal agent. Those guys are always looking for trouble."

"Where is he off to now?"

"He didn't say, and I didn't ask." Her father studied her a moment. "Heather . . ." He sighed. "Never mind. How are things going up at the Scarlatti place?"

Heather updated him on the renovations and some changes she wanted to make, as well as the wine cellar and potential sauna. "So far, so good," she said when she finished. "I need to check with Justin on a couple things. He's at the McCaffrey site?"

Her father nodded. "Brandon and Adam are out there, too. We'll be starting the Scarlatti work soon. It's good to have these large projects."

"Everything's going well on my end," Heather said.

"I've no doubt."

He followed her outside and stood in the driveway until she got her truck started. She grinned at him and waved, but he just shook his head and mouthed, "Get a new battery," as she shifted into first gear and headed out.

■ ■ ■

The house and "barn" Sloan & Sons was building for Dylan McCaffrey and now Olivia, his wife, Randy and Louise Frost's elder daughter, would be spectacular when completed. Mark Flanagan had done the design before tackling Vic Scarlatti's renovations. Both the house and barn would meld into the landscape of open, rolling fields, old stone walls and woodlands above the protected Quabbin wilderness. The property was located on Carriage Hill Road, which once wound through the now-flooded valley towns. It dead-ended at a Quabbin gate just past Olivia's destination inn, The Farm at Carriage Hill. Turning her 1803 center-chimney house into her own kind of inn had led her to contacting Dylan, who had unknowingly inherited a run-down house and overgrown yard, then a hopeless eyesore.

If only he could clean up the place, Olivia had pleaded, or let her clean it up . . .

Now they were married and on an extended honeymoon. Dylan, a very wealthy man, was still putting together what came next for him now that NAK, Inc., the San Diego–based company he'd helped grow with Noah Kendrick, had gone public, leaving them both at loose ends. An ex-NHL hockey player and a high-tech genius — not typical friends, maybe, but obviously the best of friends.

And now both were in love with women from Knights Bridge.

Heather found Justin and Brandon, her middle brother, in what would be the kitchen, its generous windows looking out at the back fields and Carriage Hill itself, the namesake for the road and Olivia's inn. Heather had hiked to the summit countless times, by herself, with her brothers, with friends. She would soak in the views of the sprawling reservoir in the valley where less than a hundred years ago the three branches of the Swift River once meandered through four small towns, now gone, a part of history.

"Brody stopped to see Pop," Justin said as he shut down his laptop. "He tell you?"

"Pop did, not Brody." Heather kept her tone matter-of-fact. "I haven't seen Brody since I left Vic's."

Her second-eldest brother stood back, eyeing her. "Anything going on out there, Heather?"

Anything going on — like Brody kissing her? Thinking about the touch of his lips on

164

hers made her feel warm, but she covered for herself with a shrug. "Not that I know of. Why? Do you have any reason to think there's something going on?"

"I don't, no," Justin said.

Brandon looked up from a nail gun he was fiddling with on a sawhorse worktable. "Does Brody?"

Heather decided to tell them. "He asked me if I've noticed any unusual incidents. I haven't."

Justin grimaced. "Why would he ask that?"

"A natural thing for a DSS agent to ask, maybe. I don't know, though. It's none of my business. I'm out there to work."

"Hold that thought," Brandon said.

He sat on a high stool at the worktable. Heather knew he was more attuned than Justin to when she was trying to hide something. Even worse were Adam and especially Christopher, both closer to her in age. Normally, she didn't mind her brothers' questions since she was open by nature and rarely had anything she didn't want to talk about with them. Her walk with Brody out to his property was one of those rare things.

Justin closed his laptop. "If Brody's concerned about Vic Scarlatti's safety or mental state, maybe you shouldn't go out there by yourself."

"I'm not by myself. Vic, Brody and Adrienne are there. I've been there alone a number of times and haven't run into any problems."

As if just to complicate her life, she saw Brody through the window in the back door.

What was he doing *here*?

So much for wanting to avoid her brothers. He had to be following her — except, of course, he'd visited her father before she'd stopped by. Still, she could feel a rush of self-consciousness that didn't bode well for the next few minutes of her life. She didn't know why she couldn't be more matter-of-fact about her reaction to him, but she couldn't. Even if she hadn't walked out to the lake with him — even if he hadn't kissed her — her emotions would be all lit up.

Justin glanced darkly at her then walked over and opened the door. "Hey, Brody."

"Justin." Brody stepped inside. He didn't look ill at ease. "It hasn't gotten any warmer in Knights Bridge since I left." He nodded to Brandon. "Good to see you, Brandon."

"Welcome home."

If there was any sarcasm in Brandon's voice, Heather missed it. She unzipped her vest. She was boiling hot, but she figured

166

she could blame red cheeks or a sweaty brow on being inside, not on having Brody Hancock show up.

"What can we do for you?" Justin asked him.

"I was out and about and thought I'd stop by. I gather Heather here told you I was in town." Brody glanced around the unfinished kitchen. "This place is something. It's Grace Webster's old property, isn't it?"

Justin nodded. "She's in an assisted living facility in town."

"And now you're building this place for Dylan and Olivia McCaffrey. Turns out Dylan is Grace's long-lost grandson." Brody ran a fingertip over a windowsill where the sink would go; it and the cabinets would be among the last items installed. "I drove down the road and checked out Olivia's new venture."

"The Farm at Carriage Hill," Heather said.

His dark eyes settled on her. "The sign with the clump of chives is her work? Isn't she an artist?"

"Graphic designer," Brandon said. "Maggie's her business partner now."

Brody gave a small smile. "Maggie O'Dunn. Glad things worked out for you two."

"Thanks. We have two boys now, Aidan and Tyler."

"That's great." Brody sounded genuinely pleased. "Noah Kendrick is about to become your brother-in-law, I hear. I kind of figured Phoebe would end up surprising everyone. Dylan and Noah are both out of town right now, aren't they?"

It wasn't a casual question. Heather knew it, and she saw that her brothers did, too. Justin stiffened visibly. "That's right," he said.

"Come on, Brody," Heather said. "I'll give you the grand tour."

He nodded. "Sure. That'd be great."

She glanced at her two brothers. "Don't let us keep you from your work."

In other words, she could handle herself. Also, the house was full of carpenters, two electricians and a stonemason in the form of her brother Adam, who was fine-tuning his work on the hearth in the main gathering room, the first stop on Heather's tour. He and Brody exchanged a polite greeting. Adam was her quiet brother, not always easy for her — or anyone else — to read, but she got his message loud and clear. He wasn't any happier about Brody showing up at the work site than Justin and Brandon were.

Their uncle Pete was downright blunt

when they ran into him in what would be the library. He grunted at Brody. "Trouble returns."

Brody grinned. "So it does. Good to see you, Pete."

"Yeah. You, too. I guess you have to behave now that you're a federal agent."

Heather led Brody to the second floor. She stopped when they reached the top of the stairs. "It's a surprise you're back here. They'll adjust."

"I don't need them to adjust," he said.

Because he wouldn't be staying in Knights Bridge, she thought. She stood at a window and pointed to the barn Sloan & Sons was building. "That's where Dylan's adventure travel business will be based. He and Noah are also talking about doing some kind of entrepreneurial education retreats there. They're both still young and have so much experience, and they know everyone. They could bring in all sorts of guest lecturers. It could be great."

"Sounds it."

She showed Brody the rest of the house. The barn could wait for another day. It was further from completion, and she needed to get him on his way before any old tensions between him and her brothers worked their way to the surface.

She walked out to his car with him. She waited for him to open the driver's door before she let her own tension rise to the surface. "Are you investigating me, Brody?"

Her question didn't seem to catch him by surprise. "*Investigating* is too strong."

"Snooping? Would that work better?"

"I'm getting the lay of the land in Knights Bridge after all this time."

"Is it because I'm overseeing Vic's renovations? Do you think whatever is going on that you're not telling me traces back to me? Is that why you invited me to walk with you out to your property?" The cold penetrated her vest and sweatshirt and the wool layers underneath. "It's not why you kissed me, is it? Because then I'd have to slap you right here and now, and someone in the house would see —"

"Heather. It's not why I kissed you."

"All right, that's something, anyway. What about my brothers? Are you investigating them? Do you think one of them is harassing Vic?"

"It's best not to speculate."

"You don't trust anyone, do you?"

"This isn't a matter of trust."

She studied him. None of the approachability she'd experienced on their walk was in evidence now. He wasn't easy to talk to.

He struck her as remote — arrogant, even. Whether it was seeing her brothers again, the tour of Olivia and Dylan's new home or her — delayed regret over kissing her — didn't matter.

"Then what is it?" she asked him.

He put a hand on the car door. "Go home, Heather."

"What — are you making sure my family isn't taking advantage of Vic? Soaking him for money, that sort of thing? You stopped by here because Dylan is even wealthier than Vic. If we're soaking Vic, we're probably soaking Dylan, too. This is where the bad blood between you and my brothers comes in, doesn't it?"

He looked up at the sky as if it could provide answers, then sighed at her. "You're taking some pretty big leaps there, Heather."

"Maybe so, but I guarantee my family wouldn't have stayed in business in Knights Bridge for all this time if we were a bunch of charlatans."

"Take a few deep breaths. You'll see where I'm coming from."

"A few deep breaths? Are you patronizing me, Agent Hancock?"

He smiled. "Never."

She almost smiled. "Good." She watched as he got into his car. "You're not going to explain yourself, are you? You've said all you have to say."

"See you at Vic's tomorrow."

He shut the door and started the engine. Heather stood back as he reversed then drove down the sanded driveway. She headed for her truck, but Justin beat her to it. "You're flushed," her brother said.

"It's the cold."

"It's not the cold. You're mad. Brody was always straightforward. It can sting, that kind of in-your-face approach. He's found a place where it works for him. It never did here."

"I'm focusing on my work."

"That's what I want to hear."

"What's Samantha up to today?"

Justin softened. "Researching pirates."

"I'm glad you two hit it off," Heather said as she climbed into her truck, pleased she and Justin were parting on a note of mutual agreement.

When Heather arrived on Thistle Lane late that afternoon, her sister-in-law, Maggie, was sprinkling sand on the front walk. She barely looked up from her task when Heather joined her. "I walked over here and didn't have any trouble until I hit this one patch of ice. It snuck up on me." She pointed to the offending spot, now covered with sand. "That's all it took. Isn't that pathetic? I went right down on my behind."

Heather noticed a streak of snow and dirt on Maggie's right hip and upper thigh. "You weren't hurt, were you?"

She shook her head. She was hatless, her dark red hair and turquoise eyes a touch of color against the snowy landscape. "I'm glad there were no witnesses. Falling while ice-skating I can explain. Falling while walking to your front door — I feel uncoordinated."

"I'm sorry. I should have thrown some sand out here this morning."

"It's not your fault. I should know to be ever vigilant in January." Maggie squinted at Heather despite the gray dusk. "I brought you bread. Oatmeal and honey, one of your favorites. It's still warm from the oven."

"Thanks, Maggie. I'm out of food, and your bread is the best. Well, anything you cook is the best. Where are the boys?"

"They're at the library picking out books. Aidan's into sea otters these days. Ask him how many hairs on a sea otter. He'll tell you. Tyler's all about pirates right now, thanks to Samantha. Brandon's taking them ice-skating on the common after they're done at the library." Maggie stretched a little, wincing. "I think I'll pass on skating

173

and take a hot bath instead. What are you up to?"

"Quiet evening."

"Alone?"

"As a matter of fact, yes."

"My mother says you and Adrienne Portale have become friends."

"We get along well. We've talked about going to a movie together, but we haven't gotten around to it."

"She seems nice, but I've only met her once." Maggie set her sand cup on a porch step. "You got sucked into a whirlwind with this renovation project, didn't you? Doing your job, and here comes Vic Scarlatti and his dramas."

Heather sighed. "Brandon told you Brody Hancock is back in town."

"Brandon didn't need to tell me. It's all over town. A federal agent with a not-so-great history with your brothers turns up, people are going to talk."

"That's understandable, but I'm just doing my job."

Maggie looked dubious. "My mother predicted Vic would need time to settle down after the life he's led. She thinks he's too young to retire, especially for a diplomat. He needs stuff to do besides look after a stray golden retriever puppy and watch you work."

"He's helping decide on wines for his wine cellar, too."

"Oh. Well, there you go. That'll keep him occupied for, what — a day? He's used to being busy and important, and now he's just another guy."

Heather shrugged, feeling the cold now. "Maybe that's what he wants."

"And maybe it's what he *thinks* he wants," Maggie said. "Or he's sincere and didn't realize he needed a transition period. Maybe he still doesn't realize it."

"Brody could be here simply because Vic's retired now and has time for company." Heather motioned toward the front door. "Do you want to come inside for a minute?"

"No, I can't stay. I left the bread on your doormat." Her sister-in-law tilted her head back, seemingly oblivious to the dropping temperature. "You were, what, twelve when Brody left town? Do you remember much about him?"

"Not really, no. Do you?"

"He was a bad boy in a way the rest of your brothers never were. He got out of Knights Bridge before he could do real damage to himself or anyone else. My mother says she asked Vic once what happened to him. Vic didn't go into detail, but

175

she figured out he'd gone into security work and hadn't ended up in prison. She didn't realize he was with the Diplomatic Security Service. Of course, she knew he still has property on Echo Lake."

In addition to being Vic Scarlatti's closest neighbor, Elly O'Dunn worked in the town offices and knew just about everything that went on in Knights Bridge. "Did Brody leave behind any broken hearts when he left town?"

"Now, why would you ask that, Heather Sloan?"

"Curiosity."

"Uh-huh. Sure. To answer your question, Brody wasn't that kind of bad boy, at least not that I ever knew. He was more of an 'it seemed like a good idea at the time' trouble-maker. He didn't have much supervision or guidance. His mother was mostly absentee during his teen years, and his father was oblivious and probably did worse things in his day than Brody ever considered doing. Brody was never arrested, but he came right up to that line a few times."

"Vic helped get him turned around?"

Maggie nodded. "Apparently something Vic said must have sunk in, and that's how Brody became a DSS agent. I never would have guessed." She started down the walk toward Thistle Lane, hopping over the treacherous spot, even though it was now sanded. She stopped, glancing back at Heather. "Brody won't be here for long, Heather. You know that, don't you?"

"Honestly, Maggie, my only interest is doing a good job on the renovations."

"Sexy, dangerous guys with an agenda don't interest you? Never mind. Don't answer. Then I'd have to tell Brandon since we keep no secrets from each other." Maggie stepped onto the narrow lane. "He and Dylan are in touch about their first adventure travel trip. I doubt Dylan will go on many of the trips himself, but he seems to enjoy the planning. I think combining adventure travel and Sloan & Sons is going to work out well for Brandon. He's happier in his own skin than I've seen him in a long time."

"That's great," Heather said.

"Yeah. This time last year, I didn't think we'd get back together." Maggie adjusted a bright blue scarf around her neck. "Neither of us misses Boston. We both love being back in Knights Bridge, raising our boys here. We never hated it here the way Brody did."

"Maggie . . ." Heather picked up Maggie's cup of sand off the porch step. "I don't want you to worry about me, okay? I'm not getting mixed up in Vic Scarlatti's life while I'm on this job. I know where my lines are."

"That makes a lot of sense to me. Enjoy the bread. My mother says hi, by the way. She asked about the puppy. Still no luck finding out if he's lost or was abandoned?"

"No luck at all," Heather said. "He can't be from town, or your mother would know."

Maggie laughed. "True."

"How does she like Southern California?"

"She says she misses the cold weather." Maggie grinned. "She was not serious."

"And Phoebe?"

"Phoebe and Noah are one of those couples who are meant to be."

It was almost dark when Maggie continued down Thistle Lane toward the library. Heather sprinkled the rest of the sand onto the porch steps and collected the bread, now barely warm under its foil wrap. Once inside, she put the bread on the kitchen counter and opened the freezer, getting out a container of some kind of soup Maggie had dropped off last week. Whatever kind it was, it would go with the bread. The country store would be open for another hour, but Heather didn't feel like grocery shopping. Maggie's soup and bread tonight, Smith's or toast in the morning.

"Works for me," she said aloud.

She sat at Phoebe's small kitchen table while the soup thawed. She debated going upstairs to fetch *The Scarlet Pimpernel*. Adventures and dangers, honor and romance — not at all like her own solid, predictable life filled with family and friends . . . but no man.

NINE

Brody stayed a few feet behind Rohan as the puppy trotted up Vic's driveway on his evening walk. It was dark, just enough light from the house to keep him from needing a flashlight. The temperature had dropped to twelve and stayed there. The cold felt good. Maybe it would clear his head. He'd awakened that morning thinking about Heather Sloan, and it looked as if he'd go to bed thinking about her.

Too much idle time on his hands.

When he'd set out for Knights Bridge, he hadn't considered that the youngest and only female Sloan was all grown up. Blue-eyed, shapely, fearless and charming.

"Damned if she didn't disarm me, Rohan."

The puppy stopped and relieved himself in the snow.

Brody grinned. "Smart dog. Take care of business and never mind anything else."

Rohan rolled on his back for no apparent reason then jumped up and dived after a small stone he'd spotted. He plopped down, chewing on the stone.

"So much for taking care of business, eh, pal? All right. Come on. Up on your feet, and let's head back."

Surprisingly, Rohan did as requested. It was a total coincidence, but Brody went with it. He hadn't had a dog since tenth grade and had never known much about the proper way to train a puppy, anyway.

He let Rohan lead him back down the driveway. Whether yesterday's mishap had taught him a lesson or he just wasn't interested tonight, the rambunctious retriever made no move for the woods and the lake. Brody didn't want to picture Heather grabbing the stuck puppy from the icy brook, but he did. That might have been when he'd first wanted to kiss her. At least he hadn't known she was a Sloan then, and his attraction to her had nothing to do with Knights Bridge history.

He'd planned to steer clear of the Sloans.

Well, plans changed.

The Sloans, however, didn't change. They were still solid, hard-working, stubborn and suspicious — at least of him.

And not for no reason.

He didn't regret kissing Heather, but he didn't plan to repeat that little maneuver, either. From her reaction, he doubted she regretted kissing him back, if only because he'd been right and they'd needed to get that out of the way. It'd been percolating between them since he'd watched her rescue Rohan yesterday.

In the end, though, they wouldn't go beyond a stolen, harmless kiss. Anything more would be madness. Wasn't happening. Heather belonged in Knights Bridge. He didn't. Nothing more to it than that.

He returned Rohan to the mudroom, but the puppy bounded into the kitchen, where Vic was chopping garlic at the counter. "You know, Rohan, my friend, I'm not your new master," Vic said, neatly hacking a garlic clove in half. "I'm your interim master. There's a difference. Look it up."

Rohan promptly sat on Vic's foot.

Brody grinned. "Twelve-week-old puppies are hard to resist."

"Golden retriever puppies are impossible to resist, period. Doesn't mean I know what to do with one." Vic set his paring knife on the counter and peeled off his chef's apron. "I'm making my mother's spaghetti sauce, but I'm missing a few ingredients, not because I can't find them in town but because I can't remember her recipe. It's been so long since I've cooked. Really cooked, not heating up something from the deli. You cook, Brody?"

"Some."

"Did you ever meet my mother?"

"Once. Little white-haired lady who thought you were the best."

"That was my mom. When was this?"

"Not long after my father and I moved out here. It was summer. You had us to a barbecue on the lake. We talked fishing. She said she loved to grill fresh trout."

"Damn . . . I don't remember. A barbecue?"

"We threw a grate over a fire in the sand."

"That's not a barbecue, Brody. That's a campfire. Anyway, I remember now. You were a pain in the ass."

"You were preoccupied with affairs of state. This is still the difference between us." Brody snatched a bit of fresh tomato Vic had already diced. "You think big thoughts and call for patience on all sides, and I get to be a pain in the ass."

"Ha. You do like things to be straightforward."

"They seldom are, even in my line of work."

Vic nodded thoughtfully. "What happened

in November wasn't straightforward, was it?"

"It still isn't."

"You left behind unfinished business. I know you hate that, but I expect you had no choice." Vic picked up his paring knife again. "How is Greg Rawlings doing?"

"He's recovered or close to it."

"That's good news, Brody. That's damn good news."

Brody didn't want to talk about November, and he couldn't — not here. He pointed at Vic's sauce-making ingredients. "Did your mother add red wine to her sauce?"

Vic's face lit up. "Wine! How could I forget? I'll get Adrienne to choose a bottle for tonight. A little for the sauce, a little for our glasses. Excellent. We're not having the sauce tonight, though. I'll never finish, and it should sit at least a day."

"Where's Adrienne now?"

"She went into town this afternoon, but she must be back by now. Probably by the fire. She's great, isn't she?" Vic peered at Brody, then sighed. "No sparks?"

"That's not why you invited me here, is it?"

"I exaggerate a few incidents so I can get you here and play matchmaker? It's a thought, but no, that's not why I invited you." Vic used his knife to scrape bits of garlic off the cutting board into the sink. "Go visit your folks, Brody. Visit Agent Rawlings. You don't get much time off. You need to enjoy it. I'm fine here. I don't know what got into me."

"Being around two attractive young women could be messing with your head."

"Could be. You know, I could try this matchmaking thing, after all —"

"Not on me," Brody said.

"How bad could it be? Things don't work out, you can go hide in some hot spot until the romantic coast is clear. Adrienne's an only child, but her mother's a barracuda. Heather — well, you know what you'd be in for if she fell for you and it didn't work out. I don't need to tell you."

"That's right, Vic. You don't need to tell me. In fact, you don't need to get involved in my love life at all."

"Do you have a love life, Brody? I don't mean a sex life. I mean a woman you want to come home to at night, a woman you want to be with when you're ninety and your parts are shriveled. You know what I'm saying?"

"I do. You're saying you wish you weren't sixty-two and alone, but you're not alone." Brody decided he wasn't having any of Vic's maudlin mood. "You've got Rohan, who is now chewing your shoe, a sure sign of true love."

Vic moaned. "That's Italian leather. Rohan!" When the puppy looked up with his brown eyes, Vic swore under his breath. "I'm not very good at being the alpha dog. Adrienne says I need to start crating him. Dogs naturally go to their den. Better than chewing an expensive shoe."

"Rohan will still chew your shoe, Vic," Brody said, heading for the back door. "He'll just chew it in his crate. See you later."

"I'm throwing a couple frozen pizzas in the oven."

"I'll be back."

Brody walked to the guesthouse in the dark, the crunch of the packed snow and sand under his feet the only sound. He should feel calm and safe here, but he didn't. He knew he was physically safe — not always the case — but he felt agitated and exposed, as if he were perched on the tip of a needle. He couldn't stay still and had nowhere to go but down.

It was emotions, he knew. Being back here. Vic and his problems, made-up or otherwise. The Sloans.

Heather and her easy wit and good humor.

Her sexy curves and deep blue eyes.

It didn't matter that she was attracted to him and he was attracted to her. Their kiss had been a little heat on a cold late-January day. A little fun — a little risk-taking — for a woman whose life had been laid out before her when she was born.

What Heather needed now was a reliable, sensible guy who loved Knights Bridge. They could build a nice, solid house in town. Have some kids. Get a dog.

Have a life together.

Brody felt himself tense as he came to the back entrance to the guesthouse. He wasn't that man. He never would be that man, not for Heather Sloan or any woman. Maybe Vic was right in pushing him toward a woman like Adrienne Portale.

Brody mounted the stone steps and opened the door with more force than was necessary. He hadn't bothered to lock it, an indication, maybe, of his opinion of Vic's "incidents."

He went inside and was relieved when his cell phone buzzed. He saw it was Greg Rawlings and answered. "What's up, Greg?"

"I'm on the case between my last couple of physical therapy appointments. This Scarlatti thing isn't urgent, is it?"

"No." Brody didn't know why he felt so

confident about his answer, but he did.

"That's what I thought. I've been reading Adrienne's wine blog. Is she as pretty in real life as her photo?"

"I haven't seen her photo."

"Okay, is she pretty?"

"Yeah. Sure."

"Not your type, huh?"

Brody turned on a floor lamp and took off his jacket, laying it across a chair. "That's not why I'm here."

"That's never stopped you before."

"We're not talking about me, Greg. How are you doing?"

"I'm getting cynical. I need distractions."

"Then you must be on the mend."

"I could go back to work now."

Brody sat on the sectional and waited for his friend and colleague to continue, but Greg was silent. It was one of those weighty silences Brody hated but had learned to wait out, at least on the job. Patience wasn't his long suit but sometimes it was the best option.

Finally, Greg heaved a sigh. "I'm the guy you don't want to be, Brody. They should have me come in to do training sessions. Here's how you screw up your personal life as a DSS agent. Works like a charm."

"A lot of people think you're a hero, Greg."

"They're fools if they do. You don't, do you, Brody? I don't have to come up there and beat some sense into you, do I?"

"You're bored."

"My big excitement today was perfecting correct spinal alignment." He muttered something unintelligible under his breath. "All right. I'll have more for you tomorrow. I think Adrienne Portale is . . . well, quite the wine lady."

"Wine lady, Greg?"

"She doesn't pitch herself as a wine expert. I don't know — what would you call her?"

"I'd go with wine expert. Wine aficionado."

"I can't say *aficionado.*"

"You just did."

"Only because I copied you. I'll forget the minute we hang up."

Greg Rawlings spoke seven languages. Brody wasn't buying into his friend's mood. "*Wine lady* might be a little patronizing."

"Ah. No wonder my wives have all left me, right?"

"One wife, and she hasn't left you."

"She's in Minnesota. I'm in New York. All

189

that needs to be said. I'll talk to you tomorrow."

Greg was gone. Brody stared a half beat at his blank screen then tossed his phone onto the cushion next to him. He stretched out his legs. He could build a fire before he headed back to Vic's and let the place warm up while he was at dinner. He could look up Adrienne's blog. He could check out the Sloan & Sons website, assuming they had one.

He did none of those things.

Even from his position on the couch, he could see the stars twinkling in the black evening sky. He pictured the surprise in Heather's eyes when she'd realized he was going to kiss her — that moment when he knew she wasn't going to tell him to back off. He could feel the softness of her mouth, the cold of her cheek as they'd stood on the shore of that frozen lake.

He blew out a breath.

He needed to get out of Knights Bridge. Soon.

By morning, Brody was refocused on finding a way to satisfy both himself and Vic that, in fact, nothing was going on with the "incidents." He wanted to clear out of Knights Bridge within twenty-four hours.

Reentry into his hometown was over and done with. Any resulting emotions were back in their cage.

It wasn't as cold as the past two days, either. Nineteen at nine in the morning. Not exactly warm, but it would get up to thirty by the afternoon. He skipped a hat and gloves when he headed outside and walked up to Vic's house.

As he rounded a curve in the driveway, he knew something was wrong. He automatically felt for his weapon, but it wasn't that kind of wrong.

Heather was to his left, just out of her truck, approaching the back entrance.

To his right, Vic was charging down the back steps holding Rohan. Rohan looked as if he were trying not to fall out of Vic's arms. Vic looked agitated, pale, in full tunnel-vision mode.

Heather immediately ran to them. "Vic, are you okay? Did something happen to Rohan?"

Vic didn't respond. Fight-or-flight mode, Brody thought, picking up his pace. He eased next to Heather and touched Vic's shoulder. "Vic. Talk to me. What's wrong?"

He jumped back, tightening his grip on Rohan. The puppy yelped, and Vic eased up. "Nothing." He choked out the word.

191

"Nothing's wrong."

"Where's Adrienne?" he asked.

Vic shook his head. "I don't know. I haven't seen her yet this morning. She was up early. I know because she made coffee." He was breathing rapidly now, his words clipped, his tone businesslike despite his obvious tension, as if he were giving a situation report after a breach of security at an embassy. "I imagine she's in her room."

Heather patted Rohan. "Here, Vic," she said gently, "let me take him."

He gave up the puppy, and she held him close, calming him, then set him gently on the driveway. He was shaky but Heather squatted down and patted him some more. He licked her hand.

Vic stared down at the puppy. "Poor little fella is picking up on my nuttiness," he said with a snort of self-disgust. "Sorry. I gave myself a fright."

"What kind of fright?" Brody asked.

Vic didn't answer. He was ashen, dressed in khakis, a sweater and fleece-lined slippers with no socks. Rohan bounded away from Heather into a snowbank. She stood and looked at Vic. "Should I call Eric?"

Vic shook his head. "No, no. We don't need to get the local cops here. We have Brody, and, anyway, it's nothing. I'm just tight as a piano wire these days. I was in the front room with Rohan and he got going in circles, and I figured I'd better get him out before he pooped on the floor. Puppies, you know? I ran to the front door with him and damned it if wasn't cracked open. I went out onto the porch and looked for footprints, but I didn't see any. We never use that door. Not this time of year. I keep it locked."

Heather frowned. "Maybe a wind gust —"

"It wasn't the wind," Vic said. "I don't know what it was. I grabbed Rohan and bolted back through the house and out here. I yelled for Adrienne, but she didn't answer. I don't know what I was thinking. A cracked door and I'm a wreck?"

Brody held up a hand. "I'll have a look. You and Heather stay here. Shout if you need me or if Adrienne turns up."

"She must be in the bathroom and that's why she didn't hear me." Vic shuddered. "Maybe the damn place is haunted."

Brody didn't respond. He took the porch steps in two leaps and went inside, heading through the kitchen and hall to the front room, a quiet, cozy fire burning, Vic's iPad and a book of crossword puzzles on his chair. In the entry, the front door was wide-open, letting in cold air. Brody noticed fresh footprints — Vic's — in the dusting of snow on the otherwise shoveled porch. Vic hadn't done the shoveling. He had a crew that came in after storms.

Brody turned as Adrienne came down the stairs, shivering, her arms crossed over her chest. "I was wondering why it was so cold. Good morning. It's —" She stopped abruptly, three steps from the bottom of the stairs. She was dressed for the day, all in black and elegant, but her skin was pale, her brow furrowed. "What's wrong?"

"Did you go through this door last night or this morning?"

She shook her head. "No. Why?"

"Vic found it cracked open. It unnerved him. He's outside with Rohan and Heather. Is anyone else here?"

"No, no one."

"No workers?"

"Not today that I know of."

"Are they sometimes dropped off, or do they always come in their own vehicles?"

"Both." She came down the last steps. "You're scaring me."

Brody softened his expression. "Just being thorough."

He escorted her back through the house and had her grab a coat and join Vic and Heather outside. Rohan was settled onto the driveway, chewing on a rock. Brody tossed Vic a jacket from the mudroom.

Ten minutes later, he'd checked the rest of the house. Downstairs, upstairs, attic, cellar.

No intruders. Nothing out of the ordinary.

He gave the all clear. They all came inside, and Brody shut the back door behind them. Rohan tried to sneak past him, but Vic tossed a treat into the kitchen and that did the trick. "He really is a cute little thing," Vic said as he joined the two women in the kitchen. "Rohan, I mean, not Brody, although I suppose — hell, I don't know. Rohan's an escape artist, but he can't open doors."

Brody went into the kitchen and stood by the counter as Heather and Adrienne sank into chairs at the table, breakfast dishes and toast crumbs not yet cleaned off. Vic paced, looking as if he'd rather be anywhere else.

"Why would an open door get to you?" Adrienne asked. "My heart's still hammering. I thought at least Brody would find a mischievous red squirrel or something."

Vic rubbed the back of his neck, obviously chastened. "I feel like a damn fool, but what can I say? This wasn't the first strange incident lately. They've all been like this. Not much, each nothing on its own. After a while, though, you start to wonder."

"Start to wonder what?" Heather asked.

Brody appreciated her bluntness and her bewilderment. It would take a lot for Heather Sloan to freak out over an open door. If it'd been her instead of Vic, she'd have shrugged it off and walked Rohan without thinking twice about it.

Adrienne was clearly as confused but not as calm. "Is this why you invited Brody here, Vic? Because of these strange incidents?"

"It's one reason." Vic glanced at Brody then sat at the square table, Adrienne to his left, Heather to his right. "I also knew he was on home leave after a rough few months on the job. I figured it was past time he returned to Knights Bridge."

Brody leaned against the counter and made no comment.

"Why past time?" Adrienne asked.

"He left at eighteen on a sour note." Vic waved a hand. "Never mind. Forget it. I'm being stupid."

Adrienne sat back in her chair. "What if these incidents aren't about you, Vic, but instead are about Brody? It's no secret you two are friends. What if someone wanted to get him here and knew you would call him if you got freaked out?" She shifted, turning to Heather. "What do you think? Do you know anyone who would want Brody back in Knights Bridge bad enough to sneak around and get under Vic's skin?"

Heather shook her head. "I don't know of anyone who would do something like that, period, for any reason."

"Yeah, too convoluted," Vic said. "People around here are more straightforward."

"You're probably right." Adrienne scooped toast crumbs into her palm and brushed them onto a plate. "When did these so-called incidents start?"

"I don't even know," Vic said. He looked spent, embarrassed. "I started noticing them after the first of the year. I've been back and forth between here and my apartment in New York since early December. If any-thing happened before Christmas, I didn't pay attention. Then all of a sudden, I'm like . . . what the hell's going on here?" He raked a hand over the top of his head. "I know it sounds crazy."

"We didn't say that," Adrienne said.

"I'm sorry you've been so worried," Heather said. "I wish you'd said something. I could have kept an eye out, but I'm not suspicious by nature — I haven't noticed anything out of the ordinary."

"See?" Vic winked. "Told you I'm off my rocker."

Brody stood straight. "It's a big house. It's old and drafty. Have you ever spent this much time here during the winter?"

"I've never spent this much time here in one stretch, period."

"Adrienne and I have been in and out a lot," Heather said. "Mark Flanagan and I have brought a few people through while we were drawing up initial plans for renovations. Maybe one of us inadvertently did something to cause some of these incidents."

"I doubt it." Vic sprang to his feet. "I've had to be evacuated from an embassy by the DSS and the marines, and I'm getting freaked out over nothing. Right now, I'm cold. I'll put on more coffee."

Brody stepped away from the counter. "I want a list of who's been here since the first of the year. Vic, Adrienne, Heather. I want you each to do your own list. Don't compare notes. Just write down everything you remember."

"Wow," Adrienne said as Brody started toward the dining room. "He's serious."

"DSS agents are accustomed to having people's lives in their hands," Vic said. "They don't screw around."

"That's not making me feel better, you know."

Brody noticed Heather hadn't said a

198

word. He opened drawers and found notebook paper and pens. He divided them up for Vic, Heather and Adrienne.

"Have coffee, jot down what you remember," Brody said. "I'll walk Rohan and be back in ten minutes."

He was in the mudroom when Vic shouted to him. "What if I have a secret lover that I don't want to admit to in front of Adrienne and Heather? What if *they* do? What if they've been sneaking guys in here —"

Brody grabbed Rohan and shut the back door before Vic could finish. It was bravado on the former ambassador's part. Vic Scarlatti cracking wise now that any perceived danger had passed.

But as Brody plopped Rohan on the shoveled walk, he wondered if he'd been presumptuous himself, thinking — assuming — that Heather had never had a rollicking love life. After all, what did he know about her? Just because there was no man in her life now didn't mean that had always been the case. For all he knew, she could have had a series of guys out here and tried out every bed and sofa with them. She wouldn't be the first woman he'd known who was into meaningless sex.

He shook his head, watching Rohan sniff a trail on the walk. Whatever Heather

Sloan's sexual proclivities, she wouldn't get away with reckless behavior in Knights Bridge. She wouldn't bring men back to a job site. Vic's renovations meant too much to her. Brody had seen that yesterday when he'd stopped by the Sloan & Sons offices — unchanged, except for computers, after fifteen years — and then when he'd stopped at the McCaffrey site. Whether she wanted to admit it or not, Heather had something to prove.

Brody wondered how many men in Knights Bridge were afraid to touch her.

He wasn't afraid. He just wasn't going to, not again — not in the way he wanted to.

A difference without a distinction, as Vic would say.

Brody shook off his thoughts and glanced at his watch. Four minutes to kill, and then he'd go see what Heather, Vic and Adrienne had on their lists. He doubted it would be much, certainly nothing that would lead to a stalker or anything remotely dangerous.

But something wasn't right on Echo Lake. It might not be dangerous, but he needed to go with his instincts and play this out. Find out what was going on.

Two more minutes.

Close enough.

He grabbed Rohan and headed back inside.

Ten

Vic had never been one to sound the alarm too soon — or too late, for that matter. If given an option, security types like Brody always preferred too soon, at least in Vic's experience. He preferred "just right." He hadn't wanted a reputation as a nervous type or a tough guy, both of which could stymie a career and, more important, put lives at risk unnecessarily.

While Brody went over their lists and Heather and Adrienne got to work on their respective jobs, Vic went down to the cellar to think about wine.

Wine was always good to think about. Much better than thinking about what a damn fool he was. He'd kept a cool head during multiple high-threat situations in his diplomatic career, but no one would remember his courage if word got out that he was wetting his pants over a few unexplained incidents at his lake house.

He pictured himself coming down to the cellar in a year or two to choose a couple of bottles of wine for dinner with friends — houseguests tired and content after a day kayaking on Echo Lake.

That was the life he wanted, he told himself as he brushed past cobwebs and turned on the overhead lightbulb. He imagined a sauna. Laughter.

A sauna really could work down here.

After a few minutes, he heard footfalls on the steep stairs, and Adrienne joined him in the corner she and Heather had selected for his wine cellar.

"Brody checked the front of the house and didn't see any unexplained footprints," she said then smiled. "Critter or human."

"Good. Excellent, in fact." Vic had to admit he wasn't surprised. He wished now he'd shut the damn door and gone about his business. "It must have been the wind, then."

"One of us could have unlocked the door and forgotten about it." Adrienne glanced around the dark corner, smiling as if she were imagining guests, dinners, wine parties and time in the sauna. "I love the idea of sitting on the front porch on a hot summer day with a chilled glass of a good pinot grigio."

"Are there any good pinot grigios?" Vic asked, trying to sound amused.

"Of course. Pinot grigio is much maligned but I have a very respectable one on my list for you."

"I'll save it for that hot summer day." Vic felt some of his embarrassment ease. "Do you think you'll still want to house-sit this summer?"

Adrienne hugged herself, obviously still cold. "I don't know."

"You're welcome to."

She smiled. "Thank you. You've been good to me." She shifted her dark eyes away from him, as if something on the old workbench had caught her attention. "Vic, did you and my mother have an affair all those years ago in Paris?"

He wasn't expecting that one. "That's not as out-of-the-blue a question as it sounds, is it?"

"I've been wondering for a while now."

"*A while* as in a few weeks or *a while* as in a few years?"

"A few months."

She hadn't hesitated. Vic cleared his throat and touched one of the old tools on the workbench. A wrench or pliers or some damn thing. He'd never been handy.

Heather would know. Brody would know, too.

"I've embarrassed you," Adrienne said quietly.

"No, no. It's not that. Caught me by surprise." He realized he'd got grease on his fingertip. Black gunk of some kind, anyway. It was something to anchor his mind on as he stalled Adrienne. He had no idea what to tell her. "I'm still recovering from the adrenaline dump after the incident with the door. Weak as a noodle."

"A fright will do that to you."

"I was more resilient when I was on the job and had real scares. Well, it doesn't matter now. Did Brody have any insights into our lists?"

"Not that he mentioned. Vic . . ."

"Talk to your mother about her past, Adrienne," he said softly.

"Not one to kiss and tell?" She smiled, but this time there was a distance in her eyes, a wariness, even. "I did talk to her. She said to talk to you."

"Then maybe the past should remain in the past." He grabbed an old rag, stiff and stained with who-knew-what, and wiped the grease off his fingers. "Maybe that's what your mother was trying to say."

"She's more direct than that. If she wanted

me to mind my own business, she'd have said so. You two met in Paris before I was born. It was before she and my father were married."

"Correct." He watched Adrienne pick up a small hammer from the workbench and smiled at her. "Not going to clobber me with that, are you?"

"What?" She seemed to need a moment to figure out what he'd said. "Good heavens, Vic, no. What's with the sick humor? No, I'm just nervous and looking for something to do with myself. Like you and that black stuff on your fingers. You're going to need soap and water for that, aren't you?"

"Probably, if not turpentine."

"Heather might have something in her truck you could use." Adrienne placed the hammer back on the workbench. "My mother wasn't the one who got away, was she, Vic? The woman you should have married — the woman you wish now you had married?"

"Your mother was engaged to your father when I met her," Vic said, sidestepping Adrienne's questions. "We weren't meant to be together."

"Forever or at all?"

"You don't give up, do you?"

"Tenacity has its place," Adrienne said

without any hint of defensiveness. "I never would have withstood the ups and downs of establishing a name for myself in the wine industry if I weren't tenacious."

"Good point," Vic said, dropping the rag on the workbench. It hadn't worked. He'd only smeared the gunk around some.

"You're dodging my questions, Vic."

He sighed. "And you're not taking the hint that I'm not going there."

She straightened, a stubborn set to her jaw. "Not confirming is confirming."

"Since when? Look, you're allowed to think what you want to think. I'm not going to argue with you, but I'm not going to talk about your mother, either. Why's this on your mind, anyway? Because you're staying here and got to thinking one day?"

"It occurred to me how alone you both are."

It wasn't an answer. Adrienne's turn to dodge, maybe. Vic grinned at her, desperate to change the subject. "I hope you're not having some fun trying to play match-maker."

She laughed, a relief to him. "Don't tempt me," she said. "Something's going on between Heather and Brody, don't you think?"

"What? Those two? Not a chance."

"Look again, Vic. Look again."

He pictured the two of them on the driveway when he'd bolted out of the house with Rohan. He hadn't noticed a thing. Had he been so self-absorbed he'd missed the sparks between them, or was Adrienne seeing something that wasn't there — like he was, or so it seemed, with his "incidents"?

Adrienne kissed him on the cheek. "I'm glad you got Brody here to help you put your mind at ease. I'm glad nothing happened this morning."

She didn't wait for him to respond and sailed up the stairs.

Vic noticed a cobweb and a spider right out of Harry Potter and went up, too.

Brody was alone in the kitchen. He'd poured coffee and sat at the table, feet up on another chair. He looked considerably less intense. "Heather took off." He set his mug on the table. "She said to tell you she's putting together sauna options for you."

"You don't think I need a sauna, do you?"

"There are needs and there are wants. A sauna would be a want."

Vic grinned, in spite of his general agitation. "Tell me that during the next nor'easter."

"I won't be here for the next nor'easter. I'm sure a sauna will come in handy. Next you'll want your own helicopter pad."

"That has a certain appeal, actually. Well, it did when I was important. Now I don't have anywhere I need to be that I would call a helicopter — certainly that anyone would send one. To be honest, I was never that important."

"But you were important," Brody said. "You had a great career. You could continue working, but you chose to retire."

"Retire to the country. Doesn't it have a good sound?"

"Depends. Are you hoping someone will try to persuade you to return to duty?"

"No. I quit cold turkey." Vic tapped the sheets of notebook paper on the table. "Anything interesting on our lists?"

"You have a milkman. That one floored me, Vic. A milkman?"

"One of life's real pleasures. It's a local dairy."

Brody was clearly mystified. He got up, took his mug to the sink and snatched the lists. "Later," he said, and left, off to do whatever it was Brody did. As many DSS agents as he'd worked with over the years, Vic had never delved too deeply into the specifics of what they did, when, why — or, for sure, how they operated when they weren't on assignment. Basically, he didn't want to know how men and women like

209

Brody thought. It might interfere with his own thinking, his ability to focus on his work.

In the past, of course. Now he had Brody's opinion on the necessity of a sauna and a milkman.

Vic headed upstairs to his bedroom, where it was quiet and he was out of earshot of Adrienne, who was again at work in the dining room. He sat on the bed and called her mother.

"Vic," Sophia said when she answered. "Adrienne texted me two minutes ago that she asked you about Paris, and you wouldn't tell her anything."

"That's right. I wanted to talk to you first." He stood, noting that gray clouds had formed over the lake. "What do you want me to tell her, Sophia?"

"Whatever you want to tell her. You're the diplomat. Adrienne is an adult, Vic. She knows I had a life before I married her father. And after, too, since he and I split so long ago."

Vic hadn't quite been *before* Adrienne's father. He'd been before their marriage, but that was splitting hairs. "Have you been happy?" he asked softly.

"Yes. Very." Sophia didn't hesitate, and her tone was brisk, as if she never gave such matters any thought. "I'm not that great a mother by Adrienne's standards, but she's turned out fine. Proof's in the pudding, right?"

She wasn't asking him, he realized. "You're proud of her."

"I'm thrilled she's able to do work she loves. Not everyone gets to. She's quite the nomad these days, but she seems to enjoy house-sitting for you. She's been out of the nest for a while now, Vic. We don't talk every week, never mind every day. We both have busy lives."

"You always liked your freedom."

"Who doesn't?"

Vic heard the impatience bordering on irritation in Sophia's voice. She'd never been one for introspection. All the thinking he'd done in recent weeks — she'd tell him he was wallowing in self-pity and should get on with his life, figure out what came next and do it. He doubted Sophia Cross Portale had ever had an indecisive moment in her sixty years. "I hate dithering," she'd told him so long ago.

He wouldn't tell her about the incidents. She'd laugh at his idiocy, and he already felt foolish enough.

Sophia wasn't the one who'd gotten away. If that was what Adrienne was hoping to hear, for whatever reason, she would be sadly disappointed.

"Look, Vic, I hate to cut this short, but I'm in New York for some meetings. Tell Adrienne whatever you think is best. That's what I did."

"We had less than a week together."

"I know. It meant nothing to either of us. It was an interlude. I've only good memories of our days together. The timing wasn't the greatest, I admit, but I suppose it should have been a wake-up call that Richard and I weren't going to work out. But we were young, and I wouldn't trade Adrienne for the world." She sniffed, taking charge. "Now. Off I go. I don't know how you retired at sixty-two, Vic. I can't believe you don't miss this."

"Enjoy your meetings," Vic said as she disconnected.

He stood at the window. The wind had picked up. He could feel the cold through the glass panes. He'd appreciate having an energy-efficient house once renovations were complete, but he'd miss the creaking and rattling of the old windows and doors — if not of turning them into a stalker.

"Ah, Sophia."

Her parting comment about his retirement hadn't been off hand. She'd wanted to remind him that she was still a player — to dig at him to make herself feel more important. He'd learned a long time ago not to let that sort of competitive jab get to him, whether from an ex-lover like Sophia or anyone else.

But he was raw from his scare that morning, and Sophia's jab had penetrated.

He remembered feeling as though he'd dodged a bullet when he'd found out she was engaged and he'd been a diversion before her wedding day. Her husband was a great guy, and somehow they'd all stayed in touch on and off despite going in three separate directions. Sophia was a special woman in many ways — witty, energetic, smart, driven — but she was also self-centered and emotionally controlling. Whatever you did or felt was fine with her provided it was what she wanted you to do or feel.

Deep down, Adrienne had to know that about her mother. Learning about his brief affair with Sophia in Paris wouldn't help Adrienne or tell her anything she didn't already know.

They'd had a hell of a time together, he and Sophia, all those years ago.

Below him in the front yard, Vic noticed Adrienne walking with Rohan. Brody joined her, but he turned back to the house while she and the puppy continued down to the lake. Vic stood by his opinion that Brody would do well with a woman like Adrienne — she would be suited to his own nomadic lifestyle as a DSS agent.

Heather was a homebody. She wasn't going anywhere, any more than one of the big old oak trees on the shore of Echo Lake was going anywhere. Sparks or no sparks between her and Brody, that was the fact of the matter.

Vic turned from the window and headed back downstairs. He'd never been much of a matchmaker, for himself or for anyone else. He'd often told himself he didn't want a permanent relationship. He'd always believed in marriage, just not for himself. It wasn't regret and loneliness chirping in his ear, throwing him off. He had friends. He could get involved with another woman.

No, he thought, it was the newness and the uncertainty of abandoning a career that had consumed him for four decades.

Had his ambivalence about retirement prompted him to imagine things? Like Sophia's barbed comment, was he exaggerating the "incidents" to make himself feel important?

He stopped at the front door. It was shut

tight now.

"All's well that ends well," he muttered, returning to his chair, iPad and crossword puzzles.

After lunch, Vic forced himself to get some air. He put on snowshoes and trudged down to the lake and back. It helped restore his mood, although he was aware Brody was keeping an eye on him. Nothing he wasn't used to from his Foreign Service days. By late afternoon, Heather had returned with her sauna options. He told her to do whatever she thought would work best. Adrienne talked her into staying for wine and hors d'oeuvres.

All in all, the day was turning out far better than it had started.

They gathered in the dining room. Adrienne, Heather, Brody and Vic. Adrienne had set the table with Wedgwood china Vic had brought down from his parents' house after their deaths. She lit two slender white candles in silver candlesticks that he didn't recognize. He assumed she'd discovered them in the back of some cupboard.

"I collected several local artisan cheeses and handcrafted wines available at the country store in town," Adrienne explained, gesturing to her array on the dining room table. "We have an aged cheddar, a soft goat's cheese, a hard goat's cheese and a blue cheese, plus assorted accompaniments — grapes, apples, crackers, olives, roast peppers."

"Looks great," Vic said. "Thanks for doing this."

Adrienne beamed. "As you can probably tell, I'm enjoying myself." She pointed to three wine bottles lined up behind the food trays. "We'll be tasting a variety of wines from the local Hardwick Vineyard and Winery. I adore their Massetts Cranberry. It's an award-winning blend of ninety-percent white grapes and ten-percent cranberries."

Vic picked up the bottle and noted the clear red color of the wine and the classic New England house on the label. "Festive," he said, placing the bottle back on the table.

"It's wonderful to see small wineries take hold in rural New England," Adrienne said. "I want to do the different wine trails and visit as many vineyards and taste as many varieties of wine as I can."

"It's all fascinating," Heather said.

Vic noticed she went easy on the wine, no doubt because she had to drive home on back roads in the January dark. He also noticed that Brody stayed close to her and when she got ready to leave, offered to walk out to her truck with her. Vic tried not to grit his teeth, but those two . . . there was just no way.

Heather slipped her vest on. "I'll be fine. The bears are still hibernating, and the driveway's freshly sanded."

"Not worried about a bad guy who likes to leave doors open?" Vic asked with a self-deprecating grin.

"No, but I don't mean to make light of your worries."

"Please do," he said. "I'd rather be over-reacting than be dealing with a real stalker."

Adrienne sampled a bit of her artisan cheddar and apple. "Brody, do you think you should move from the guesthouse into one of the guest rooms here? They aren't well furnished, but I'm sure we could figure something out."

Vic didn't give Brody a chance to answer. "No need to go to any trouble. We can get Brody here in seconds, but it won't be necessary unless I sleepwalk and fall down the stairs in the dark." He tried to keep his tone light, but he felt his heartbeat race at the prospect of another incident. Having Brody at the guesthouse helped, and it was enough. Setting him up in a guest room would only escalate the internal tension —

in other words, the made-up fears — that Vic had been trying to quell all day. "There's no reason for alarm," he added, more for his own benefit than anyone else's.

Adrienne pointed her wineglass at Brody. "Do you agree?"

He shrugged. "I do."

"I guess we wouldn't be here enjoying wine and cheese if you thought there was any reason for alarm. Are you sure there's nothing to these incidents?"

Vic raised a hand. "I got ahead of myself, I'm embarrassed to say. That's all there is to it."

"But what if that's not all there is to it?" Adrienne set her glass on the table and splashed in more wine. "What if these incidents of yours are for real but you're not the target? Brody, either. What if whoever is responsible is after Heather or even me?"

"Why would either of you be a target for something like this?" Brody asked evenly.

Adrienne sipped her wine. "I don't know. I have a popular wine blog, and people can be weird and nasty on the internet. The Sloans are well-known in town. They could have enemies."

"Everyone has enemies," Vic said. "I don't know how someone would get in here and do the things I've mentioned. The hang ups on the phone are easy to explain, but the other stuff — I'm just nuts is all."

Heather helped herself to a slice of apple. "Did our lists produce anything of interest?" she asked Brody.

"Not at first glance," he said.

Adrienne seized on his answer, almost spilling her wine. "There you go. What if a local guy who knows the house — knows the lay of the land around here — has been sneaking in here? What if it's about the property itself, some grudge rekindled by the renovations?"

"Now we're deep into the land of speculation," Vic said. "We'll keep Brody's number handy and call or text him if anything happens, or just shout from the back door. Heather, what about you? You live alone. I hope we're not making you nervous with our talk."

"Not at all. I'm within shouting distance of three of my brothers. Brandon lives in the village, and Eric and Christopher are both on duty tonight."

Vic thought he saw Brody smile — or maybe it was something between a smile and a grimace. He'd never understood the dynamics at play in Brody's relationship with the Sloan boys. Hadn't tried to understand. He'd tried, simply, to help Brody figure out what he wanted to do with his life besides go fishing and get into trouble.

Adrienne polished off the last of her wine. "All these brothers. Wow. Honestly, Heather, I don't know if you realize how lucky you are to come from a big, tight-knit family. I didn't even have a pet growing up."

"Having five brothers has its advantages." Heather smiled her bright, unaffected smile. "But I can handle myself. I'm also within reach of a baseball bat."

Vic saw her remark went up one side of Brody and down the other, but his young DSS agent friend recovered almost immediately. When Heather started out to the kitchen, Brody went with her. She didn't argue.

Adrienne raised her eyebrows. "I know I've had too much wine — which isn't like me — but I'm not seeing things. Our two Knights Bridge natives are very interesting together, aren't they?"

"Interesting. Yes. Apt description."

Vic grabbed his wineglass. He was partial to the Yankee Girl Blush, perhaps because it was nicknamed "summer in a bottle." He'd been cold all day despite the slightly warmer temperature and his reluctant snowshoe trek. He blamed his dour mood more than

220

January in New England.

"Anything I should know?" Adrienne asked.

He'd lost her train of thought. "About what?"

She sighed. "Heather and Brody."

"Oh." He made a dismissive motion with his glass. "Wine makes my mind wander. I don't know anything you don't know about Heather and Brody."

"Heather is so open and optimistic. It's her roots here in Knights Bridge, I think. That big family of hers. She knows who she is. She knows where she'll be when she's eighty. I don't. I don't know where I'll be eight months from now." Adrienne sank into a chair at the table and looked out at the black night. "Brody's had a rough time recently, hasn't he?"

"He's had some tough assignments the past few years. His choice, and he's good at what he does."

Her dark eyes lifted to Vic. "He must be accustomed to keeping his emotions at bay. Has he always been like that? Controlled, careful, hard to read?"

Vic shook his head. "He used to be a troublemaker."

"When he was growing up here? He's ripe for falling for someone like Heather, isn't he? The path not taken." Adrienne reached for a couple of green olives. "Do you think she's ripe for falling for him?"

"Adrienne . . ."

She grinned. "You look like I just stabbed you with a fork. I'll be quiet."

"What about you and Brody?" he asked.

"Me and Brody? Now, there's a thought that hadn't occurred to me." She popped the olives into her mouth and shook her head as she wiped her fingers on a cloth napkin. "Not a chance."

"Why not?"

She stood again. "Some things aren't meant to be, Vic, and that's one of them." She peered under the table. "What happened to Rohan?"

"He vacated the premises for a spot by the fire."

"He's so spoiled. I'll take the last of my wine and join him. What about you, Vic? A quiet dessert wine by the fire on a cold winter night?" She smiled, hooking her arm into his. With her free hand, she snatched up one of the wine bottles. "This is your new life, you know."

"It's a good one."

"You sound as if you're trying to convince yourself. Once you settle in here and get a few hobbies, you'll be fine. I predict you're going to want to keep Rohan, though. He'll be excellent company."

"Should I buy a pipe and a tweed jacket, too?"

She laughed. "I thought you already had a pipe and a tweed jacket."

Vic appreciated Adrienne's laughter, but when they reached the living room, she had drifted into a thoughtful silence. She set the wine on a side table and sat on the floor next to Rohan, sprawled out on the hearth, and stroked his soft fur. Vic sat in a chair. He could hear the wind, which had picked up over the past hour, buffeting the old house, whistling through the trees and rattling the windows.

Adrienne reached up for the wine and poured some into his glass. He noted she hadn't brought her glass in with her. "Here you go, Vic. More wine"

"Thank you." He smiled and raised his glass to her. "Cheers."

But after two sips, he knew he was done for the night. Totally beat. Adrienne kissed him on the cheek. "I'll see you in the morning, Vic. I'm glad you're okay."

He didn't know what to say. "Yeah. Sleep well."

By the time he stumbled up to his bedroom, he was too tired — too inebriated, maybe — to notice that Rohan had followed him. Next thing, the cuddly little beast was on the bed. Vic didn't have the heart or the energy to kick him out and take him back downstairs. They could start proper puppy training another day.

"You pee in my bed, mister, and we'll have words."

Rohan responded by collapsing onto the right side of the bed, where, in past years, a fetching woman might have slept.

Vic took off his shoes and clothes and crawled under the duvet in his shorts. Would he ever have another woman in his life? He'd long known, and accepted, that he wouldn't have an Ozzie-and-Harriet family, much to his mother's disappointment. His father's, too, but he'd recognized that his only son was a workaholic with a wandering eye and would have been a lousy father and husband.

But he was in his sixties now, and the idea of one special woman in his life had an appeal it hadn't even five years ago.

Or was he deluding himself?

The wind was still whipping around out in the dark.

As he settled into his pillows, he felt something warm and wet on his cheek and realized Rohan had licked him.

My new life, Vic thought. Yes, indeed.

ELEVEN

Heather almost fell off the couch in Phoebe's living room when she woke up automatically at six. She didn't remember falling asleep on the couch and had a moment of panic. Had she drunk *that* much wine last night? As she sat up, her elbow caught *The Scarlet Pimpernel* on the cushion and knocked it onto the floor.

"Oh, right."

She'd stayed up reading because she'd been preoccupied with thoughts of the federal agent up at Vic's house. She'd needed something else to occupy her mind, and Sir Percy Blakeney and his alter ego — the daring, mysterious Scarlet Pimpernel — had done the trick.

Phoebe would be proud, Heather thought as she stumbled into the kitchen, made coffee and stared out at the backyard. In the warm-weather months, it would be filled with flowers. Now icicles dripped off trellises and stone pots. Phoebe had expected to live here on her own and retire as the Knights Bridge librarian. Then Noah Kendrick had swooped into her life at a Boston costume ball.

Phoebe's unlikely swashbuckler.

Heather smiled, thinking of her friend, in love with a billionaire, expert fencer, high-tech genius and thoroughly decent man.

For reasons that now escaped her, Heather had convinced herself that Brody would kiss her again last night when he walked with her out to her truck. It didn't happen — decidedly just as well — and she'd found herself home alone with *The Scarlet Pimpernel.*

She poured her coffee then remembered she didn't have milk. She wasn't particularly hungry and could wait and have coffee at Vic's, but she wasn't going up there feeling groggy and out of sorts. Never mind wanting to appear professional and in control in front of Vic, her client, she needed to be properly fed and caffeinated dealing with his federal-agent guest.

Another morning for Smith's, even if it meant encountering some combination of her brothers while she was still feeling groggy and out of sorts. Better a couple of Sloans than Brody Hancock, who was in full-on DSS agent mode. That was what she'd concluded last night, anyway, after another fifty pages into her book.

She headed up to her bedroom to get dressed. She'd fallen asleep in her clothes, but she wasn't rewearing them for the day. A hot shower improved her energy level, and clean clothes at least helped her feel as if she could survive Brody's scrutiny. She had nothing to hide, and if someone was trying to get under Vic Scarlatti's skin, it wasn't her or, she was almost positive, anyone on the list she'd done for Brody.

She wasn't sure if her shower and fresh clothes would make her impervious to her physical attraction to him, but maybe a good breakfast would help.

When she headed out, laptop and clipboard in hand, Christopher, her youngest brother, was on the front porch, about to ring the doorbell. She and her youngest brother were thirteen months apart in age, each the least likely in the family to argue. As far back as Heather could remember, Christopher had always wanted to be a firefighter. It had been a straight path for him, if not always an easy one.

"I just finished my shift and decided to walk over here," he said. "I was looking for some company at breakfast before I hit the sack. Join me?"

"Sure. I was heading in that direction myself."

He jumped into her truck with her. He had on jeans, a frayed canvas jacket and boots but no hat or gloves. He didn't look cold, just tired.

"Rough night?" Heather asked as she started the engine.

"Not too bad. I need to catch up on some sleep." He peered at her, alert, despite his obvious fatigue. "You don't look so good yourself."

"Hey, I haven't had coffee yet. I'm still half-asleep. I was up late reading."

"Reading?"

"Yes, Christopher. Reading. A lot of people like to read."

"I like to read," he said.

"What's the last book you read?"

"I don't know. Oh, yeah. *King Lear.* It's a play not a book, but it counts."

Heather gaped at him. "*King Lear,* Chris?"

"Yeah. I was taking one of Ava O'Dunn's theater friends to see a production of *King Lear* in Amherst. I figured I'd better read it first. I didn't want to look like an ass or fall asleep because I didn't know what was going on."

Ava was one of Phoebe's younger twin

sisters, both theater graduate students without a shred of snobbery in them. Heather considered all four O'Dunn sisters — Phoebe, Maggie, Ava and Ruby — friends. She stopped her truck at the intersection of Thistle Lane and South Main. "Ava's an incorrigible matchmaker. Why don't I know about this woman?"

"Because we didn't hit it off. Didn't even make it through *King Lear.*" He didn't sound the least bit upset. "She told me I was bored and should go home. I wasn't bored with the play, but I did go home."

"You were bored with her," Heather said, knowing her brother. "She was a snob?"

"Class-A snob." He settled back in his seat, stifling a yawn. "Ava claims she warned me, but I think she and Ruby had a bet whether I'd make it through *King Lear* with this woman."

Heather tried to bite back her amusement with Christopher's story but sputtered into laughter. "I'm sorry," she said.

He grinned. "Don't be. I've had worse dates. How 'bout you?"

It wasn't, she suspected, an idle question. "I haven't had a date in a while. I've been busy."

"The Scarlatti renovations. Going out there today?"

"Right after breakfast."

"Watch the weather. It's supposed to turn nasty later."

She'd been so preoccupied with waking up on the couch and thinking about Brody and his lists that she hadn't checked the weather. Chris was always aware of the weather and his surroundings in general.

She pulled up in front of Smith's, but she and Chris ended up ordering breakfast sandwiches to go. She dropped him off at his apartment down the street from the restaurant.

"Twenty minutes with you, Chris, and you didn't once mention Brody Hancock."

"Didn't need to. He's why you were up late reading."

"You can't possibly know that."

"Yes, I can," he said with his usual confidence. "Mind the weather."

He shut the passenger door and sauntered off with his breakfast sandwich. Heather continued out to Echo Lake, noticing the sky was overcast — no lavender-streaked sunrise today. She parked in her usual spot but didn't see anyone. Just as well, she thought. If she saw Brody now, in the cold gray morning light, would she think about their kiss down by the lake, or yesterday when he was in DSS-agent mode? Had her evening alone and her night on the couch purged her of her attraction to him? She had no idea. Normally, she wasn't indecisive, but she was right now.

Best, she thought, to go with the flow and try not to think too much. It wasn't as if Brody would be sticking around Knights Bridge. One in-the-moment kiss wasn't about to change anything for him — or for her. Once he was on his way, they would both put his brief return to his hometown and their inconsequential kiss on the shores of Echo Lake behind them.

Maybe her overheated attraction to him was a wake-up call that she needed to pay attention to her social life. She couldn't be like the black bears in the dense woods on the other side of the lake and hibernate all winter.

She headed inside. No one was in the kitchen, but she could hear voices toward the front of the house. The coffee in the pot was fresh, or fresh enough. She poured herself a cup and sat at the table, determined to get Vic a hard-and-fast start date for work by the end of the day. The wine cellar and now the sauna shouldn't cause any delays.

Brody entered the kitchen from the hall. He had on his jacket and said nothing as he made straight for the mudroom.

Heather barely looked up from her laptop. "Good morning, Brody."

"Good morning, Heather. I didn't want to disturb you."

"Quiet night?"

He had his hand on the doorknob but turned to her, his gaze settling on her. "Yes. Very quiet."

"That's good, right?"

"Depends on your point of view," he said, then headed out.

It was a good five seconds before Heather breathed again, and even then, it wasn't a decent breath. She'd stepped into that one. Couldn't she have asked him if he'd had a good breakfast? Why ask about his *night*?

He'd meant to get to her. She knew that much. Brody Hancock, she decided, didn't do or say anything that wasn't deliberate and totally under his control.

Not a thought she needed as she was about to head back down to the dank, dark cellar. She grabbed her laptop and clipboard, determined to focus on her work, even if it was now clear that their quick kiss hadn't gotten anything out of the way — for Brody or for her.

A midday trip out to Frost Millworks and

the Sloan & Sons offices — mercifully empty of Sloans — and Heather was back at Vic's place by three o'clock. Adrienne was in the dining room, cleaning out the built-in cupboard ahead of renovations, sorting books, photo albums, dishes, decks of cards and outright junk into neat piles.

"Vic's down in the cellar, rethinking the sauna," Adrienne said, sitting cross-legged on the floor.

Heather resisted a moan. "He's giving up on it?"

"Oh, no. He's now considering whether he should turn this place into a day spa to give himself something to do." Adrienne smiled. "Don't worry. It's a whim. He said he didn't sleep well. Retirement jitters, and Rohan got him up twice in the middle of the night."

Heather made no comment on Vic Scarlatti's approach to puppy training. She would concentrate on finalizing plans for the sauna and the extensive work on the house's three porches.

Which led her to the front door and, ten minutes later, down the porch steps to a shoveled walk that wound through pine trees to the guesthouse. The promised storm was getting started as a cold drizzle. She wanted to be on her way before it turned to freezing rain, but first she needed to see Brody.

She debated for two seconds before she knocked on the side door.

"It was the hardware," she said when he opened the door. She pointed vaguely back toward the house. "Vic's door yesterday. He might have shut it tight, but there's a shaft that's worn-out."

"A shaft that's worn-out," Brody repeated, his tone neutral.

Heather nodded. "It's nothing you'd notice right away. I was checking my order and saw that it was shot. We'll have to replace the door. Frost Millworks can do a copy of the original. It's too far gone to fix."

"I see. Can't have a worn-out shaft."

She stopped still, then put a hand on her hip and sighed at him. "You know I have five brothers, right, and have heard everything? There isn't one smart-aleck remark you can make about shafts and such that will make me blush. Not one." She stood straight, noticing his smile. "That was your point, wasn't it? To see if I'd blush?"

"Just having a bit of fun. Come inside. Tell me about this shaft."

"There's nothing more to tell. I don't know if someone's messing with Vic's head with the other stuff he says has been going on, but it makes perfect sense that the door wouldn't stay shut. Anyway, I wanted to let you know." She glanced behind her, the telltale sheen on the walk suggesting the drizzle was already turning to freezing rain. "I should get going."

"Too late. You won't make it to your truck, never mind back to town."

"You don't have sand?"

"Not enough to handle freezing rain." He stood back and opened the door wider. "Why don't you come inside and wait for the freezing rain to change over to snow? I've been stuck out on that back road in ice. It's not pleasant."

"What did you do?"

"Left the car and walked home. There was soft snow on the side of the road. I managed not to get hypothermia. I suppose you'd have someone you could call if you got stuck."

"Could," Heather said. "That doesn't mean I'd want to."

He gave the door a jiggle. "In or out?"

"In."

He grinned. "You make it sound as if I just invited you into the wolf's den."

"I have things to do. I don't have time for an ice storm."

"Life in Knights Bridge," he said.

"Not all the time."

She stepped past him into the warm living room. Even trying to get back to the main house posed a challenge in the rapidly deteriorating conditions, but so did waiting out the freezing rain alone with Brody. She saw he had a cozy fire going in the woodstove. A blanket and pillow were stacked on one end of the sectional.

"Better view out here than in the bedrooms?" she asked.

"Simpler to sleep on the couch."

"You must be hit by memories at every turn."

He winked. "Just the ones I haven't blocked." He opened the lid to the woodstove, checking the fire. "I offered to make dinner tonight. I should be able to get up to the house by then. Adrienne said she'd choose a wine. Vic said he'd set the table. Why don't you join us?" He smiled. "You can help cook."

"My father and brothers didn't warn you about my cooking abilities yesterday, did they?"

"We didn't get into that particular subject." He shut the stove lid without adding another log to the fire. "You're not much on cooking?"

She shrugged. "I don't mind it. I'm just

not that good at it, at least according to my family and friends."

"Let me see. I'm going to guess that you don't follow directions. Am I right?"

She pulled off her vest and tossed it onto the back of a chair. "Directions? You mean there are directions?" She grinned at him. "I have to be very precise in my work. I treat cooking more like an art. Maggie, who's a caterer, says that's great, but I should have the basics down first, then experiment."

"And you think you do have them down."

"I'm learning by doing. I've never poisoned anyone."

"I have, but they all lived."

Heather laughed and unzipped her sweatshirt. With heat from the woodstove, the small house was toasty warm. She took off her sweatshirt and tossed it on top of her vest.

"I've been wondering what you wear under that sweatshirt," Brody said then nodded to her. "A Sloan & Sons T-shirt. I should have known."

"It's a hand-me-down from Adam. Works. Were you expecting lace?"

He stepped away from the woodstove. "Do you ever wear lace?"

"I'm more partial to sequins."

"I can see you in sequins," he said. "And lace."

"Sure. Why not? I do get out of my steel-toed boots every now and then." She tried to ignore the surge of heat in her veins. It wasn't just the fire in the woodstove, either. "Do we ever get to see you in a tuxedo?"

"Only if the job or a friend's wedding requires it." He motioned toward the kitchen. "I have soup makings. I grabbed what looked good at Hazelton's and figured I'd toss it into a pot and see what happens."

Heather noted he'd used Hazelton's, the local name for the Swift River Country Store. "No directions?"

"Experience."

He was visibly relaxed as he went into the kitchen. She followed him, not as relaxed herself. He had an assortment of vegetables lined up on the counter, and one of Hazelton's fresh baguettes.

Brody handed her a paring knife. "I don't blame you for being on guard with me."

His words caught her by surprise. "Should I be?"

"No. Not in the way you're thinking. I'm not here to stir up trouble or play out teenage nonsense. Seeing your brothers again . . ." He opened a drawer and withdrew another knife. "Time's passed."

239

Heather placed a cutting board on the counter and selected a few carrots to chop. "I'm used to butting heads with my brothers. It doesn't surprise me when other people do, too. They're straightforward, and they can be very stubborn, but they don't hold grudges. I think they're not sure what you're up to."

"With their little sister or with Vic?"

"You're not up to anything with me except making soup in the freezing rain."

He peeled the loose skin off a yellow onion. "Is that what you're telling yourself or telling me?"

"Stating a fact."

"Evidence for this fact?"

"Carrots, onions, paring knives and the weather." She pointed with her knife at the stove. "Big soup pot on the front burner."

"That's solid evidence, but you don't know what's going on in my mind. I could be thinking about this onion, or I could be thinking about . . ." He set his onion on his cutting board. "Other things."

"Nope. I'd know."

"The five-brothers thing again?"

She shook her head. "You'd cut your finger if you were thinking about other things. Also, you're a federal agent. You can't let your mind wander."

"Ah, yes. I'm on home leave, though."

"Technically, maybe, but you wouldn't be here if Vic wasn't worried about someone messing with his head." When Brody didn't respond, she finished chopping a carrot and turned to him. "Well, am I right?"

"I'd have come back here sooner or later, because of my five acres on Echo Lake that no one wants."

"If you built a lake house there, someone would bite."

"Volunteering Sloan & Sons?"

"It doesn't have to be us. I think it would be easier to sell your property if it had a house on it. Your original house had a well and a septic system, didn't it?"

Brody hacked his onion in two. "Yes, but we're making soup. We're not talking about septic systems." He leaned toward her. "Even if that is routine talk at the Sloan house."

"Better than talking about lace and sequins."

"So you say."

There was a sexy huskiness to his voice that launched her heartbeat into another fit. Heather tossed her chopped carrots into a colander and rinsed them in the sink. Brody made short work of his onion. Together they chopped, sliced and rinsed the vegetables and got them simmering in the soup pot. He indicated they would add white beans and herbs later.

"If I tried to throw stuff together like this," Heather said, "I'd end up feeding it to Elly O'Dunn's goats."

"That's because you'd be throwing it together. I have a plan."

She shook her head at him. "No, you don't."

He grinned. "A rough plan, then."

"That I can believe."

He went to the back door and flipped on the outside light. Heather stood next to him and saw that the walk and driveway were encased in ice from the freezing rain. "I can handle sleet," she said. "Freezing rain is downright treacherous."

"We won't be going anywhere for a while," Brody said. His phone dinged on the table, and he grabbed it, glancing at the screen. "Vic says not to bother with dinner. It's not worth risking a broken wrist trying to make it to the house. He and Adrienne will have grilled cheese."

"We could make it without falling," Heather said. "I imagine you've been in more dangerous situations than carrying hot soup and bread in an ice storm."

He was tapping keys on his phone. "But

we don't have to carry soup and bread in an ice storm, and I just told Vic it was a good idea, and he and Adrienne should enjoy their sandwiches."

"You haven't hit Send yet."

He popped a key with his thumb and grinned at her. "Now I have. Shall we put another log on the fire while we wait for the soup?"

The wintry mix continued while the soup simmered and the fire settled into a slow, hot burn. Heather sat on the sectional — well down from Brody's blanket and pillow — while he stood at the tall windows and looked out at the lake. She wasn't sure what he could see given the bad weather.

"No moon and stars tonight," she said.

"No." He turned to her, his eyes as dark as the night sky behind him. "A friend of mine has been looking into Adrienne's background."

Heather sat up straight. "Why?"

"A precaution."

"Has he been looking into my background, as well?"

"No need."

"You've done it yourself." She sank deep into the soft cushions. "Well, that's annoying. Did you look up my bank accounts and discover I have an insatiable appetite for —" She stopped, waved a hand. "I thought I'd think of something on the fly, but I can't. Chocolate, maybe, but I buy most of it with cash. I'm not in debt. There you have it. As I've told my brothers countless times, I have no secrets. Now you can tell them it's true."

"I didn't look up your bank accounts, Heather."

She thought she detected a hint of humor in his tone but there was none in his expression. She picked up a throw pillow that felt as if it'd been on the couch for at least as long as Brody had been away from Echo Lake. "Did you tell Adrienne you've been checking her out?"

"Not yet, no."

"So these incidents Vic told you about — they're enough to warrant an official investigation?"

"I wouldn't go that far." He walked toward her but didn't sit down. He fingered her sweatshirt on the back of the chair next to the couch. "Adrienne's mother was in Paris on business when Vic was at the embassy there. That's how they met. She was Sophia Cross then. She and Adrienne's father were engaged, but he didn't go to Paris with her."

"Sounds straightforward. Nice the three of them have stayed in touch all these years."

Brody didn't react to her comment. "Adrienne tapped into her parents' connections this past year while she's been wandering the world studying and writing about wine. She got in touch with Vic when he was winding down his last assignment in New York and ended up house-sitting for him here in Knights Bridge."

"None of that's a secret," Heather said. "She's told me that from the start."

"Has she mentioned any friends?"

"Anyone who might want to mess with Vic's head, you mean?"

Brody waited a beat before he responded. "Anyone at all."

"Adrienne seems to have a lot of friends, but I don't know of any who've stayed here. She's treating house-sitting like her personal retreat — a chance to strip away distractions and focus on her work and what comes next for her. I got the impression she's doing well but is a bit overwhelmed."

"Does having Vic here change things for her?"

Heather shrugged. "I imagine it does. It's not something we've talked about. He's figuring out what to do with himself when we start tearing up the house for renovations. He could stay here or at his apartment in New York, travel, visit friends." She took a breath, trying not to look agitated. "Did you decide to take advantage of the storm so you could interrogate me?"

"I'm not interrogating you. We're just talking."

"*Just talking* wouldn't make me break out in a sweat. Damn."

His mouth twitched. She thought he might smile outright, but he didn't. "I'm here to help a friend. That's all."

"Well, you can be intense, you know."

"I'm not trying to be intense," he said calmly.

"I'd hate to see you try. I don't mind if you need to ask me questions. I mind . . ." She shook her head, stopping herself. "I'm just going to leave it there is what I'm going to do."

He came around from the back of the chair and sat next to her, patting her thigh and, finally, smiling. "Why censor yourself now?"

"A good a time as any to start thinking before I speak."

He laughed. "Might as well give it a shot."

She angled a look at him. "You haven't laughed much recently, have you, Brody?"

"I suppose I haven't. It's been a busy few months."

"I won't pretend I can imagine what *busy*

means to you. This friend who's helping you — he's a DSS agent?"

"For now. He's recovering from injuries. Helping me gives him something to do."

"What happened?" Heather asked quietly.

"A bad day at work."

"What does that mean?"

Brody glanced at her, no sign of laughter now, just the return of his intensity. "You're persistent, aren't you?" He didn't wait for an answer. "Greg — that's my friend's name — was securing a site and ran into guys with guns. He took a bullet in the shoulder, but he'll be fine. He is fine."

"He'll be able to return to work?"

"Physically, yes. The rest is up to him."

"And you? Were you there?"

Brody rose and walked over to the windows, staring out at the storm. "We got him out." He looked back at her. "That's all that matters."

"This is why you're on home leave? At least part of why you decided to come back to Knights Bridge?"

"Maybe. I haven't thought much about it."

"Not a time for deep thinking, I suppose. You do what you have to do and let the emotions sort themselves out later." Heather got to her feet and walked over to him at the windows. She could hear the crunch of ice outside as the freezing rain changed to sleet. "You have a dangerous job, Brody."

"Construction can be dangerous." The glint of humor was back in his dark eyes. "Ever drop a hammer on your toes?"

"Brody . . ."

He stood close to her and brushed a few stray hairs off her face, tucking them behind her ear. "Everything's good, Heather. No problems. Okay?"

"Sure thing. Dropping a hammer's right up there with bullets flying."

"You can trust me," he said softly.

"Trust you how? No . . . never mind." She reined in her reaction to him — to his touch, his intensity. "I'm sorry about your friend Greg, and I'm sorry you went through a tough time. If there's more you want to say, I'll be happy to listen. I'm not going to wilt." But she knew he wasn't going to say more, not tonight, maybe not ever. "Seeing you in action, though — even just over a door that swung open — you can be very scary, Agent Hancock. I mean, seriously."

"That's the idea."

"A good thing I'm not up to anything."

"I suspect you're up to a lot."

"You keep suspecting." She pointed a

finger at the windows. "Sleet's changing over to snow now. That's a good sign. In the time we've been chatting, my brothers have all texted me to see if I got home all right."

"Did you tell them I was just about to fluff up the comforter?"

"I did not."

He laughed and kissed her on the forehead. "Soup's ready."

TWELVE

With the changeover to snow, Heather was
able to get out after dinner. The soup wasn't
half-bad. Brody didn't detect any reluctance
on her part to leave. She had on her sweatshirt and vest and was on her way to the
door, telling him she didn't need a shovel
or sand to get to her truck, it was just a
couple inches of snow, the ice underneath
was no longer a problem . . .

"I'll go with you," he said, interrupting
her midstream.

She stopped at the door. "Thanks, Brody,
but I live here. I deal with storms all the
time. It's okay —"

"You'll manage. I know." He grabbed his
jacket and shrugged it on. "I'm heading up
there, anyway. Figured I'd see if Vic and
Adrienne need a hand with Rohan. Vic will
have to get used to storms if he's retiring
here. I'm guessing he hasn't gotten them
down yet."

"I saw to it he has sand. I didn't want to get stuck out here, but I didn't think about stocking the guesthouse."

"What little sand there is here wouldn't have helped in the freezing rain, but it will get us to your truck." He pulled open the door, standing back to let her go first. "You've already fallen in a brook this week."

She rolled her eyes. "You don't give up, do you?"

"Never."

"I think I like that about you." She stepped past him then paused, turning to him with a smile. "*Think* means I'm not positive."

He grinned and followed her outside. She grabbed a number-ten can of sand and he grabbed a shovel, trying to remember the last time he'd shoveled snow.

Over dinner, they'd talked about Knights Bridge, people they knew in common, the changes in the area since his departure. Elly O'Dunn's goats, her first one purchased after the death of her husband ten years ago in a tree-cutting accident. Patrick O'Dunn had taught Brody how to use a chain saw. Brody had never been a part of town the way Heather was, but he appreciated their conversation. For one thing, it kept him from telling her more about what his world was like now. She didn't need to know.

251

It also kept him from carrying her into one of the bedrooms. The beds weren't made, but that wouldn't have stopped him. Her, either. He was confident she had gone on about the schoolteachers they'd had in common to distract herself from conjuring similar images of him sweeping her off to bed.

Not that the living room floor wouldn't have done.

He smiled at the thought.

He was fairly certain she'd exaggerated about the text messages from all five brothers.

The walk to her truck was a notch under treacherous, but the plow had come and gone and the driveway was in decent shape. Vic had left the back door light on. The snow had dwindled to fat, intermittent flakes.

Heather got her scraper out of her truck and started clearing off the windshield. Brody got another scraper out of Vic's car and helped with the opposite side of the windshield. The sleet and freezing rain had left a crust of ice under the snow, but it had been a fast-moving, relatively light storm, not as bad as predicted. Heather would have no trouble returning to Thistle Lane.

When they finished cleaning off her truck,

he opened the driver's door for her. She tossed her scraper in back. "Thank you for your help," she said, turning to him. Her cheeks were flushed from the cold and exertion, her eyes a midnight blue in the dim light. "And thank you for dinner. The soup was great."

"Your carrots made all the difference."

She laughed. "It's hard to screw up a carrot. See you tomorrow?"

"I'll still be here."

"Brody . . ." She put out a gloved hand and caught a few snowflakes, then smiled at him. "I never get tired of studying snowflakes. Thank you for tonight. It was a good idea for me to wait out the worst of the storm."

"Be careful driving home."

"Always."

He returned the scraper to Vic's car and waited until Heather was safely out onto the back road. If not for the quick improvement in the conditions, tonight could have ended quite differently. What if she'd been stranded with him in the guesthouse until morning?

No point going there in his mind since not only hadn't it happened, it wouldn't have, either. It would have to be a hell of an ice storm to keep the Sloans from coming to the rescue of one of their own, whether or not Heather was stranded with him.

Brody sighed and went inside, passing Rohan lapping water in his bowl in the mudroom and headed to the front room. He found Adrienne sitting cross-legged on the floor in front of the fire.

She smiled up at him. "I'm glad the freezing rain and sleet changed to snow. I'd rather have a foot of snow than a quarter-inch of ice. Where's Heather?"

"She's on her way home."

"Vic went upstairs after dinner. Headache. He thinks it's the low pressure from the storm, but I think it's the pressure of retirement. He wants to matter, and he isn't convinced he does anymore. That's what these incidents are about, isn't it? He's ratcheting up normal occurrences so he can feel important again. I guess it can happen to any of us."

Brody said nothing as he sat in Vic's vacated chair.

Adrienne stretched out her legs and wiggled her bare toes in front of the fire. "If you'd told me this time last year — when I was in Portugal, mind you — that I would be sitting here in wool socks, I'd have laughed in your face."

"It's an odd time of year to choose to be

here," Brody said.

She shook her head without hesitation. "Not for me. I've never experienced a New England winter, and it doesn't get better than here on Echo Lake. You should see Knights Bridge decorated for Christmas." She made a face, catching herself. "Never mind, I forgot that you have seen it."

"Not in a long time."

"I doubt it's changed." She planted her palms on the floor behind her and leaned back, her eyes on the flames. "Keeping up this place is a lot of work. I wonder if Vic realizes how much. It's one thing to air it out a couple times a year for a quick visit. It's another actually to live here. He's going to need more help."

"He's lucky he can afford whatever help he needs," Brody said. "Tell me more about how and why you contacted him. Why now, Adrienne?"

She frowned up at him. "What do you mean?"

"I assume you had other options besides house-sitting for Vic Scarlatti. What prompted you to get in touch with him versus someone else — another of your parents' friends, a friend of your own?"

"I'm not responsible for freaking Vic out."

Her tone was neutral, but Brody sensed

she was struggling not to come across as defensive, someone with something to hide. He shrugged. "Maybe I'm just making conversation."

She gave him a weak smile. "It doesn't sound like making conversation. It sounds like asking questions." She sat up straight, tucked her knees under her chin and wrapped her arms around them. "Sorry. I'm not used to people asking me questions. My parents never do, and I don't have any brothers and sisters looking over my shoulder. Not like Heather. I can't imagine having five older brothers. Were you all friends growing up?"

"We were." Brody left it at that and smiled at her. "Now who's asking questions?"

"Can't blame me for trying. You're not going to give up, though, are you? Okay, to answer your question, I've been going nonstop for months and months. Work, friends, family, travel, life."

"And?"

She shot him a look. "You can tell there's more? They teach you that in DSS school or whatever it's called? Never mind. I probably don't want to know. I had a bad breakup with a guy. I finally realized I needed to slow down and get my head together, figure out who I am and what I want to do with my life — or at least the next year. I was in New York. I introduced myself to Vic, and he told me about his place here and retiring. I suggested I could house-sit while he geared up for renovations. It made life easier for him and for the architect and Sloan & Sons, and it was great for me."

"Who's the ex-boyfriend?" Brody asked.

"You do cut to the chase, don't you? It's no one you know. He owns a wine shop in New York. Upper West Side, near Columbus Circle. He doesn't know Vic. He doesn't know where I am now, in case you're thinking he's stalking me. He doesn't care where I am or what I'm doing, and I don't want him to care."

Brody considered his response. "I'm sorry you've gone through a difficult time."

"I appreciate that." She faced the fire again, but not before he saw the tears glistening in her eyes. "His name's Thad, by the way. Thad Bowman. He made a ton of money in the stock market before he turned thirty and decided to quit and open up a wine shop."

"How long did you two see each other?"

"Almost a year. We met at a Christmas party. He was drinking a merlot I loathe. I should have known then we weren't meant to be." She glanced up at Brody again, tears on her lashes but not any longer in her eyes. "What about you? How many broken hearts have you left behind since you became a DSS agent?"

He smiled. "Maybe I'm the one with the broken heart."

She returned his smile. "Somehow I doubt that."

Brody left her by the fire and headed back to the guesthouse. His fire in the woodstove had died down, but he didn't revive it, preferring the cooling air as he sat on the sectional and called Greg Rawlings.

Greg already knew about the ex-boyfriend on the Upper West Side. "Thad Bowman is what my dear departed grandmother would call a piece of work. I have other terms that would have offended her."

"You've talked to him?"

"No. I went to his wine shop and saw him in the back room, looking important. My guess is he'll get bored with wine and move on to the next conquest. It's quite the shop, though. We're not talking the corner liquor store where I grew up."

Brody could see stars over Echo Lake now, the sky already clearing after the storm. "What are you up to now, Greg?"

"Doing my PT stretches because I didn't

do them earlier. I was checking out this wine merchant. It's good I'm in the city that never sleeps since I don't, either."

"You need your seven to eight hours."

"Yep. How're you sleeping now that you're back in your hometown, or shouldn't I ask?"

Brody thought of Heather and ground his teeth. Nothing about his return to Knights Bridge was turning out to be simple or straightforward. "Stay in touch."

"I see *shouldn't have asked* was the right answer. I struck a nerve, didn't I? Which is it, the jilted wine expert or the hometown girl who knows how to use a nail gun?"

Brody pretended not to hear and disconnected, but he still had his phone in his hand when Greg texted him.

It's the hometown girl.

You need sleep. Try chamomile tea.

I'd be kicked out of the DSS for sure.

Brody didn't respond. He got up and walked over to the tall windows. No one would kick Greg Rawlings out of the DSS for drinking herbal tea. Greg had bigger issues than temporary insomnia.

As he looked out at the dark lake, Brody

remembered his father grumbling about winter. "I'm not sticking around Knights Bridge, Brody. Once you graduate, I'm out of here. Take my advice and get out, too. There's nothing in this town for either one of us. Nothing."

It was one of the few pieces of good advice his father had given his only son.

Brody hadn't bothered with the blinds and drapes and woke up to bright sunlight streaming through the windows and sparkling on the freshly fallen snow. Coffee, toast, a shower and clean clothes, and he was off, duly noting it was one hell of a cold morning. He'd already noted the two soup bowls in the sink from last night. That stung him more than the frigid temperatures.

Heather, Heather.

Why couldn't Justin have been overseeing renovations? Not as fun as his sister by a stretch but much less complicated. He and Brody sure as hell wouldn't have chopped veggies and had soup together last night.

The walks and driveway were crunchy with snow, ice and sand, but Brody saw that Heather had just arrived, a van following right behind her. She jumped out of her truck, talking to him as if they'd parted two minutes ago instead of twelve hours. "It was

260

slow getting home last night, but the roads are in good shape this morning. We'd never get anything done if we hung around waiting for good weather." She nodded to the van as her brother Adam got out. "Adam and I are discussing the stonework for Vic's house. The outside work will have to wait for warmer weather."

"Brody," Adam said. "Still here, I see."

"Yeah. I'll try not to overstay my Knights Bridge welcome home."

Adam grinned but the fourth Sloan sibling had little else to say as he and Heather got to work, all that Sloan focus and energy well in evidence this morning. Brody went inside, helped himself to coffee and found Vic reading *War and Peace* by the fire.

"It was in a box of books I brought here years ago from my folks' place," he said, holding up the tome. "My father left school at sixteen to help earn money for the family. He worked hard and did well, better than he ever expected. He and my mother wanted my sister and me to have a good education. I found a set of encyclopedias, too. Now all that stuff's on the internet. It's not the same."

"No incidents this morning?" Brody asked.

Vic's cheeks reddened slightly. "No, unless you want to call fighting with Rohan over a tennis ball an incident. I'm going to read a few chapters and check another box. I'm not unpacking anything because I'll just have to pack it up again for the renovations." He placed the book in his lap and pointed at a yellowed page. "I wrote notes in the margins. A precursor to my life with the Foreign Service, perhaps."

"Adam Sloan is here."

"The stonemason Sloan. I keep trying to imagine this place finished. It'll be grand, don't you think?"

"Definitely."

Vic narrowed his eyes on Brody. "You'll come back to see it, won't you?"

"I haven't planned that far out. I don't know what I'm doing this afternoon, never mind a year from now."

"You've always liked spontaneity in your life. You can have your pick of assignments after the past few years. Any thoughts?"

Brody shook his head. "Not right now."

"All right," Vic said. "I'll read my book and leave you alone. One day it wouldn't hurt for you to talk to someone about your life, you know. What you want, who you are, what you've done."

"I'll do that, Vic."

"Oh, you will not. You're about as introspective as a hunk of cordwood, and opening up — acknowledging your human vulnerabilities — goes against your personal code."

Brody frowned, trying to suppress a grin. "I've been called a lot of things, but a hunk of cordwood?"

"I didn't call you cordwood. I was making an analogy. Obviously, I'm not Tolstoy when it comes to words." Vic waved a hand. "Never mind. Rohan could use some fresh air."

"So could I now."

"Good. His leash is by the back door. He needs to get used to it."

"You're okay, Vic?"

"Yes. I feel like the boy who cried wolf for calling you, but there's no wolf about to show up. You don't have to stay on my account. You're welcome to, of course, but if being here is causing problems for you, feel free to be on your way."

"No problems."

Vic scowled. "I knew that's what you'd say. I had hoped coming back here would be good for you, even this time of year."

"It is good. Thanks for having me."

"Seriously, Brody?"

"Sure."

Vic pointed a finger at him. "You're full of

it, and you know it. Cocky bastard. Go away."

Brody grinned and returned to the kitchen. Heather was there with Adam and Adrienne, all three about to descend into the basement, presumably to discuss stonework having to do with the sauna and wine cellar. Brody didn't need details. He grabbed Rohan and the leash.

It wasn't any warmer outside, but the puppy didn't seem to notice. Brody snapped on the leash. Rohan looked offended at first then bolted toward the lake.

"Not that way," Brody said. "The snow and ice will wear you out. We're taking a different route."

They walked out to Brody's land. Rohan handled the leash reasonably well. When they reached his lakeside acres, Brody unsnapped the leash and let the puppy ramble. He could see himself out here on a similar winter day, shoveling snow, wondering what he would end up doing with his life. He'd known he didn't want to be a fishing guide in the Florida Keys like his father.

He made a fist-size snowball and tossed it onto the road. Rohan dived after it.

Brody laughed. "Can't forget you're a retriever, can we?"

He looked out at the lake again, the sky

clear and as blue as in his dream before Vic's call.

He could see Heather out here with him the other day. Feel how much he'd wanted to kiss her.

He turned from the lake and whistled for Rohan. Heather's life was in Knights Bridge with her family.

His life wasn't here. It never had been, and it never would be.

When Brody got back, he saw Vic alone down by the lake, his shoulders hunched against the cold. Maybe wishing he'd bought a condo in Lisbon, Brody thought, taking a wet, muddy Rohan with him to the guesthouse. He cleaned him up, gave him a bowl of water and let him collapse in the living room. He debated starting a fire in the woodstove. He could also pack up his car and get out of here. Heather's truck, he'd noticed, was still in the driveway, but Adam's van was gone.

Brody got out an old Risk game he and the Sloans had played as teenagers. He'd brought a few things up from the cabin before he'd demolished it. Vic had left the boxes untouched in a closet, no surprise to Brody now that Vic had told him about *War and Peace* and the encyclopedias.

He set the game on the coffee table. When they were kids, Heather had wormed her way into a game with Justin and Brandon. It was a warm summer night, and they had set up on the Hancock cabin porch. She rode her bicycle up from the O'Dunn place and arrived sweating, hair tangled, pink rubber bands on her braces. Brody remembered being annoyed.

She was different now. Way different.

He was relieved when his phone rang. He needed a distraction. But he recognized Heather's number on the screen. Not the distraction he had in mind. He answered. "What's up?"

"Do you have a second?"

"I do. I have many seconds. Rohan and I are here with my old Risk game."

"You and my brothers always shut me out except for one time."

"I remember. You were ruthless."

"Conquering the world."

Brody smiled at the memory. "What can I do for you?"

He heard Heather suck in a breath. "Adrienne has a bunch of Vic's old photos out in the dining room. I think you should come have a look."

"I'll be right there."

As he grabbed his coat, he got a call from

Greg Rawlings. "Our Adrienne Portale isn't quite who she says she is," Greg said.

"Meaning?"

"She's a wine expert. That part's true. Her mother is Sophia Cross Portale, a woman Vic met in Paris thirty years ago. Also true."

He sounded more animated, more like the old Greg. Brody opened the front door. "Her father?"

"That's where it gets interesting. Richard Portale isn't Adrienne's biological father. I don't know how long he and Sophia have known, but Adrienne has only known for the past six months. She's in quote-unquote emotional turmoil."

"Who are you quoting?"

"Friend of a friend of a friend who knows all of them — the Portales and our good ambassador. You know how it works. We operate in a small world."

"Adrienne thinks Vic is her father," Brody said.

"Yep."

"Is he?"

"Don't know. If he is, he doesn't know. I'm sure of it. This woman — Sophia — sucks the oxygen out of every room she's in. Self-absorbed but irresistible. Knows what buttons to push. I've been known to not resist that type myself. You get sucked in for a few days, and then you find yourself rotting on a beach, being pecked by seagulls. You check your wallet and your body parts to make sure everything's intact. It usually isn't."

"Nice image, Greg. So Adrienne Portale could be the daughter Vic never knew he had."

"Or she contacted him because she needed space from her mother and wanted to find out about her life in Paris."

"All right. Thanks."

"Adrienne was in the midst of this emotional turmoil when she got mixed up with this rich idiot in New York with the wine shop."

Brody stepped outside, a stiff breeze kicking up snow. "Got it."

"What you don't know, Agent Hancock," Greg said, "is that in an effort to bind Mr. Bowman to her, Adrienne bought a golden retriever puppy."

"Rohan is hers?"

"Yep. Your abandoned rider of Rohan is hers."

THIRTEEN

Heather sat at the dining room table while Adrienne fingered one of the photographs scattered in front of them. "I was trying to find photos of Paris when Vic and my mother met there before I was born," Adrienne said. "I got a little carried away."

"I've never been to Paris," Heather said, picking up a photo of a dark-haired woman with the Eiffel Tower rising behind her. "My friend Jessica Frost used to dream about going to Paris. She talked about it all the time. She works for Frost Millworks, another family-owned business here in town. Anyway, she finally went with Mark Flanagan."

"Vic's architect? I didn't know he and Jessica Frost were an item."

"Mark and Jess got married in September."

"Oh, right." Adrienne gave a feeble smile. "I'm starting to get all these small-town connections down."

Heather set the photograph back on the table. "You haven't told us everything about why you're here, have you, Adrienne?"

"Wine and nostalgia."

"Nostalgia for a time before you born? How does that work?"

She noticed that Brody had entered the room. Adrienne didn't look up from the photos spread out in front of her but had to be aware of him. With one finger, she slid a picture across the table to Heather. "A young Vic Scarlatti with a young Sophia Cross, my mother," Adrienne said. "What do you think?"

Heather shook her head. "Adrienne . . ."

"No, no, go ahead, Heather. Please. It's all right. Take a look." Adrienne raised her gaze to Brody. "Do you want to take a look, Agent Hancock?"

"I don't need to," he said.

"I thought not from your expression when you came in here. Your investigation has borne fruit, as they say. It's tough to hide anything from your lot, but my mother managed to for a very long time. All my life, in fact." Adrienne returned her gaze to Heather opposite her. "Vic could be me in that picture, couldn't he?" She managed another weak smile. "Except for the men's clothes, of course."

The expression on the younger Vic Scarlatti . . . the stance . . .

Heather slid the photo back to Adrienne. "You believe Vic is your father," she said.

"The resemblance isn't as strong now as it was when he was younger. It's not enough by itself, I know." Adrienne cleared her throat, obviously struggling to control her emotions. "I'm sorry I didn't say something sooner."

"Did you know?" Brody asked quietly.

"I suspected. Technically, I still don't know. My mother won't confirm or deny that she and Vic had an affair in Paris, and I haven't . . ." Adrienne gulped in a breath, fighting tears. "I didn't say anything to Vic at first. I wanted to get to know him better. I didn't want any drama about biology affecting our relationship. I only asked him about an affair the other day. He squirmed and didn't give me a straight answer." She pushed back her chair and sprang to her feet. "Now I've made a complete mess of things."

"Where's Vic now?" Brody asked, staying on his feet.

"Upstairs going through another old box," Adrienne said. "He's been brooding all day. He's in the middle of a major life change with retirement, and now here I am, the long-lost daughter."

Heather collected some of the photos and returned them to their box. "Do you think he has any idea, Adrienne?"

"I don't know. He's so innocent in some ways. It wouldn't occur to him that my mother would deliberately not tell him she came home from Paris expecting his baby. I accept that she did what she thought was best. I don't know if he will." Adrienne cleared her throat, her eyes on the Paris photo. "My dear mother."

"Did anyone else know?" Heather asked.

"My father, you mean? The man she stepped out on six weeks before they were married? No. He didn't know. She didn't tell him the truth, either. He found out, though. We don't have compatible blood types. That's how I figured it out, too, but only six months ago. He figured it out years earlier but never said a word to me. I didn't understand the divorce, why he pulled back from me. As far as I was concerned, he was my father."

"I'm sorry, Adrienne," Heather said. "It sounds as if you've had a lot to work through."

"I know it could be worse. I truly do." She touched another photograph of her mother, this time on a Paris street. "I sort of like being the product of my mother's Paris fling with an up-and-coming American Foreign Service officer. She never would have married Vic. I see that now. They were two lions. They would have torn each other to pieces."

Brody leveled his dark eyes on Adrienne. "Vic's odd goings-on —"

"My doing. All of them, including the hang ups. I wasn't trying to upset him or anything. I was torn, confused, trying to figure out if I was crazy and just wanted him to be my father or if he actually is my father. I've been sneaking around here, searching for clues. Proof. I didn't want him to know." She waved a hand. "The front door, though — that wasn't me."

"It was worn hardware," Heather said.

"What about Rohan?" Brody asked.

She crumpled into tears and sank back onto her chair. "I got him when I was with Thad. You know about him, don't you, Brody?" She waited for his curt nod before she continued. "It was one of those dumb impulsive things. I hoped Thad would want to stay with me if we had a puppy, but he didn't. I couldn't keep Rohan on my own, and I thought it was too much to ask Vic to have a puppy here."

"You pretended to abandon him," Brody said.

She nodded, sobbing now.

Heather noticed a muscle work in Brody's tight jaw. "Adrienne, you have to tell Vic everything," he said.

"I know. I'm sorry." She wiped her tears with her fingertips. "I was about to tell him when I started sorting through these old photos. It all became real to me. What I've missed, what he's missed. How deceitful I've been these past few months. Oh, Heather. I can't believe I've withheld the truth from you all this time. You deserve a better friend."

"I'm having a hard time being angry," Heather said. "And I'm glad we're friends."

Vic entered the dining room from the hall. He was ashen, his breathing ragged, as if someone had just tried to strangle him. "You're not responsible for anything your mother and I have done, Adrienne. Not any of it."

She knocked over her chair as she jumped up. She ran out of the room, crying, begging everyone to leave her alone.

Vic winced, rubbing the back of his neck. "She and I are definitely related with the waterworks," he said, his voice cracking as tears streamed down his lined cheeks.

■ ■ ■ ■

Heather appreciated the burst of cold air when she finally headed out to her truck. She wished she hadn't witnessed the deeply personal scene in the dining room, but the lines between friendship and business had been blurred from early on with her work out here. She'd hit it off with Adrienne the first time they'd met in December, and she'd always liked Vic Scarlatti. She'd never once considered his life would turn out to be *this* complicated.

"Heather," he called to her from the back steps. "Hang on a second." He crossed the driveway to her. "Thanks for waiting." He wasn't wearing a coat. He shivered, looking surprised, as if he suddenly remembered it was winter. "I wanted to tell you how sorry I am about all this. I don't know what more to say."

"You don't have to say anything, Vic."

"I wonder if we should consider putting the renovations on hold. It's a huge project, and now — I'm reeling, to be honest. I need time. Can you work with me on this?"

"Of course. Let's talk tomorrow."

He seemed barely to hear her. The wind blew through his gray hair. "Maybe I should sell this place. Maybe it's too late for me, and all my plans and hopes and dreams were for a younger man. A different man, perhaps a man I never was."

"I don't know about that, Vic, but your house needs a certain amount of updating, regardless of anything else."

He smiled. "Practical Heather. We could ditch luxuries like a sauna and wine cellar but keep necessities like a new heating system?"

"We could, but it's never a good idea to make big decisions about a house when you're in the throes of an emotional upheaval. You were never here with Adrienne's mother, were you?" Heather immediately held up a hand. "I'm sorry. That's none of my business."

"It's okay. Sophia and I were together for a few days in Paris, and we've stayed in touch over the years. I've stayed in touch with Richard, too. I wouldn't call either one a close friend, but I was happy to do what I could for Adrienne when she contacted me. Having her house-sit worked out for both of us. I never expected . . . I never saw any resemblance . . ." He broke off with a heavy sigh, the revelations of the day obviously weighing on him. "Neither Sophia nor Richard has ever been a guest here."

Heather nodded without comment and pulled open her truck door.

"I'm not the man I thought I was," Vic said half under his breath. "I'm a damn heel. I never asked Sophia . . . I never . . ." He seemed unable to continue.

"I'll come by tomorrow, and we can go from there."

"Thank you."

He spun around and headed back to the house. Heather got in her truck and noticed her hands were trembling when she started the engine. Sloan & Sons had dealt with last-minute cancellations and major cutbacks of big projects and would handle whatever Vic decided to do, but she hoped he would continue — not just for her sake or even for his. She'd fallen in love with his quirky 1912 house on Echo Lake. She wanted to see it updated so that it could last another hundred years. If Vic abandoned renovations altogether, he'd be talking to a wrecking crew in another ten years. The place would be condemned. The opportunity to save it — to turn it into one of the gems of Knights Bridge — would have passed him by.

When she reached Thistle Lane, she went inside just long enough to change clothes and grab her ice skates. She needed to burn off her emotions. Witnessing Adrienne's pain and embarrassment and Vic's anguish — his gut-wrenching recognition that the daughter of an old friend was *his* daughter — had affected Heather to her core.

Then there was Brody.

She broke into a run as she crossed South Main onto the town common. It wasn't smart to think about Brody Hancock. Watching him interact with Vic and Adrienne had reminded her that he wasn't in Knights Bridge for any other reason besides helping a newly retired senior Foreign Service officer, a man like countless men and women he was dedicated to protecting.

He was a *federal agent*.

He wasn't the kid who had played Risk with her brothers — who'd had some epic fight with them and left town, determined never to return.

Her young nephews waved to her from the skating rink. "Aunt Heather, Aunt Heather!" seven-year-old Aidan called to her. "Are you going to skate with us?"

"You *have* to, Aunt Heather," five-year-old Tyler said.

She laughed and sat on a bench to change into her skates. "Yes, I'm going to skate with you."

Brandon, their father, was with them. She

278

decided to wait to mention the potential problems with the Scarlatti renovations. First things first, and right now, she needed to be with her family and friends.

"Mind if I join you?"

Heather reined in her reaction to the sound of Brody's deep voice behind her. She glanced up at him and noted the pair of skates in his hands. "It's a public rink. You can skate anytime you want."

He grinned. "Now, there's a warm welcome."

"I didn't mean —"

"I know." He came around the bench and sat next to her. "I thought I'd check on you and whisk you off to skate. Then I saw you on the common."

"Like minds."

"Sometimes."

She introduced Brody to her nephews. They'd overheard their parents mention he was a federal agent and somehow were under the impression that meant he was a spy — not that they knew quite what a spy was. "Are you spying on Aunt Heather?" Aidan asked.

"Your aunt is going to help me remember how to skate," Brody said. "How would that be? You can help, too."

The boys loved the idea that a spy might

not be able to skate. Tyler took Brody's hand. "I'll show you. You won't fall."

"I'll help, too," Aidan said, taking Brody's other hand.

He skated off with the two boys, but his strides were strong and smooth.

Brandon eased in next to Heather. "Doesn't look rusty, does he?"

"Not even a little."

"Hell, Heather," her third-eldest brother muttered.

"What?"

He shook his head. "Never mind. I don't want to know."

"I only noted that his skating isn't rusty."

"Yeah. That's not all you noted. Go on. Skate."

Heather knew better than to keep protesting. She would only dig a deeper hole for herself. She tightened the ties on her skates and headed out onto the ice, the portable lights creating shadows as the January dark settled over the village. She greeted friends, slowly picking up her pace, making sure she had her balance and her mind was on skating and not wandering off to thoughts of her day on Echo Lake — or to watching strong, sure Brody Hancock skate with her nephews. They joined her, Aidan and Tyler claiming success in reminding their new friend how to skate. Brandon motioned to the boys from the bench — time for dinner and homework — and they reluctantly skated off, but not before turning care of Brody over to Heather.

He slid his arm around her waist. "Now you can be the one to keep me from falling."

"And how would I manage that?"

"More ways than you know." He leaned in close to her. "You can start by putting your arm around me."

"Ah. Makes sense." She eased her arm around him, noticing the firm muscles in his back, his warmth. "My brothers think I'm too trusting, you know."

"Is that what you think?"

"Sometimes."

"Maybe it's better than thinking you're going to step on a snake at every turn."

"Is that what life is like for you?"

He didn't answer as they skated around the perimeter of the rink. She was aware of her brother Eric arriving with his girlfriend, a local paramedic, but Heather didn't pull away from Brody. There was no use pretending she wasn't attracted to him. She had always known where she belonged, but right now she just wanted to be with him, a prospect that was straightforward and undeniable and felt right, but was also strangely unnerving.

They skated back to the bench. Brody showed her a text he'd received from Vic.

Rohan's tearing up the back room. Adrienne's packing. I'm drinking Scotch.

"Go, Brody." Heather smiled. "I have a couple more chapters to go in *The Scarlet Pimpernel.*"

FOURTEEN

Heather finished *The Scarlet Pimpernel* and then stayed up watching a house-and-garden network show. By morning, she had a better grip on yesterday's revelation about Vic and Adrienne if no better grip on her attraction to Brody. Anesthetizing herself last night hadn't helped her dismiss the flutter in her stomach when she thought about them skating arm in arm. But it was madness. What would a man like Brody Hancock do in Knights Bridge? What would she do in his world?

Time to return to reality. No more fantasies, no more pretending something could be that couldn't.

When she arrived at Vic's, she half expected to find that Brody had left last night. With the mystery of Vic's "incidents" solved, why would he stay? Instead, she spotted him down by the lake with Rohan.

A subdued Vic was at the kitchen with an

untouched mug of coffee and plate of toast. "Adrienne cleared out at first light. She's going to stay with friends in New York. I tried to talk her into staying here, but she wouldn't listen to any arguments. She offered to take Rohan with her, but I insisted she leave him since she doesn't have her own place." He gave Heather a grim smile. "I'll have to get those puppy training books, though."

"This must be difficult for both of you."

"Yeah. Thanks. I'm still all over the place with the renovations. I don't know what the hell to do."

"I'll collect any odds and ends I've left here," Heather said. "You'll need to make some decisions, but I can give you some time."

"Hours, days, weeks?"

She smiled. "Not weeks."

"Unless I want to pay through the nose," he said, not making it a question. "It's okay. I'll figure out what comes next. Right now I keep thinking . . ." He paused, clearing his throat. "I remember Sophia sent me a picture of Adrienne when she was three months old. You know that baby smile? No teeth, no problems." He raked a hand over his head and swore under his breath. "It kills me. What I missed."

"I'm sorry, Vic."

"I was such a driven jackass back then. If I'd known Adrienne was mine . . ." He shook his head. "I can't believe I'd have walked away from her. I wouldn't have. I know I wouldn't have."

Clearly he wasn't convinced. "Is there anything I can do?" Heather asked.

He gave her a ragged smile. "Ignore my whining."

She started into the mudroom. "We can talk paperwork once you figure out what you want to do. I won't be long here."

He nodded. "Right. Thanks."

She noticed torn-up newspaper and a stolen throw pillow in Rohan's bed. He was sprawled out, dead asleep. She left him and went down to the cellar. When she reached the workbench and turned on a light, she discovered a note under a hammer, handwritten in flowing cursive on three-holed notebook paper.

Dear Heather,
I'm sorry to leave without saying good-bye. Thank you for your friendship. Vic will come to his senses about the house. The sauna and wine cellar will be perfect. The wine list I developed is for real.
 I wanted to hate him but I couldn't. I

can't. He's a good man. I hope he sees that. Right now we both need time . . . like a good wine.

Knights Bridge is a special place. You're so lucky to know who you are and where you belong.

Your friend,
Adrienne

Biting back tears, Heather folded the note and tucked it in her vest pocket. She hadn't bothered taking off her sweatshirt and vest since she didn't plan to stay more than thirty minutes.

She heard heavy footfalls on the steep cellar steps. Too heavy to be Vic.

Brody joined her in the dusty corner. "Back in the cobwebs."

"Better than snakes. No stiff muscles after ice-skating?"

He shook his head. "Your nephews took good care of me. Heather . . ."

"You're heading out," she said. "Now?"

"In a few minutes."

"Vic's going to be lonely. I noticed Rohan's tearing things up in the mudroom."

"He senses the emotions."

"I imagine so." Heather picked up a clipboard she'd left on the workbench. "Well, I should get rolling. It's been good to see you again. Winters are long in Knights Bridge. Gossip over your return will get us clear through mud season. You saw the raised eyebrows last night skating, didn't you?"

"No," he said. "And neither did you."

"I assumed they were raised. I admit I was too busy trying to keep you from falling. I felt you teeter a few times."

He smiled. "I didn't teeter."

"No way, huh?"

"I didn't say that. Heather . . ." He slipped his arms around her. "What am I going to do about you?" Before she could get a decent breath, never mind respond, he lowered his mouth to hers. "I can't stop thinking about you. I don't want to stop."

"Is that why you're leaving?"

He didn't answer as his mouth found hers. It wasn't a gentle, lighthearted kiss this time. Not one to get it out of the way. He lifted her, tightening his hold on her. She threw her arms around him and opened her lips as their kiss deepened. He was going away, and she wasn't holding back now. With tools, dust, grease and cobwebs in the cellar and Vic Scarlatti upstairs, there was no chance she and Brody would go too far.

But she wanted to, she realized. Oh, she wanted to.

Somehow he got his hands under her sweatshirt, vest and T-shirt and onto the small of her back. His hands were rough, the skin warm as he drew her against him. She could feel his arousal. Her head spun with a thousand different sensations, not any of them conflicting. Her mind, body and soul were one in wanting to make love to this man.

Now, here, anywhere.

He sat her on the workbench, whispered her name as he pulled back. He kissed her cheek, her forehead, as he slipped his hands out from under her clothes and skimmed them up her arms, into her hair.

Finally, he held her face in his hands and looked into her eyes. "I expected a lot of things when I agreed to come back here, but I didn't expect you."

"You expected a crazed stalker and a bunch of mean-assed Sloans."

His mouth twitched. "Something like that."

"You're not that convenient for me, either. This federal agent who lives all over the world. This guy who hates my hometown and got run out by my brothers over some fight about pumpkins."

"The fight wasn't about pumpkins. The fight involved pumpkins."

"Pumpkins." She gulped in a breath, realizing her throat was tight, and she was on the verge of breaking into tears. "Brody." She draped her arms over his shoulders and lifted her mouth to his. "I could fall in love with you, you know."

"I know." He kissed her softly. "Be well, Heather."

"Where are you going, or can't you say?"

"I promised to visit my folks in Florida."

"A dose of warm weather will make Knights Bridge seem unreal."

"I doubt that."

"Adrienne and Vic can figure things out from here. It might not be easy, but it doesn't involve the Diplomatic Security Service."

"You're under my skin, Heather. That's not changing."

She made a face. "That sounds like a fungus."

He laughed and scooped her up off the workbench and set her back on the floor. "You're a breath of fresh air. You have a good life here," he said. "I'm not going to screw that up."

"You can't. I don't care how well armed you are, my brothers would come after you if you screwed up my life." But she couldn't sustain her teasing and took his hand into hers. "You don't need to worry about me, Brody. I know you're not likely to pick a safe follow-on assignment to this last one, which obviously wasn't safe. You like the action, and you're good at what you do. Go where you're needed."

He squeezed her hand but said nothing.

"I'm not fragile. I'm not jumping ahead, either, even if it sounds like I've got us . . ." She shook her head. "Never mind. I just don't want you to worry that I can't handle what you do for a living."

"It's tough to worry about someone as relentless and open as you are."

"Is that a compliment?"

"It's a fact. I'll see you soon, Heather." He tucked a finger under her chin and kissed her on the forehead. "I'm not going to see palm trees and suddenly forget you. Be good. Stay out of the cobwebs."

When Heather emerged from the cellar, the kitchen was empty, and Rohan was still asleep on his bed in the mudroom. She slipped outside and walked a little ways down the driveway toward the guesthouse, but she already knew Brody's car wouldn't be there. Still, she felt a jolt of emotion that she couldn't identify when she saw it wasn't. Loss? Regret? Hope? She didn't know. She only knew that what had happened in the cellar wasn't an end. It was a beginning.

Then again, she'd been wrong before. Once Brody crossed the Knights Bridge town line, he could have come to his senses and decided returning to his hometown had been a mistake that he need not repeat.

That didn't mean she couldn't leave town, go find him . . .

Heather shook off the thought.

She walked back to her truck and drove out to the Sloan homestead and the Sloan & Sons offices. No one was around. Beaver, once her dog and now the family dog, a mix of German shepherd and black Lab, was rolling on his back in the snow. She grabbed a homemade blueberry muffin from a plate set out on the meeting table. She sat on a folding chair. She would call about getting a new battery for her truck and do what work she could. She didn't know what would happen with Vic's renovations, but she didn't need to know this afternoon. Let him get his feet under him after yesterday.

She was into her second muffin when her brother Christopher stopped by. "I thought I might find you here," he said. "I heard Adrienne Portale and Brody Hancock left town, and that Vic Scarlatti is in a state over something but won't say what."

"You're a firefighter, Chris. How do you

know these things?"

He grinned. "Elly O'Dunn is home from California."

"That explains it."

"A couple of friends and I are going back-country snowshoeing this afternoon. Want to join us?"

"Thanks, but I've got a few things I need to do here."

"They don't involve moping, do they?"

She made herself smile. "No moping."

He helped himself to two muffins and headed out.

Normalcy, Heather thought.

Her life.

She made the call about her truck battery. As she hung up, Justin arrived from the Mc-Caffrey job site. The Echo Lake gossip would have reached him, too, but he didn't bring it up. "Why don't you join Samantha and me for dinner tonight?"

"I wouldn't want to intrude."

"It's her idea." He grinned at her. "You two can talk pirates and rogues."

FIFTEEN

Vic tolerated Smith's if he stuck to the turkey club or went for breakfast, but he knew better than to say anything since it was a Knights Bridge institution. He arrived in the morning at prime Sloan time. The uncle and three of the brothers — Justin, Eric and Adam — were at a table up front. Vic thought he'd missed Heather, but then he saw her at the counter, chatting with a waitress.

He sat on the vacant stool next to her. She gave him a bright smile. "Well, good morning, Vic. Isn't this early for you?"

"*Early* isn't the word. It's still night by my accounts."

He'd woken up in a dark, rotten mood but struggled not to take it out on anyone else, especially Heather. He was aware of her brothers casting him not-quite-suspicious looks. He didn't blame them. He would do the same in their place.

Heather's waitress friend set a mug of coffee in front of him without being asked. He supposed he looked as if he needed a jolt of caffeine. He'd had a rough night. He was ragged. But he had made some decisions, and he had a plan.

He drank some of the coffee, black. "I want you to keep going on the renovations as planned. No changes."

Heather narrowed her eyes ever so slightly. "You're sure?"

"Positive. They'll help me sell the place if it comes to it. I bought it for a song twenty years ago and own it outright. It'll be fine."

"If that's what you want to do, then I'll resume work today."

"It is what I want to do."

"A twenty-four hour pause barely counts, you know."

He smiled but said nothing. He ordered a sausage biscuit and drank more of his coffee. Behind them at the table, the uncle — Vic was fairly certain Pete was his name — got to his feet, laid a few bills next to his plate and headed out, stopping to kiss Heather on the cheek. He grunted a hello at Vic and left.

"Deep down Uncle Pete is a sweetheart," Heather said.

"How deep down?" She laughed, but Vic

could see her heart wasn't quite in it. "Heather . . ." He lowered his voice. "I never should have called Brody. I'm sorry if he hurt you."

"He didn't hurt me, Vic."

"You're half in love with him, aren't you?"

She turned on her stool, almost facing him. "It doesn't matter one way or another, does it? He's gone, and I have a job to do for you. I'm looking forward to it. All is well. I promise."

"You don't have to convince me. Love is a great thing, but it doesn't happen for everyone — and it rarely happens at a convenient time. You and Brody would be a disaster for each other. I don't have to tell you that, do I?"

"*Disaster* is a little strong, don't you think?"

"No, actually I don't. I know what Brody's life as a DSS agent is like, and I know what your life here in Knights Bridge is like. Your lives are, in a word, *incompatible.*"

The pain in her eyes took him by surprise. It wasn't a reflection of his own pain, any kind of projection on his part. "I know, Vic," she said quietly. "I do."

He went still, instantly hating himself. This wasn't some esoteric conversation over coffee early on a January morning. This was real. This was a young woman who had fallen head over heels for a man she knew would never fit into her life in Knights Bridge. As she picked up her mug, Vic saw the strain in her face. She'd obviously had a bad night herself.

He was so mad at himself he could have thrown his mug through a window. He glanced at her brothers and swore Justin was about to get to his feet, perhaps to throw *him* through a window.

"My apologies, Heather. I had no right to say that."

"It's okay." She seemed relieved when the waitress returned with her breakfast of scrambled eggs and toast. "Brody's your friend. You steered him into a career he obviously loves. A lot of people in town thought he'd come to a bad end. He's done well. He has time to add some romance to his life."

"So do you," Vic said. "But I'm the last person you should trust on matters of the heart. I should get my own life in order before I comment on anyone else's."

"Did you come to breakfast just to tell me you've decided to go ahead with the renovations?"

"Not just. I'm leaving for New York today. I'll be there a few days, at least. Elly O'Dunn has agreed to keep Rohan while I'm gone, but if you could look after the house now that Adrienne . . ." He faltered, just saying her name. "Since you'll be up there."

"Of course I'll look after the place."

"There's not much to do beyond calling me if it burns down."

He thought he saw a flicker of a smile as his sausage biscuit arrived. He took it with him, waving at the Sloan brothers as he paid for his biscuit and coffee and headed out. He didn't know the Sloans well. The truth was, he didn't know anyone in Knights Bridge well. He had people in from time to time to do odd jobs, and he had someone plow and take care of the yard, someone clean, someone bring cordwood and stack it. In twenty years, he'd never been to a single town event, not even the Memorial Day parade or a school bake sale. He knew Elly O'Dunn the best of anyone but only because she was his closest neighbor and was willing to do things for him.

Things needed to change, he thought as he stepped outside, noting that at least the damn sun was up now.

He climbed into his car and opened up his biscuit. It was as close to perfection as a biscuit could be. Who was he to look down his nose at this place?

Things didn't need to change. *He* needed to change.

He finished his sausage biscuit on his way back to Echo Lake. Adrienne had left her list of selections for his wine cellar on the dining room table, returned the rest of the photos to their box and lined up five wines in the built-in cupboard, each with her notes about its qualities.

Her goodbye to him, he realized.

He was already packed. He dragged his suitcase out to his car. As he put it in the trunk, he could see a peek of the snow-covered lake, glowing pink in the early-morning sun. Who was he kidding? He loved this place. A few dull cocktail parties in New York would get him back to himself and appreciating his chosen retirement life-style.

Not to mention Sophia was in New York, and she'd invited him to lunch at her favorite French bistro.

Sophia Cross Portale was older but as beautiful as the day Vic had met her in Paris thirty years ago. She was already seated at a table for two when he arrived at the cozy bistro she'd chosen. They exchanged a sterile kiss, and he sat across from her at a little round table by a window.

298

"I ordered a bottle of wine," she said. "I hope you don't mind."

"Not at all."

"I figured I'd go for a bottle after the last twenty-four hours. We polished off a few bottles of wine when we were together in Paris, didn't we, Vic?"

He tried to smile, to appear as cool and unshaken as she was. "More than a few."

"It was a good time. It was my first hint that Richard and I weren't going to work out, but I chalked our fling up to — I don't know. My last gasp of single life. I told myself that it didn't mean anything. I loved Richard and while I liked you a lot, I knew you were no more interested in marrying me than I was in marrying you."

Vic sat back as a waiter poured sparkling water.

"I'm sorry if that sounds unfeeling," Sophia added.

She wasn't sorry, he knew. She was just stating the facts. "It doesn't."

"We never talked about Paris after you found out about Richard."

"It seemed wrong to bring it up," he said.

"I appreciated your discretion. I didn't at first. You'd run from me at a dinner or cocktail party, and I'd think you hated me — that I'd done some terrible thing in suc-

cumbing to human temptations and frail-
ties. I wasn't married to Richard yet when
you and I were together. When we did get
married, I tried to make our marriage work.
He did, too. It seems like ancient history
now."

Vic glanced down at the handwritten
menu. His sausage biscuit seemed ages ago,
part of another life. "Time marches along,"
he said quietly.

"Yes, it does. When I got pregnant . . ."
Sophia fingered her water glass. "I knew the
baby was yours."

He raised his gaze to her. "You never had
any doubt?"

"I never had any reason for doubt," she
said, not meeting his eyes.

"I see." He didn't know what else to say.

"Do you hate me, Vic?"

"I don't hate you, no. I hate myself. I
should have done better by you."

"It was my decision not to tell you and
Richard, and then not to tell Adrienne. I
thought it was the right choice for everyone." She waited as their server poured their
wine, leaving the bottle. As he retreated, she
picked up her glass. "But it was my choice
to make. You do see that, don't you, Vic?"

"I'm not here to second-guess you, Sophia. You were in a tough position."

"Women have been in worse positions than I was, then or now. I had a husband, a career, a good income. I might not be the mother Adrienne wishes she had, but I did the best I could. I'm a grown-up, Vic. I was then, and I am now. I made choices."

"We all do."

"I'm not a monster."

"No, you're not. Sophia . . ."

She drank some of her wine, again avoiding his gaze as she set her glass down. "I wish Adrienne had left well enough alone, but once she figured out Richard couldn't be her biological father, she was determined to scratch that particular itch. She didn't tell me at first she was house-sitting for you in Knights Bridge. I thought she was staying with friends in New York."

"You refused to tell her I was her father."

"I believed — I *believe* — it wasn't the right thing to do, to tell her."

"What about telling me?"

"I thought I was doing you a favor by not telling you."

She set her glass down, the color in her cheeks deepening, reminding him of Adrienne. Their daughter. Contrary to her belief otherwise, Sophia was a woman of strong feelings, but she liked to pretend she was above strong emotion — that it was a weakness. She detested emotion in others. Vic remembered her telling him in Paris that she wasn't going to be one of those "weepy women." He hadn't known what she was talking about then. He hadn't cared, either. He'd been too keen on keeping her in his bed for as long as he could. Looking at her now, he could see that Sophia Cross Portale was simply afraid of herself. Maybe it had taken being in Knights Bridge — seeing Adrienne, Heather, Brody — to recognize what was so obvious to him now.

"It's good to see you, Vic," she said. "I'm not going to interfere with whatever you and Adrienne decide to do. Your relationship is for you two to sort out."

And that was that. They ordered lunch. She told him about her life and work. "I'm nowhere near retiring," she said not once, or even twice, but three times. She was in a five-year relationship with a corporate executive she described as "handsome, stable and reliable." She got along with his grown sons.

She asked him nothing about his own life, but he didn't mind. What was there to say? He hugged her goodbye, noting that she was still lithe and fit, but he had no reaction to her. She went back to her hotel. Vic watched her march down the street. He shook his head, marveling at how he could have had a child with this woman, and started walking in the opposite direction. He didn't stop for hours. It was one of those good, long New York walks that he often did when he was there for any length of time. They cleared his head. He'd let problems simmer, and when he came back to them, he could see them in a new light. Not personal problems — diplomatic problems. He'd paid no attention to personal problems. Really, he hadn't thought he had any.

He returned to his apartment, which he'd had for longer than his place in Knights Bridge. When he'd found it, he thought he lacked for nothing because his building had an elevator and a doorman. He'd lived in so many different places in his life. New York had always been his anchor, but Knights Bridge — how could he explain it? His little town that time forgot was his soul. It was always there, solid, beautiful and home in a way no other place was.

He wanted Adrienne to know she would always be welcome in Knights Bridge. He wanted to have a presence in her life, but only if it was what she wanted. Now, though, he wondered if he would ever see her again — if, having learned he had a daughter, he would have to learn to do without her.

SIXTEEN

Greg Rawlings lay sprawled on a sofa that was so big it made even him look small. He was a muscular man with dark red hair — what was left of it — and the kind of piercing eyes that scared the hell out of people. He didn't have to say a word. Brody had met him during his first weeks on the job. Greg was already something of a legend then, but the past few months had taken a toll.

He sat up, yawning. "Pizza, beer and a TV remote. Life doesn't get better, Brody." He patted his abdomen. "Still have my six-pack abs, though."

Brody sat on the edge of a chair that was covered in cat hair. Greg had already explained that the cat didn't like strangers and was in hiding. It was his niece's cat, but she was in college and couldn't have him in her dorm room. Therefore, her parents — Greg's brother and sister-in-law — were minding the cat. They owned the small apartment where Greg was staying during his recovery and marital troubles. He'd agreed to look after the cat while he was there. Not necessarily to clean up after him.

On the job, there was no one more thorough, more exacting, more disciplined than Diplomatic Security Service agent Gregory Rawlings.

Brody eyed his friend and colleague. "You happy, Greg?"

"Not wired that way. How was Florida? Your folks doing okay?"

"They're fine. Florida was warm and sunny."

"I like warm and sunny. So tell me why I married a woman from Minnesota, who thinks seventy-eight degrees is hot. Your old man has the life, doesn't he? Fishing guide in the Keys. I could do that if I don't go back on the job. Think he could use a partner?"

"He could use one, but that doesn't mean he wants one."

Greg sat up straight. "Independent cuss like you, Brody?"

"My father and I do have some things in common. I found him working on his boat. The damn thing looks like it'll sink. He said it's seaworthy."

"Any boat can sink," Greg said. "Look at the Titanic."

Brody got to his feet. "You're in therapy for your moods, aren't you, Greg?"

His friend grinned. "My moods are great. How are yours? What about your mother? Isn't she working as a fairy or something at Disney?"

"She's a hostess at a restaurant at Disney World. She doesn't wear a costume. She's doing well. Thanks for asking."

"Are your folks proud of you, or do they wish you were in Florida, too?"

"I'm not in this job to make my parents proud."

"But they *are* proud?"

"My father said he's proud. My mother asked me if I had a woman in my life."

"You tell her about your hometown girl?"

"I did not," Brody said, keeping his tone even.

Greg tossed the television remote onto a coffee table with two empty beer bottles and one empty pizza box. Brody had been relieved there weren't more bottles and boxes.

His friend looked past him, his eyes glazed over. "The woman in my life is in Minnesota. She's not coming back, Brody. I want her to be happy, and she can't be happy with me. I figured that out before she did."

"You made it a self-fulfilling prophecy."

"We tried couples' therapy on my last home leave, did I tell you? My idea, even. I still can't believe it. It was before I got shot, obviously. After that — I don't know. Doesn't matter. I don't give up easily, but Laura and I grew too far apart. She's not the same woman I married. I'm not the same man. That would be okay if we'd changed together, but we didn't." He waved a hand. "Whatever."

"I'm sorry, Greg."

"About what? I'm good. She's good. Kids are good. We'll adjust. People get divorced all the time. Time to move on." He cleared his throat and jumped to his feet, agile for a man his size and despite a near-fatal bullet wound. "That was the cat hair in my throat. I'm not emotional."

"You do need to vacuum this place."

He pointed to the kitchen. "Vacuum's in the utility closet if you feel the urge."

Brody collected the empty beer bottles and pizza box and brought them to the kitchen. He got a pitcher of tea out of the refrigerator, filled two glasses with ice, added the tea and brought the glasses into the living room.

He handed one to Greg. "Vic Scarlatti is in New York," Greg said.

Brody nodded. "I heard."

"Your mother ever have a fling with him?"

"Never. I didn't ask. She volunteered the information. She said he's not her type despite his fluency in French. I didn't try to follow her logic. She hasn't been back to Knights Bridge since my high school graduation."

"Why would she go back? Especially in winter. Did you tell her you went back?"

"I told her I was checking on the land, figuring out whether now was the time to sell it. She knows there's more to it."

"Mothers. They just want to know we're happy. Also that we're not in jail. Also that we're not bleeding on a dirty floor in some nasty, dangerous place where we'll die like a rat and they'll never see us again." Greg sat back down with his tea. "But that could just be my mother."

Brody felt himself start to relax. "I've met your mother, Greg. She's like you. She doesn't have the worry gene."

"She's moving into this place next month. She sold her house. She told me if she finds one cat hair, she's sending it to me. She doesn't care where I am." He grinned. "She wants to paint the walls apple-blossom pink.

She likes to pretend she's a sweet old lady."

"She is a sweet old lady in her own way."

"She says I need more balance in my life."

"Funny," Brody said, "my mother said the same thing."

"They never give up. There's no such thing as balance with our approach to our work and the tough assignments we take on. It's not the job, Brody. It's us."

"You're going back in," Brody said, not surprised.

"Yep." Greg put his feet up on the coffee table. There was no hint of self-pity or pain — physical or emotional — in the teal-blue eyes that settled on Brody. "And my intel says you're getting promoted, Agent Hancock. They want you in London."

Brody said nothing. He didn't doubt Greg's *intel*. After seventeen years in the Foreign Service, Greg Rawlings had sources everywhere and legions of people who trusted him, for good reason.

"You can have a family in London," Greg added, his gaze still on Brody.

"I can have a cat, too, but I don't have one, any more than I have a family."

"What about the hometown girl? Wouldn't she be interested in London? Scones, palaces, gardens, Harrod's."

Brody pictured Heather in Vic's cellar, her

blue eyes shining as he'd held her. He felt his throat tighten with a mix of emotions that had become familiar over the past week in Florida but that he was no closer to untangling. He wasn't sure he wanted to. Just let them sort themselves out on their own and go away.

"We've got some mop-up work to do first," Greg said, voice matter-of-fact.

Brody pulled himself out of his thoughts. "When?"

"No start date yet but soon. Saddle up, my friend."

"In the meantime, do you know where Adrienne Portale is?"

Greg's face split into a wide grin. "Of course."

When Brody left the soon-to-be apple-blossom-pink Mrs. Rawlings's apartment, Greg had out the mop, broom and vacuum. Add a bucket of hot water and a sponge, and Brody figured there was hope. Half of what his friend had been coping with in recent months was the death of his marriage and the realization that he had to learn to be a different kind of father to his teenage son and daughter. He could no longer pretend he was the devoted husband and father who was always there for his wife and kids, even when he was thousands of miles away and out of touch for weeks at a time. That had been part of the problem. The pretending. The insisting he was always there when he wasn't. The facts were otherwise, but he'd refused to believe them because they challenged his view of himself. Meanwhile, his wife and kids had been living with the reality, drifting away from him and his illusions.

Or so Greg had explained when he and Brody split a beer before Brody left.

Brody hadn't followed all of Greg's logic but, as he drove into Manhattan, he was confident his friend had turned the corner and was fine. Brody didn't know anyone more resilient than Greg Rawlings, but a bullet wound and a divorce were a lot to handle at one time.

He parked half a block down the street from Thad Bowman's Upper West Side wine shop. He and Greg had decided he should start there. Adrienne was staying with a mutual friend a few blocks away. Odds were she was making a stab at getting back together with her ex-boyfriend.

In a few minutes, she emerged from the shop, a red wool hat pulled over her dark hair and her black coat buttoned against the damp, gray afternoon. She stopped short when she saw Brody. "What are you doing here?"

"Checking to see if you're all right. As a friend. No one sent me."

"Vic or the DSS, you mean." She glanced back at the wine shop then shifted back to Brody. "It was a mistake to try, but I had to know."

"You wanted to be sure you two didn't break up because of your turmoil over your background."

"I was obsessed with finding out if Vic was my biological father." She bit her lower lip, pausing before she continued. "I'm not proud of everything I did, but I never meant to hurt anyone. I guess I felt I was the one who'd been hurt. Lied to, denied the truth. But my mother was in New York for a few days and we talked and . . ." Adrienne crossed her arms on her chest, as if she needed to hug herself. "I have a better understanding of why she made the choices she did."

"What are you going to do now?" Brody asked her.

"Wallow or deal with things, I guess. I miss Rohan and Echo Lake. And I miss Vic. I can't explain. I didn't think it would be this bad. I don't know what to do." She smiled. "Wallow awhile longer, I guess."

"You'll figure it out." Brody nodded to the wine shop. "This guy Thad — you can do better."

Some of the tightness seemed to go out of her, and finally she laughed. "I appreciate that, Agent Hancock. Thank you."

"Vic decided to go ahead with renovations."

"Do you think if I told him I want to be part of his life, he would listen?"

"Vic's got his faults, but he always listens."

Adrienne tilted her head back, studying him a moment. "You feel you owe Vic, don't you? That's what this visit is about, isn't it?"

"Nah. I'm just hoping you'll finish stocking his wine cellar."

"Are you ever serious?"

He winked. "I'm always serious."

He left her and drove down to Vic's street in the low fifties between First and Second Avenue. Brody didn't love driving in New York, but it didn't intimidate him. He found a parking space, checked with the doorman and took the elevator up to Vic's fourth-floor apartment.

Vic had set a battered suitcase by the front door. "I'm leaving for Knights Bridge in the morning. Elly O'Dunn says Rohan misses me. He misses Adrienne, too, but there's nothing I can do about that."

"You should invite Adrienne to dinner tonight, before you leave."

"*Should* is a bad word, Brody. You shouldn't use it." Vic grinned, but the strain was evident in his face. His grin evaporated. He glanced around the small apartment. "I should give up this place. It's served its purpose in my life."

"You'll be happy in Knights Bridge?"

"Happier than I would be anywhere else." He clapped a hand on Brody's shoulder. "Come. I have no alcohol in here, but I have a bottle of San Pellegrino and a lime. Let's have a drink together. You can tell me about your promotion."

"You've been talking to Greg," Brody said.

"He called a little while ago. He knew you'd be stopping by. He wanted me to tell you that his place is now spotless. I assume you know what that means?"

"It means the Greg we know is back."

"That's a good thing, I suppose. Let's talk, Brody. I'm sick of figuring out bathroom fittings and discussing puppy poop."

"Poop, Vic?"

"You expected more colorful language?" He grinned again, clearly more himself as he led Brody back to the kitchen. "I'm ever the diplomat."

■ ■ ■ ■

It was after dark when Brody arrived back in Knights Bridge. He slowed as he passed the town common on Main Street. The skating rink was lit up, and he saw Heather with her two nephews, all three laughing as they skated in crazy zigzags, arm in arm. The only Sloan brother he noticed was Eric, not in skates as he stood by the bench. He looked right at Brody and shook his head, as if he'd known Brody would be back sooner or later. Brody waved at the Knights Bridge police officer and continued on his way.

He didn't go into Vic's house. He went straight down to the guesthouse. His blanket, sheets and pillow were still stacked up on one end of the sectional, his old Risk game still on the coffee table.

He stood at the windows. The snow on Echo Lake gleamed in the light of the full moon. A stiff wind blew through the trees, creating shifting shadows on the lake.

Plans for the mop-up operation were moving fast.

He didn't have much time.

He went outside and got back in his car.

SEVENTEEN

Heather was surprised when Eric walked with her from the skating rink back to Thistle Lane. He hadn't skated, of course, but she'd stayed out on the ice for over an hour, burning off energy after work. "I hear it's full speed ahead on the Scarlatti renovations," he said as they made the turn at the library, lit up for an evening program.

She nodded. "We're in good shape, although I had one of those days of one problem after another. The usual annoyances."

"Surprises, delays and Adam the perfectionist?"

"I tell myself that we want a stonemason who is a perfectionist."

"I guess so," Eric said with a grin. "Vic's still out of town?"

"Mmm. He's at his apartment in New York. He's still deciding where he wants to stay when we start tearing apart the house.

It doesn't matter to me since he's available by email, text and phone."

"What about Adrienne Portale?"

"I haven't heard from Adrienne since she left Knights Bridge."

Heather hadn't told anyone, including Eric, that Adrienne was Vic's daughter. It wasn't her story to tell.

He slowed as they came to Phoebe's house. He was in jeans and a leather jacket, not his uniform. "I wish you'd told me Brody was looking into a series of unexplained incidents that had Vic concerned."

"I didn't know much until it was over."

"A man like Vic doesn't have just the occasional plumber mad at him, Heather." Eric stopped at the end of the shoveled walk out to the lane. "Neither does Brody."

"All's well that ends well, right?"

"This time."

"Brody's job is protecting people like Vic. If there'd been any real danger, he'd have —"

"Protected you, too?"

Heather felt her cheeks flame and was glad for the darkness. "Dealt with the situation," she said. "It's water over the dam at this point, Eric. Why are you bugging me about it now?"

"I'm not bugging you, Heather. I'm talking to you. Brody's a good-looking guy with a dangerous job. Some women fall for that type."

"I imagine they do."

He didn't budge. "You know what I'm saying."

"I do, and you don't have to worry. Brody's visiting his parents in Florida."

"And then what?"

"I don't know. Call him and ask him." She motioned toward the house. "I succumbed to a Valentine's Day display at the country store and bought two chocolate hearts. Want one?"

Eric scowled. "No, Heather, I don't want a chocolate heart."

"They're fresh. They're not leftover from last year. It would be a real opportunity for you to save me from myself."

"I give up," her eldest brother said. "If anyone can handle a federal agent with time on his hands, it's you."

"Are you ever going to tell me about the fight you guys had with Brody?"

"It would serve no purpose."

"No arrests were made," she said, trying to prod him into talking.

"Correct."

"That means there's no record of the incident I can look up."

"Right again."

"Okay. You won't talk. I'll tackle Justin next. Then Brandon. Then Adam. Then Christopher. Take you in order."

"You do that. Meanwhile, enjoy your chocolate hearts." Eric started down Thistle Lane. "If you need me, little sister, you know where to find me."

"You know I hate being called *little sister,*" she yelled back to him.

He didn't bother turning around. "I know."

She went inside and helped herself to one of the chocolate hearts while she heated up stew Maggie had dropped off, taking pity on her long day after hearing about Adam's nitpicking — which he would call his specifications. What was especially annoying was that he was right.

She saw she had an email from Vic. He was alerting her that he would be returning to Knights Bridge tomorrow.

She emailed him back: Excellent. Safe travels!

The past week had been quiet without him and Adrienne at the house. Heather had tried to tell herself that Brody hadn't been in Knights Bridge long enough for her to miss his presence, but she knew better.

Even Rohan was away, if only down the

319

road at the O'Dunn house. Heather had stopped to see him several times. Elly had tried to extract information about what was going on up on Echo Lake, but Heather had stuck to describing progress on the renovations.

She ate Maggie's stew and her second chocolate heart. Despite her sugary indulgence, she felt in control and normal, at least on the surface. As she'd buried herself in work and her routines since Brody, Vic and Adrienne had all left Knights Bridge, she'd noticed a strange emptiness in her that she'd never felt before. As excited as she was about Vic's renovations, she recognized that a part of her had been going through the motions this past week.

It was the aftermath of coming so close to falling in love with Brody Hancock.

All there was to it.

She left her bowl in the sink, tossed her chocolate wrappers and went to the back bedroom where Phoebe had brought dresses she'd discovered in a hidden attic room at the library late last summer. Most were copies of gowns from Hollywood movies from the 1930s through the 1960s. Phoebe had discovered the Edwardian gown in the collection and had worn it to the costume ball where she'd met Noah.

Never mind reading another of Phoebe's musty books, Heather thought.

She would try on Hollywood dresses.

An hour into her marathon of trying on dresses, Heather heard footsteps on the front porch. She assumed it was one of her brothers and pulled open the door, only to discover Brody standing on the front porch. He was wearing his suede jacket, unbuttoned over a navy blue sweater and jeans, and scuffed boots. He looked her up and down, biting on his lower lip, not saying a word.

Well, what was there to say?

She could have picked a sleek, sexy dress Grace Kelly or Audrey Hepburn had worn in one of their movies, but no. Oh, no. She'd decided to have a little fun and had slipped into a copy of the dress Billie Burke wore as Glinda, the Good Witch in *The Wizard of Oz.*

"Where's your magic wand?" Brody asked finally, his mouth twitching with humor.

"It's here somewhere."

"I knew there had to be one."

"There's no hat, though. I looked. Just the magic wand." She pointed to her shoulders. "And the wings. I'm not sure what they're all about. Do you remember Glinda having wings?"

"Ah . . . no."

"I didn't, either." She opened the door wider. "Would you like to come in?"

"No Munchkins and Flying Monkeys?"

"Nary a one."

"Then I'll chance it."

Brody entered the small house, and Heather shut the door behind him. From her Sloan & Sons T-shirts to Glinda. There had to be a middle ground, but apparently not tonight.

"Do I want to know why you're wearing a dress out of *The Wizard of Oz*?"

"Because the dresses from *Gone with the Wind* are too small."

"That's a reason."

"And it's funny. Me as Glinda. Don't you think that's funny?"

"*Funny* isn't one of the words on the tip of my tongue, no."

"The woman who sewed the dresses used to work at the library. She left Knights Bridge for Hollywood ages ago. She's coming back in the spring. She and Ruby and Ava O'Dunn are cooking up stuff. I think Samantha's involved now, too, and probably Maggie."

"I see."

He obviously didn't, but Heather was

breathless. "How was Florida?"

"Warm and sunny, as you predicted."

"Well, welcome back. I should change back into my jeans and sweatshirt. The dress is old, and the seams and zipper aren't guaranteed to hold. Then I'd be in a mess, wouldn't I? Not that I'm worried. You've dealt with worse messes as a DSS agent than a Good Witch dress coming apart . . ."

What was she saying? She glanced around the small living room, the love seat and chairs piled with dresses. "I need to find that magic wand so I can shut myself up."

"Heather."

"It itches, too. The dress, I mean. I don't know about the magic wand."

Brody stepped closer to her. "Heather," he said quietly.

"I'm sorry but you have *no* idea what it's like to be standing here in pink chiffon."

"As true a statement as I've ever heard."

She motioned with one hand toward the stairs. "I'll only be a minute, although it's one of those dresses that's probably easier to get on than to get off . . ." She caught herself. "Never mind. I'll just go now."

She started up the stairs but tripped on the hem of her gown. Brody was there, grabbing her by the waist before she could hit the steps.

"It's yards and yards of chiffon," she said. "I don't think I've worn a long dress since I was a bridesmaid for Brandon and Maggie's wedding. I do wear dresses, though. And I know how to use a needle and thread. My grandmother and mother taught me how to sew quilts."

She didn't know if he heard a word she said. He had her off her feet and up the stairs before she could take a breath and babble some more. Why couldn't he have warned her he was back in town? Why had he surprised her? It wasn't just that he'd caught her in a ridiculous dress. She could have been eating her chocolate hearts or doing the dishes and she still would have reacted this way.

It was being near him again, she knew.

"I thought for sure you'd come to your senses and not come back," she whispered when he set her on the floor at the top of the stairs.

"I came to my senses and did come back." He touched a knuckle to her cheek. "I missed you."

She found herself glancing through the open door into her bedroom, her unmade bed visible from the top of the stairs. She tore her gaze away and waved a hand. "I should get this dress off."

"No argument from me."

"Brody . . ." She touched her fingertips to his lips. "I missed you, too."

She ducked into her bedroom. He stood on the threshold, watching her as she eased off the detachable Glinda wings. He leaned against the doorjamb. "Easier putting this thing on, wasn't it?"

"I made a game of it." Her fingers hadn't been shaking then. She set the wings on a chair. "You could help with the zipper. Once you get it started, I can manage."

He stepped into the bedroom and walked over to her. "Will you turn me into a frog if I tear something?"

"My magic wand is downstairs, remember?"

"Glinda could have told Dorothy right from the start that she could click her heels together three times and go back to Kansas. I think she used her to get rid of the Wicked Witch of the West for her."

"Clicking her heels wouldn't have worked if Dorothy hadn't believed it would."

He lifted her hair at the nape of her neck. "She had to get the hell scared out of her a few times to really be convinced there's no place like home."

Heather felt his fingers on her skin as he found the pull for the zipper. She couldn't

breathe properly with the tight-fitting bodice. She'd had to dispense with her bra to
get into the thing, but she didn't tell Brody
that. "I'm not an expert on *The Wizard of
Oz,*" she said.

"I'm not, either. I'm just making stuff up
off the top of my head to keep myself from
ripping this dress off you. I don't want you
to have to explain a shredded Glinda dress
to your friends."

At this point, Heather thought, she almost
preferred explaining a torn dress than staying in it another minute — and not just
because it was tight and itchy. Her skin was
on fire from Brody's touch. "It's tedious
work, I know. It's an invisible zipper, and
it's old. I had trouble with it."

"I'm not having trouble with the zipper.
That's not why I'm running out of patience." As if to prove his point, she felt the
zipper slide a few inches down her back.
"It'll be easier if I unzip it all the way, don't
you think?"

"I should warn you . . ."

"You don't have to," he whispered. "I've
already figured out you don't have anything
on under this damn dress."

"I must remember you're very observant."

The zipper was down, and the bodice was
off, revealing her breasts to the cold air and

his gaze. The rest of the dress quickly followed, a heap of pink chiffon in the middle of the floor. Brody stepped over it, taking her in his arms. He carried her to the bed and laid her down on her back, kissing her with a gentleness she didn't feel anywhere else in his body as her hands skimmed down his shoulders and arms to his hips.

"I want to make love to you," he said between kisses, as one hand smoothed down her side, over her hip and slowly, tantalizingly, between her legs. "But I'll leave if you want me to."

She eased her hands around to the front of his pants, unbuckled his belt, if not efficiently at least successfully. She managed the button next then tackled the zipper. Her pulse quickening, a thousand sensations tingling her skin, she tucked one hand inside his pants. He was hot, hard. She felt his fingers slide into her own heat, and she let her moan be her answer. She didn't want him to leave. She wanted him to stay and make love to her.

His clothes came off, cast onto the floor with her dress, and their mouths and tongues and teeth followed their fingers over their heated bodies, tasting, teasing, plunging them into a kind of incoherency Heather had never experienced. When he thrust into her, she knew she wouldn't last and threw her arms over her head, giving herself up to the searing pleasure and faint pain of having him inside her, driving deep, relentless. Finally, she clasped her arms around him and let the climax take them both, until they collapsed together onto her now-warm sheets.

It was a long time before the air felt cool again. Brody sat up, using his fingertips to push a few damp strands of her hair from her face. "Why didn't you tell me?" he asked softly.

"I knew you'd figure it out."

"Heather . . ."

"I don't have *no* experience. Just not a lot of experience." She took his hand and sat up. "I'm not fragile, Brody."

He smiled and kissed her on the forehead. "I noticed."

They got dressed and went back downstairs. Brody helped pack away the rest of the dresses. He found Glinda's wand. "Greg Rawlings and I could have used this in November. We were in a tough spot. Couldn't click our heels together and get back home, either."

"That's when Agent Rawlings was wounded?"

Brody nodded. "He's a good friend and a guy with regrets. A failed marriage and two teenagers he hardly knows. It's his doing. He'd tell you that himself."

"Does it have to be that way with the work you do?"

"No. We know agents — men and women both — who have solid marriages and happy family lives. That doesn't mean there are agents who aren't on that road."

"What road are you on, Brody?"

He kept his dark eyes on her. "You don't see me with a wife and kids, do you?"

Heather sat on the love seat. "This home leave has been difficult, hasn't it?"

"It just got better." But his humor evaporated, and he sat next to her, putting a hand on her knee. "It was a close call back in November. It's been intense.

"I was looking for a distraction when Vic called with his problems."

"Does he know what happened to you and Agent Rawlings?"

"Some. Not the details."

"Vic's always had faith in you," she said quietly.

"There were times he was the only one who did, and even I didn't understand why. He's not perfect, but he's a good man. He's loyal, and he believes in people."

"You're more skeptical?"

"A lot more skeptical."

"Your work — this mission — it's still intense, isn't it?"

"It's unfinished," he said.

Heather felt her mouth go dry. She placed her hand over his on her knee. "I don't want to be a home leave distraction, but if I am —"

"You're not. I've never felt what I'm feeling right now. It's not going away. That much I know."

"Things have happened fast between us. I mean, sex before we've even had a candlelit dinner together."

"We had wine and hors d'oeuvres at Vic's. There were candles as I recall."

She smiled. "So there were." Her breath caught in her throat. "Brody . . ." She couldn't finish, wasn't sure what she meant to say. "Do what you have to do, okay? Don't worry about me." She made herself smile again. "I've got loads of people who worry about me."

"They want the best for you."

"Always. No doubt in my mind."

"What is the best for you, Heather?"

"Workwise? I'd like to get into interior design. Justin is supportive. I haven't talked to Pop about it. He hates debt, but I think he'd be fine if I can prove to him the educational expense won't break the bank. My mother would be happy if I would learn to cook, but there's not much hope of that." Heather paused, realizing she'd been talking fast. She squeezed Brody's hand. "That's the road I'm on, but I don't have to stay on it."

He got to his feet, pulling her up with him. He slid his arms around her waist and kissed her softly. "We'll have lots of candle-lit dinners together." He stood back from her. "I need to get up to Vic's." He winked at her. "Trust me. Word is already out that I was here for longer than it takes to help you with the dishes."

"Let's hope no one knows about my Glinda dress."

He was grinning as he left, and that was something, Heather thought as she put away one last dress, the sleek Audrey Hepburn dress from *Breakfast at Tiffany's.* Olivia Frost had worn it to the September costume ball where Phoebe and Noah met. Heather knew there was no *way* she would fit into that one. But as she returned from the back room, she felt hot tears in her eyes. She'd seen the intensity building in Brody as they'd put away the dresses. It was unmistakable. Their lovemaking *had* been a diversion. Now he was getting back into the mind-set he needed for his return to his work.

She might be a natural optimist, but she couldn't fool herself. She would never regret the past few hours, but she wouldn't be designing a house for Brody Hancock on Echo Lake anytime soon.

Eric and Justin were at Smith's when Heather arrived for breakfast. Almost simultaneously they pointed to one of the two empty chairs at their table. She gave them a cheerful smile as she sat down. "Great morning, isn't it?"

"We know Brody Hancock's back in town," Eric said.

Justin eyed her over the rim of his coffee mug. "How was your visit with him last night?"

"How do you know?"

"Brandon walked the dog on Thistle Lane and saw Brody's car parked in front of Phoebe's house."

"Brandon doesn't have a dog."

"He doesn't?" Justin shrugged, unrepentant. "Oh, well."

"To answer your question, Brody stopped by to let me know he was back in the guesthouse at Vic's place." She tried to ignore the rush of heat to her cheeks; tried even harder not to think about making love to Brody . . . the feel of him inside her. She seized her coffee when it arrived.

"Heather," Eric muttered. "Hell."

Justin pushed the cream pitcher to her. "Forget you don't take your coffee black?"

"One of those mornings."

He rolled his eyes. "Yeah, right."

"Brody's coming off a high-stress, dangerous assignment, isn't he?" Eric asked.

Heather dumped cream into her coffee. "I've gathered that, yes. There was a firefight. A friend of his was shot. He's making a full recovery. I think there are still loose ends with whatever happened."

"Loose ends," Eric repeated, his jaw visibly tight.

"You don't want to be a diversion for a guy like that, Heather," Justin added.

Justin had a reputation as the bluntest of the Sloans. She usually could match his directness with her own, but this morning, she didn't know what to say. She wasn't any better at talking about feelings than her brothers were, and she woke up in the gray light of dawn, her sheets still tangled from last night with Brody, her bed empty, and she hadn't known what she felt.

She didn't know why she thought breakfast at Smith's would help.

Eric pulled his coffee in front of him. "We don't want to see you here with a broken heart when Brody goes back to work."

"I don't want that to happen, either," she said. "But if it does, I'll handle it."

Justin winked at her. "Good, because he's tougher to beat up than he used to be."

It was a joke, but Heather saw his point. "I appreciate your concern, Justin. Yours, too, Eric."

"But we can butt out," Justin said.

She shook her head. "You can trust me."

"I do. I don't trust Brody, though."

"It's not because of the past," Eric said. "It's because of the nature of what he does. Being a DSS agent isn't just a job for Brody. It's who he is. You can see that the minute you meet him."

Justin pushed back in his chair. "For the record, Brandon didn't see Brody's car last night. We haven't even talked to him. Eric and I made that up to get you talking, so don't nail him to the wall."

"All you had to do is ask me about Brody."

Eric shook his head. "You'd have stonewalled us. We had to surprise you." He leaned toward her, serious now. "There are a hundred guys you could see, and Justin and I wouldn't bat an eye. Brody isn't one of them. This isn't a regular guy you're falling for, Heather."

"I know that," she said without any defensiveness.

Her eldest brother got to his feet. "I'm not saying anything else on the matter, but if you ever need to talk, or a shoulder to cry on . . ." He grinned suddenly. "Call Maggie."

He tossed a few bills on the table and left. Justin nodded to the waitress, who refilled his mug. He added cream and waited for her to withdraw before he spoke. "Your work isn't a hobby, Heather. If you want responsibility, it comes with commitment."

"Fair enough."

"Did Brody tell you he worked for us before he left town? Pop hired him."

Heather shook her head, hiding her surprise. "I didn't know."

"Brody lasted two weeks."

"What happened?"

"Ask him." Justin held up a hand. "I don't know myself. Pop won't talk."

"Did he quit or was he fired?"

"Don't know."

"Was this before or after the big fight you all had with him?"

"Before. It seemed like a big fight at the time. Now . . ." He drank some of his coffee, his blue eyes taking on a warmth that reminded Heather of what a good man her second-eldest brother was. "It doesn't seem like anything at all."

He left without finishing his coffee.

Heather ordered a breakfast sandwich to go. It turned out to be a good idea since she passed her youngest brothers — Adam and Christopher — as she headed out. She could tell they were in interrogation mode, too.

Or maybe just curious, she thought, climbing into her truck. Just as she had been when Justin was falling head over heels for Samantha Bennett, a woman no one in Knights Bridge had expected to be the right match for him. But instead of whisking him off to adventures all over the world, treasure-hunter Samantha had found a home in Knights Bridge, a place where she could be herself and feel settled.

As Heather started her truck, she noticed it was a cloudy, dank, gray morning that fit her mood. Knights Bridge had never been home for Brody. Getting her out of her Glinda dress last night wasn't going to change that.

She looked out at the town common and the classic houses that ringed it. Could she ever leave this place to be with him? Had

Justin asked himself that same question when he'd fallen in love with Samantha, or hadn't it occurred to him? Was it a given for her brothers, working for Sloan & Sons, living here in their hometown?

Brandon appeared out of nowhere and tapped her window. She rolled it down. "You startled me."

"Thought you had that glassy-eyed look. Anything on your mind?"

He'd obviously talked to either Justin or Eric, maybe both. "Breakfast."

"Right. Maggie said to tell you she's trying new recipes tonight and making enough food for an army if you want to come by." He kept his gaze on her. "You can bring a guest if you want."

"Thanks. I'll see how the day goes and let Maggie know."

Brandon stood back, and Heather rolled up her window. As she started out of the village, the sun tried to break through the gray. She smiled, taking it as a sign even if it wasn't one, and ate her breakfast sandwich as she reviewed her to-do list for the day and focused on her work.

EIGHTEEN

It hadn't been a dream.

The acres of pink fabric. The magic wand. The frustrating zipper.

The warm soft skin of Heather's back as he'd finally slid the zipper down to her waist, knowing he wanted to make love to her.

Brody hadn't known they would go that far, but they had.

He should have guessed she was inexperienced and have gone easy, but he hadn't. He hadn't even realized what was going on until she'd dug her fingers into his back. By then it was too late — and not just for him.

"Oh, yeah," he said. "Last night wasn't a dream."

He walked up to the main house. Much of the snow and ice had melted with a few warm days while he was away, but he wasn't fooled. It was early February. The New England winter was still in full swing.

Vic had arrived from New York. Heather's truck was there along with several other trucks and vans. Brody noticed the Sloan & Sons logo on a couple of them. He saw her on a side porch with a group of men, including her brothers Justin and Brandon — an indication that they were getting serious about the work on Vic's house.

Brody left them to their meeting and went into the kitchen.

"I couldn't invite Adrienne to dinner last night," Vic said from the table. He had *War and Peace* opened in front of him but didn't seem to be making much progress.

"All the things you've done your life, Vic, and you chickened out on a simple dinner invitation?"

"Totally. You've never seen such cold feet." He jumped up, grabbed his jacket. "The place isn't the same without Rohan. Never thought I'd say that. I'm going down to Elly's to pick him up."

"He needs a home."

"Yeah. Yeah, he does. All this bouncing around isn't good for him. I told Adrienne I would see to him. She's got enough to worry about, poor kid."

Brody saw that Vic had washed out Rohan's bowls and set them on the counter to dry. "Maybe Elly's been able to teach Rohan some basics."

"Like not chewing my cashmere scarf? I found it in his bed. Little rascal."

"He's not going to stay little."

"Good." Vic shrugged on jacket. "Brody . . . I know you have a lot on your mind. I just want to say one thing to you, and then I'll stay out of it. You don't owe anyone. Not after all you've done. You don't owe your parents, the Sloans, Knights Bridge, the stupid, mixed-up troublemaker you used to be. You don't owe me."

"I appreciate that, Vic."

"No, you don't. You're gritting your teeth. That's okay with me, provided you take my words to heart." He pointed a finger at Brody. "You do not owe anyone. Do you hear me?"

Brody yawned. "Sure, Ambassador Scarlatti. I hear you."

"I had a professor who threw anyone who yawned out of class. He regarded yawning as insolent and rude." Vic sighed. "When I say *no one,* Brody, I mean no one — including Greg Rawlings and the entire Diplomatic Security Service. You've done your part. There are countless ways you can put your training and experience to good and honorable use if you so choose."

"If I quit, you mean."

"If you decide to move on, is what I mean. You're young, but you've done more in ten years than a lot of agents do in twice that. Have a life before it's too late." Vic snatched his car key off the table. "I know I'm jumping the gun, but I also know you. Give Heather a chance to fit into your life and for you to fit into hers. Don't assume it's impossible and push her away."

"I have no idea what you're talking about, Vic."

Vic frowned. "You two *are* involved, aren't you? Good heavens. I hope you're not unconsciously getting back at the Sloans through her."

Brody picked up the dog bowls. "Go fetch Rohan."

"You're an all-in type. I know, because I am, too. You think that will hurt Heather. You think she belongs here in Knights Bridge."

"Everyone thinks that, Vic, including you."

"I admit I didn't see the sparks between you two until they were about to burst into flame, but now that I do —" He sighed. "Let her decide where she belongs."

"Do you think there's any doubt?"

"I don't think it's as black-and-white as you obviously do," Vic said. "She's not a home-leave fling for you, Brody. I can see it

341

in your eyes when you talk about her. But you're going to let her believe she doesn't matter to you, aren't you?"

Brody ignored Vic and set the dog bowls on the floor in the mudroom. "I want Heather to focus on renovating this place."

Vic had followed him into the mudroom. He nodded thoughtfully. "I see." He placed a hand on the doorknob. "You can want whatever you want, Brody, but Heather is a Sloan, and she will do as she damn well pleases. You like her independent spirit. Don't try to tell me you don't."

"I won't, then."

"Adrienne is worldly and nomadic. I thought maybe you two . . ." He opened the door. "She knew she wouldn't stay here. That's why she pushed me to get puppy training books out of the library."

Brody could see the anguish in the older man's eyes. "What are you going to do, Vic? Immersing yourself in renovations will only take you so far. You need a plan for the next thirty years."

"I thought about writing my memoirs, but nobody gives a damn. I'll do something else. It'll be fun to train Rohan. I've always wanted a dog."

"You haven't always wanted a dog."

"You're leaving. You've got that look.

When?"

"As soon as I hear from Greg Rawlings."

"I thought he'd been shot."

"He's all better."

The Sloan & Sons vehicles departed all at once after an hour, leaving only Heather's truck. Brody went out to the front porch and found her staring down at the frozen lake. "We're expecting another storm this weekend," she said without looking at him. "Could be the biggest of the season."

"I saw the forecast."

She glanced at him. "Will you be here to see it?"

"I don't know."

"Is this what your life is like — not knowing where you'll be day to day?"

"Not always, no. It is right now because of a particular situation."

"The one that led to your friend Greg getting shot." She inhaled, turning back to the lake. "What really happened that night with my brothers? Did you vandalize a job site?"

"Depends on your point of view."

"Were there mitigating circumstances?"

"I was eighteen and angry."

She shook her head. "It wasn't that simple."

He stood next to her at the rail. He could see shadows on the snow-covered lake. "It

343

was a practical joke that wasn't really a practical joke, and it got out of hand. I was pissed off at the world."

"You didn't hurt anyone?"

"Not physically, no. I never knew how much of a mess you can make with a couple dozen pumpkins. I cleaned it up, left town and got my act together."

"I didn't know you worked for Sloan & Sons until this morning. What happened?"

"I got fired."

"My father fired you," she said, not making it a question.

"One of those things."

"And you come home and discover we're doing Vic's renovations."

"It made sense. You guys are the best in the area. I never asked or expected Vic to hold grudges on my account."

"You never expected to be back here. You could have sold your land without ever stepping foot in Knights Bridge."

"That's true. I wiped the dust of Knights Bridge off my feet when I left. Vic didn't know your father fired me. I never told him, and I knew Jack wouldn't. It doesn't matter, Heather. Not after all this time. Vic helped me in countless ways, but he never called me to task the way your old man did. He said I had potential and was wasting it screwing around."

Heather smiled. "Sounds like Pop, except I bet he was more colorful."

"I needed a wake-up call. I needed to be held accountable in a way my parents couldn't and Vic never would. Your father was right to dump my ass, but it was hard to see that at the time."

"Vic?"

"He helped me figure out that I might make a place for myself in the Foreign Service, and I saw that I needed college to do it right. He and your father pointed me in the right direction, but it was up to me to take the steps I needed to take. I got my degree, and I became a DSS agent."

"And here you are, back where you started."

"My parents were never happy here, but they could have been on a beach in Fort Lauderdale and they wouldn't have been happy at that time in their lives. Knights Bridge isn't what made them miserable."

"You have nothing to prove to anyone here, Brody."

"Neither do you."

"To my brothers, you mean?" She grinned. "Damn straight."

He could see that her good humor didn't reach those deep blue eyes of hers, but he heard his phone ding in his pocket. He knew what the message was, but he got out his phone and glanced at the screen, anyway. The message was typical Greg Rawlings.

Be in Boston in six hours. Bring your toothbrush.

In his years as a DSS agent, Brody had never had to leave a woman behind. He'd seen to it that was never a possibility. He'd kept an emotional distance that he'd told himself protected any woman who might think she was in love with him, but it also protected him.

Now here was Heather Sloan, watching him with her eyes narrowed.

He tucked a finger under her chin and tried to put the distance into place, but instead he kissed her. He didn't give a damn who walked onto the porch. Vic, Rohan, one of her brothers.

Finally, he stood back. "I have to go," he whispered.

She touched his cheek with her fingertips. "Be safe, Agent Hancock." She smiled. "I'll be here when you get back."

NINETEEN

Heather drove into town for a few errands and gave Brody enough time to get his things together and leave without her as a distraction. When she returned, he was gone. She had a brother who was a police officer and two brothers who were firefighters. They'd had close calls, but she'd known where they were, what they were doing. Would Brody be able to tell a wife more than he'd told her?

She shook off the thought and got out of her truck as Vic arrived with Rohan. The puppy bounded to her, jumping, licking her hand. She laughed in spite of her raw emotions. "Hey, Rohan. I saw you just yesterday at Elly's, remember?"

"He's excited to be back on his home turf," Vic said, grinning as he joined her in the driveway. "He's grown, hasn't he? It's barely been a week, but I swear he's looking more dog than puppy."

"He's beautiful."

Rohan leaped onto the remains of a snow-bank and found a rock he'd left behind. As he settled down to chew it, Elly O'Dunn pulled her Subaru in behind Vic's car and got out, her red hair — dyed at this point in her life — brightening the gray light. "I knew he'd be happy to be back here," she said, obviously delighted. "He missed you, Vic."

"He's Adrienne's dog. I said I'd see to him, but I shouldn't get attached."

"You already are attached, and he needs a master. Adrienne pretended to abandon him because she knew you would take him in and provide him a good home. I did what I could, but it's up to you to train him. You can't keep spoiling him."

"Spoiling him? How do I spoil him?"

"Let me count the ways," Elly said with an incredulous laugh. She glanced around as if looking for someone. "Where's Brody? I thought I'd say hi. I haven't seen him since he left town all those years ago."

"He had to leave," Heather said, surprised at the catch in her voice. "Something came up with his work."

"Nothing good, I'm sure." Elly reached down and patted Rohan. "I'm glad we have men and women who can do the work he does. They keep people like Vic safe so they can do their jobs."

"They're indispensable," Vic said. "Brody's one of the best."

Elly stood straight. "Being called away at the last minute —"

"He'll be home before we know it." Vic didn't sound as confident as Heather suspected he meant to. He turned to her. "How was the meeting of the Sloans? You all are going to be able to juggle the McCaffrey job with this one?"

"Absolutely," Heather said, relieved at the change in subject.

"The girls and I thought we'd see a wrecking crew out here before you ever got around to renovations, Vic," Elly said. "It'll be wonderful having this place fixed up. Did I hear you're adding a sauna?"

"I am, indeed. I added it at the last minute, but our Heather here didn't bat an eye."

Elly laughed. "Don't forget your neighbors when it's up and running."

"Adrienne . . ." Vic knelt down and snapped a leash on Rohan. "She hasn't returned any of my calls or emails."

From Elly's expression, Heather could see that Vic's neighbor and friend knew that his house sitter had turned out to be his daughter. He'd have told her. Elly was like that — people told her things. She watched Rohan heel next to Vic. "What a good dog," Elly said. "Vic . . . you have to be patient with Adrienne. I can understand her reluctance to talk to you right now. She's embarrassed, and she's confused. She needs time."

"She must wish she left well enough alone and never contacted me."

Heather had never seen him look so pained, so at a loss. "Vic . . ."

Elly didn't seem to notice Vic's mood, or wasn't indulging it if she did. "Adrienne can't unring that particular bell, can she? Neither can you. She has to decide what to do with what she knows, and to make peace with how she handled it." Elly leveled her turquoise eyes on her neighbor of twenty years. "Leave her alone, Vic. Give her the time she needs, and live with whatever she decides." She smiled, heading for her car. "Ambassador O'Dunn speaks."

"You'd have made a damn good Foreign Service officer," Vic called to her.

"It's raising four daughters — not to mention a whole bunch of goats." She paused at her car, her expression softening. "You know where to find me if you need help with Rohan." She gave an exaggerated shiver. "I miss Southern California already."

Vic watched her climb in behind the wheel, pull the door shut and start down the driveway with a wave. He sighed at Heather. "Elly's a dynamo. Doesn't mince words. She and Brody's mother were friends, before Patrick O'Dunn died and before the Hancocks divorced. I don't think they've stayed in touch. Sometimes . . ." He inhaled deeply. "Sometimes you have to wonder at the twists and turns in life."

Heather smiled. "I know the feeling."

"Ah, yes. I'm sure you do."

Heather arrived at Maggie and Brandon's Gothic Revival "gingerbread" house off the town common in time for what her sister-in-law was calling Mediterranean night. She pointed at the array of foods on her kitchen counter one by one. "Here we have grilled eggplant with lemon juice, spinach with coriander, hummus, three kinds of olives, tabouleh, stuffed grape leaves and sundried tomatoes. You invited Vic and Brody, didn't you? You got my message?"

Heather helped herself to an olive. "I got your message and invited Vic. He said to thank you but he's tired from his drive up from New York this morning."

"Another time, then. What about Brody?"

"He had to leave." Heather glanced at her

watch. She wondered if he was on his flight. She made an effort to smile. "Duty called."

"Oh. You mean he's on some kind of mission?"

"Yes."

"I see. And he didn't give you any details, so it must be dangerous." Maggie paled slightly. "Heather —"

Eric had come in through the back door. "These guys are careful and well trained," he said then slung an arm over Heather's shoulder. "Brody isn't the wild pumpkin-smasher he used to be, is he, little sister?"

Aidan squeezed between Heather and his mother. "I hate olives," he said.

Maggie scoffed. "How do you know if you've never tried one?"

"I've tried them a million times, Mom. It's Tyler who won't try them."

"Because you gag instead of letting him make up his own mind."

The rest of the Sloan family descended on Maggie and Brandon's house.

After dinner, Brandon got out his Risk game. Justin, Adam and Christopher joined him. Eric passed since he had to be on duty soon. Brandon invited Heather, but she declined. She knew they were making a point. She didn't have the memories of Brody Hancock as a teenager that they did.

They were reminding her that he wasn't a sexy stranger who'd wandered into town.

But he wasn't that to her, either.

"We used to play Risk with Brody," Justin said. "He was a total hard-ass. No prisoners."

"I remember," Heather said.

Justin looked surprised. "Really? Most of the time you were sulking in your room."

"I remember he played Risk with you guys. I don't remember if he was a hard-ass." She pulled out a chair at the kitchen table where they'd set up the game. "And I never sulked. It's not a Sloan trait."

Brandon grinned at her. "You kicked our butts when you did play with us. Wait until you and Brody play Risk and he sees what a devious world conqueror you are."

Heather laughed. "You guys don't hold a grudge against him?"

"Never did," Adam said. "You can't hold grudges in a big, healthy family."

"That doesn't mean we weren't wary of Brody's return to town," Justin added.

The Risk game broke up early when Aidan and Tyler persuaded their uncles to take them ice-skating. The boys had their arguments set. It was Friday night. The rink was open until ten on Fridays. They could stay up. They'd make everyone hot chocolate.

Maggie declined to join them. "I'm staying here to put up my feet and read while it's quiet."

Her husband kissed her on the top of her head. "It won't stay quiet."

She smiled. "It never does." She looked at Heather with concern. "Do you want to stay? I've got ice cream in the freezer."

"No. Thanks, though. Enjoy your quiet time."

Heather walked with her nephews and brothers to the common but continued on to Thistle Lane. When she approached her house, she saw a car in the driveway, and for a moment thought it might be Brody. Which, of course, was impossible, and also not the case. For one thing, the car was sleeker, newer and had Massachusetts plates.

Noah Kendrick and Phoebe O'Dunn stepped out and waved to Heather. She waved back and picked up her pace. "Noah, Phoebe — what a wonderful surprise. Welcome home!" She reached the driveway. "It's great to see you."

"You, too, Heather," Phoebe said. "We just got in."

On Noah's private jet, no doubt. Heather motioned toward Phoebe's darkened house.

"You two can stay here. I can stay with my folks or one of my brothers. It'll take me two seconds to pack."

Noah shook his head. "We wouldn't hear of it, Heather."

He was fair-haired and deceptively fit, a master fencer as well as a high-tech genius. He was driven, but also kind — and obviously in love with Phoebe, his turquoise-eyed, redheaded librarian.

"We're staying with my mother," Phoebe said. "We're only here for a few days. We're discussing wedding plans." She smiled. "Noah and I are engaged."

Heather clapped her hands together in delight. "Congratulations! That's wonderful. I'm thrilled for you both."

She brought them inside. She was relieved she'd tidied up and the place didn't show any obvious signs of Brody's presence.

Noah slipped his arm around Phoebe. Definitely a man in love, Heather thought. And Phoebe . . . she smiled at him in such an intimate way that Heather could see her friend's love for this man was more than up to the massive changes in store for her. Phoebe had settled into a fulfilling life on Thistle Lane and her work as the library director. Now she was engaged to a billionaire.

But to Phoebe, Heather knew, Noah was simply the man she loved. The rest didn't matter.

They chatted for a few minutes, catching up on Knights Bridge goings-on. Elly had already filled in her eldest daughter on Brody's return but not the reasons. As fast as news traveled in their hometown, people did have their secrets and could be discreet, and Heather had no intention of discussing Adrienne's relationship to Vic.

"There was nothing to these incidents?" Phoebe asked.

"Nothing."

"What's Brody like now?"

Heather's mouth went dry. She saw Noah narrow his eyes on her. She suspected he wasn't nearly as clueless about people as he liked to believe — and liked everyone else to believe.

She decided on a vague answer. "He's good, I guess. You just missed him. He left today."

"Is he coming back?" Phoebe asked.

"I don't know. Anyway — is there anything I can do for you?"

"We hear Adrienne Portale is house-sitting for Ambassador Scarlatti," Noah said.

"Not at the moment. Do you know her?"

"*Of* her," Phoebe said.

Noah nodded. "We understand she's quite the wine enthusiast."

"She is," Heather said. "I'm not an expert, of course, but she put on a couple of wine tastings and talked to me about wine. She's been helping Vic with a wine cellar. She obviously loves what she does."

"I got the impression from my mother that Adrienne is at a loose end right now," Phoebe said.

Heather nodded. "That's true."

"I'd like to talk to her," Noah said. "If she's interested. Could you arrange an introduction, Heather?"

"I'll do what I can," she said.

Noah had an uncanny knack for choosing the right people to do what he couldn't or didn't want to do, and he was intensely loyal. His friendship with Dylan McCaffrey went back to kindergarten. Dylan had been an ex-hockey player sleeping in his car when Noah had tapped on his window and begged him to help him with his fledgling high-tech company.

After Phoebe and Noah left, Heather called Adrienne's cell phone and left a message. She would call back or she wouldn't, but Heather had a feeling that whatever Noah had in mind could be just what her new friend needed right now.

What do I need?

Heather let the question hang unanswered in her mind and went over to Phoebe's bookcase. She chose a frayed copy of *Assignment in Brittany* by Helen MacInnes.

She had a good life, but for the first time — the first time ever, she thought — she felt a tweak of what she could only describe as loneliness.

How was that even possible?

She took her book up to her empty bed. As she turned the first page, she received a text message. She assumed it was one of her brothers, but it wasn't.

Wheels up in ten minutes. All good there?

All good. Rohan is back at Vic's.

I heard. He peed in the dining room. Vic had to clean it up himself.

Heather smiled, trying to picture Brody as she typed.

Life on Echo Lake.

Gotta go.

Be safe.

Always.

She knew he was gone. She held her phone tight in her hand, as if somehow that brought him closer to her. After another minute, she set her phone on her nightstand and opened her book.

He stared at the unfamiliar watch on his wrist. Three hours ago he had stood on English soil. Three hours ago he had been Martin Hearne, British Intelligence agent.

Perfect, Heather thought, and continued to read as the wind picked up outside with the brewing weekend storm.

TWENTY

The storm picked up steam Friday night and raged through Saturday, finally dwindling to flurries before the sun broke out midday Sunday. With almost two feet of snow dumped on Knights Bridge, the roads were edged with tall snowbanks and evergreens drooped with heavy wet snow, any green branches barely visible under the white. The sky turned blue, and when Heather arrived on Echo Lake, its beauty took her breath away.

She was there on a Sunday because Adrienne had called.

Heather found her friend in the driveway with Rohan and a pair of snowshoes. "Elly O'Dunn will be here any minute," Adrienne said. "We're going to snowshoe out to the state forest. Vic is grumbling, but he's joining us. Heather . . . I'm so sorry I've been out of touch. I needed time."

"It's good to see you, Adrienne."

She set her snowshoes on the plowed driveway. "I'm not staying. I want to see about Rohan and then go back to New York. I have a friend's couch I can sleep on."

"Do you want to talk to Noah first?"

Adrienne frowned. "Noah?"

"Did you get my message?"

"No. I saw you'd called but I didn't listen to your voice mail. It's a bad habit. Are we talking about Noah Kendrick?"

"He and Phoebe are in Knights Bridge."

"Oh. Elly said she was bringing one of her daughters. It must be Phoebe. Do you think Noah will be with her?" Adrienne knelt down, pulling off her gloves and tightening the ties on her boots. Finally, she looked up at Heather. "You know Noah's winery is incredible, don't you?"

Heather smiled. "I've heard it has huge potential."

Adrienne smiled back, rising. "Wonder who told you that. Oh, Heather. I'm not going to get ahead of myself, but I would love to talk to Noah. Did you bring your snowshoes?"

"I keep a pair in my truck. It's okay, though. You all go on." Heather tried to think of an honest if incomplete excuse. "I did a lot of shoveling this morning."

"Ugh. One of my least favorite winter

chores." Adrienne laughed as Rohan got hold of one of her boot laces and loosened it. She patted him on the head. "Don't worry, buddy. You're joining us. You don't have to tear into my laces." She squatted down again and retied the lace. "Vic said Brody was here overnight and then left on Friday. Think he'll be back?"

"I don't know why he came back last week," Heather said.

"Don't you?" Vic asked, joining them. He set his brand-new snowshoes on the driveway and stabbed the poles into a snowbank. "I can't believe I let myself get talked into snowshoeing. In any event — Heather, you must know why Brody stopped here."

"Something to do with you, I assume," she said.

Vic shook his head. "Nothing to do with me. My dear Heather, Brody came back because of you. He knew he was leaving, and he wanted to see you first."

"He said that?"

"Of course not. Brody doesn't talk that way. But it's the deal."

"I like it," Adrienne said with a smile. "You and Brody, Heather. I like it a lot. It's complicated, though, isn't it?"

Vic snorted, dismissive. "The Sloans aren't hothouse flowers. Heather will adjust.

And no one's tougher than these DSS agents. If there's a will, there's a way."

Adrienne turned to Heather. "You know who you are. That will help, whatever happens with you and Brody. I've struggled on that score."

"Are you still struggling?" Heather asked her.

She smiled. "Less and less."

"I'm struggling with these damn snowshoes," Vic muttered. "Which one is right and which one is left, or doesn't it matter?"

Adrienne laughed, shaking her head. "I have no idea."

Elly and Phoebe arrived, and Elly got Vic straightened out. Heather waited until they set off down the as-yet unplowed road to Brody's property, where there were trails to the north shore of the lake. Then she walked down to the guesthouse. She didn't go inside but instead stepped into the deep snow on the porch. She wondered where Brody was right now, and if he thought about Knights Bridge and Echo Lake — if they helped or were a dangerous and unwelcome distraction. Or if he'd slipped back into his old life, and didn't think about his hometown at all.

By the end of the week, Heather knew she

was ready to get her first crew out to Vic's house that Monday. Vic had decided to stay in his guesthouse during the renovations and give up his apartment in New York. Adrienne was exchanging emails with the manager at Noah Kendrick's winery about how her skills and enthusiasm could help take their labels to the next level. In the meantime, she was snowshoeing every day and working on Vic's wine cellar. Not once had she mentioned her relationship to him to Heather. It was as if Adrienne had buried that knowledge until the time was right to take it out and figure out its impact on her life.

Heather was in the guesthouse, checking on the heat per Vic's request when she heard a vehicle arrive. She thought it might be Noah, but in another minute, she saw a man at the back door. Her heart jumped, but it wasn't Brody. This man was thickset, with close-cropped hair as red as any O'Dunn's.

"Greg Rawlings," he said when she opened the door. "Brody's friend."

Heather felt her heart jump. "Something's happened?"

"What?"

"Brody . . ."

"He's not here? I thought he'd be back in

Knights Bridge by now. That'll teach me to think."

"I'm Heather Sloan, by the way. I don't live here. I'm overseeing renovations on Ambassador Scarlatti's house."

"Right. I know." Greg glanced around, as if noticing his surroundings for the first time. "Nice place. There's a ton of snow out here if you haven't noticed. Damn." He looked again at Heather. "Have you heard from Brody?"

She shook her head. "Not since he left."

"Right." The burly DSS agent shrugged. "Sometimes you can't communicate. Where's Vic? I heard he's growing kale these days."

Greg obviously knew that Vic had come up behind him on the small porch. "In your dreams, Agent Rawlings. I recognized your car. How are you?"

"Alive. Did my survival a couple months ago cost you money in the pool?"

"Gallows humor," Vic said.

"How's your daughter?"

"You go near her, and I'll call the cops."

"I am the cops. Relax. I'm off to parts unknown, and she's too young for me."

"You're healed?"

"Cleared for hazardous duty."

But he'd obviously expected Brody to be

there. Heather could see Vic was concerned, too. She brought them into the guesthouse kitchen. "If something happened," she said, addressing the senior DSS agent, "you'd know, wouldn't you?"

"To Brody you mean? You bet. I'd know."

"Then where is he?"

"I don't know. We went our separate ways a couple days ago. He mentioned stopping in Washington. I didn't think he was serious."

"Oh, dear," Vic said. "A new assignment brewing?"

Greg ignored him. "I'll throw my stuff in a guest room with a view. Vic, no law against building a fire down by the lake, is there?"

"A fire? Why would —"

"No? Good."

Greg disappeared down the hall. Vic turned to Heather. "Brody and Greg go back to Brody's first days as a DSS agent."

Heather understood what he was saying. Brody Hancock and Greg Rawlings had a friendship and a bond based on work that she, and even Vic, if less so, could never fully understand.

"Knights Bridge won't make Brody happy any more than it did his parents, will it, Vic?"

"I've offered to buy his land here a number of times. He's never so much as named a price. Echo Lake is home, Heather. His parents only came here as adults. They were unhappy together, and they didn't like Knights Bridge. They focused on themselves and their own wants and left Brody to his own devices. It didn't get better after they divorced."

"No wonder he cleared out of town." She fingered the dishes he'd left in the strainer. "What if going on this mission brought him to his senses, and he doesn't come back here? Greg would know if something was wrong, wouldn't he? If Brody was in danger —"

"Greg would know, yes. Absolutely." Vic studied her a moment. "Heather?"

She shook off her questions. "The heat's fine in here, Vic."

He hesitated then nodded. "Good. I love this place, but I hate to be cold."

Heather went straight back to Thistle Lane and tried on the Cleopatra dress in Phoebe's back room, because, well, why not? The dress was too tight, but not way too tight, but it wasn't as much fun as the Glinda dress — even before Brody had arrived and helped get it off.

What an evening that had turned into.

She forced it out of her mind and examined her reflection in a full-length mirror on the door to the closet where most of the long-hidden dresses were now stored.

"All I need is a snake," she said aloud.

No way, though, would she pass for either Cleopatra or Elizabeth Taylor.

She peeled off the dress and carefully hung it back in the closet then slipped into jeans, a flannel shirt, wool socks and boots. This was who she was, she thought, glancing at her reflection. She was the sixth and youngest sibling — the only sister — of the hardworking Sloans of Knights Bridge, Massachusetts, a small, pretty town on the edge of the Quabbin Reservoir.

She liked her life, and she had nothing to prove.

But she didn't want to think Brody had decided that whatever was going on between them wasn't in his best interest to pursue. She didn't want to get some perfunctory text from him telling her he was in a faraway, undisclosed location.

We had fun, but time for you to find yourself a regular guy.

Maybe she wouldn't get a message at all. Maybe he'd just disappear, thinking that was what was best for her.

She hated it when people tried to decide

what was best for her.

She knew she was leaping well ahead of any facts and being negative, which wasn't her style. She grabbed her jacket and headed outside, ignoring the dark, the cold and the mounds of snow as she walked down to the library and on to the skating rink.

Justin was there, watching Samantha skate with Aidan and Tyler. He grinned at Heather. "You can tell Sam's grandfather explored Antarctica, can't you?"

"The cold doesn't seem to bother her, and she's a natural on ice."

"I see you didn't bring your skates."

Heather shrugged. "I just wanted some air and company."

Her second-eldest brother eyed her. "Brody back?"

"His DSS friend Greg is. He's bunking in Vic's guesthouse. Apparently Brody made a detour to Washington."

"Makes sense, given what he does for a living."

"Yep. Makes perfect sense."

"You never tell us what you're feeling, Heather, but you don't have to. You wear your heart on your sleeve. We're not going to get into the middle of whatever is going on between you and Brody, but we're here for you, no matter what. Just want you to know that."

She angled a look at him. "We? You mean you guys have all talked?"

"Not Adam," Justin said. "He never says much, but he's with us."

"The pick-Heather-up-if-she-falls-apart brigade?"

"You're not going to fall apart. Hell, Heather, can't you just say thank-you?"

She grinned at him. "Thank you." But her grin didn't last. "I mean that, Justin. I admit it'll be spectacularly awful if I never hear from Brody again."

"But that's not going to happen." Justin smiled as Samantha spun toward him on her skates. "Not right now, anyway."

"You say that with such confidence."

He handed her his phone. On the screen was a text from Chris.

Just saw Brody turn down Thistle Lane. Where's Heather?

She could barely contain herself as she returned the phone to Justin. "Tell Chris I'm on my way to Thistle Lane."

"Don't run," Justin said, grinning. "You don't want to slip on the ice and break an ankle. That would mess up your reunion."

She pointed a finger at him. "You guys

370

need to stop spying on me."

"Who's spying? It's a small town. We see things."

There was no explaining to him, and Heather had to admit she and her other brothers had exchanged calls and text messages when Samantha Bennett had come to town last fall looking for pirate treasure.

When Heather reached Thistle Lane, Brody's car was in the driveway. She didn't see him on the porch, but then remembered she hadn't bothered to lock the door. She ran up the steps.

He opened the door. "Evening, Heather."

She smiled. "Evening, Agent Hancock."

She went inside. He shut the door behind her. He still had on his jacket, and she noticed dark circles under his eyes. Wherever he'd been, it hadn't involved much sleep.

"I was hoping I'd catch you trying on another dress," he said, easing his arms around her.

"You missed your chance. I was Cleopatra an hour ago. No snake, though."

"Can't be Cleopatra without a snake." His mouth found hers. There was no fatigue in his kiss. "I like you just fine as you are."

"I'm not sure I know you just as you are, but it doesn't matter." She put her arms around him. "I'm glad you're here."

"Back on home leave, at least for now."

"I met your friend Greg. He said he was going to build a fire down by the lake."

"He doesn't stay still for long."

"You two are a couple of rugged guys. I wasn't sure you'd come back to Knights Bridge."

"I was," Brody said, drawing her closer.

"You've had a rough time, haven't you?"

"It all worked out."

Heather touched her fingertips to his jaw. "Go and be with your friend, Brody." She smiled. "I'm not sure I trust him with matches."

"Smart woman." This time, their kiss was deep, lingering. Finally, Brody stood back and kissed her on the forehead. "I'll see you tomorrow."

TWENTY-ONE

The next morning was overcast and cold, but Heather noticed the sunrise was earlier, a sign winter was winding down. Mud season would soon be upon them. She smiled to herself as she started up Vic's back steps. She didn't know if he'd ever been in Knights Bridge during mud season. Brody had, of course, but she doubted it was one of his fonder memories of his hometown — although mud season did spell the end of the darkest days of winter.

She pushed open the back door, expecting Rohan to rush her, but he wasn't in his bed or at his bowls. She unzipped her vest, wondering where Vic, Adrienne and the two DSS agents might be. She'd sneaked into Smith's early for a breakfast sandwich, which she'd eaten while walking back to Thistle Lane. She hadn't wanted to join her brothers or anyone else for breakfast and sit there pretending she'd slept well and wasn't preoccupied with what was going on between her and Brody. Neither, she told herself, would distract her from doing her job.

She went into Vic's kitchen, frowning when she saw a chair overturned. Then she noticed shards of clear glass by the stove, as if someone had cleared off the counter and smashed whatever wineglasses were there onto the floor.

She got out her cell phone as she edged into the dining room.

It was worse there. Chairs upended. Photographs and Adrienne's wine-cellar notes swept off the table onto the floor. In the living room, it was the same. Shelves emptied of books, magazines and knick-knacks. A footstool on its side. Something — a vase, maybe — smashed on the hearth.

She hit Eric's number. He answered on the first ring. "What's up, Heather?"

"Something's wrong at Vic's. It's a mess. It's like someone tore apart the place in a rage. I don't know if there was a fight or what."

"Where are you?"

"Living room. I don't see or hear anyone else. I'll check upstairs."

"Don't check anywhere. I'm on my way. Get into your truck. Lock the doors."

"Brody and his friend Greg are here some-where."

"They were at Smith's for breakfast. They should be back there soon. Wait for them in your truck. Got it, Heather?"

"Got it."

As she disconnected, she heard men's voices in the kitchen. Before she could get her next breath, Brody and Greg were through the dining room and into the living room.

"Whoa," Greg said, taking in the mess. "Somebody was pissed."

"It was like this when I got here," Heather said.

"Where are Adrienne and Vic?" Brody asked.

She shook her head. "I don't know."

"I'll look for them," Greg said, then melted into the entry.

Heather noticed a photograph by itself on the mantel, otherwise cleared of its usual display. She lifted it for a closer look and saw it was of a dark-haired woman and a girl on a summer day. They were on a lake-front, sitting on a boulder with their feet in the water as they smiled at the camera.

"That's Adrienne," Heather said as Brody stood next to her. "She can't be more than ten. The woman must be her mother."

He tapped the photograph. "You recognize the spot, Heather?"

She took a closer look. "It's the cove out by your old place, isn't it?"

"I used to fish off those boulders with my father."

"Where did this picture come from?"

"I've never seen it before. I would have been living here when it was taken, but I don't remember a mother and daughter showing up. My father's a sociable guy, but he didn't have much company out here."

Greg returned with Adrienne, sniffling, her face splotched from crying as she cuddled Rohan in her arms. "I found them out front," Greg said. "She doesn't know where Vic is."

Adrienne pointed to the photograph in Heather's hand. "I showed that to Vic last night. I remember going to a pretty lake with my mother on our way home from a trip to Boston, but I didn't know where the lake was until I came here in December. Something about it got to Vic. He didn't say a word when he looked at it. He just went upstairs and shut his door."

"Bedroom's a wreck, too," Greg said.

"Do you think Vic is responsible for tearing up the place?" Brody asked.

Adrienne gave a small nod. "He must be.

I got up early. Everything was fine, at least down here. I went to help Elly with the goats, I got back to this," she said, going pale as she glanced around the trashed room. "I checked inside and outside, but Vic isn't here. I was about to call you guys when Greg found me."

"Looks like Ambassador Scarlatti had himself a dark night of the soul," Greg said, then shrugged. "Or a dark morning, anyway. Same difference out here." But his teal eyes were serious as he turned to Brody. "His car's still here. He must be out in the woods somewhere. You and Heather know the terrain. Want to see if you can pick up his trail?"

"I've got snowshoes in my truck," Heather said.

"Snowshoes," Greg said. "I'd rather jump out of a helicopter."

Brody ignored him. "You and Adrienne wait here, in case Vic turns up on his own or we need a formal search-and-rescue team."

"My brother's on his way," Heather said.

Greg frowned at Brody. "Brother?"

"Cop. There are five brothers. Expect them all."

Heather went with Brody into the kitchen. He grabbed a pair of snowshoes and poles hanging above Rohan's bowls in the mud-room. She followed him out through the back door. They stopped at her truck, and she got her snowshoes, poles and a first-aid pouch.

They didn't put on the snowshoes. She and Brody would walk out along the road first.

Heather tucked the first-aid pouch into her vest. "If Vic wasn't in his right mind and didn't dress for these conditions . . ."

"He'll be cold," Brody said.

They headed onto the road out toward the cove where the photograph of Adrienne and her mother had been taken. Heather knew she didn't need to explain the dangers of hypothermia to Brody. She checked the side of the road but saw only animal prints. Wild turkeys, deer, rabbits.

Brody pointed to a footprint visible on the plowed road. Heather nodded. "It's got to be Vic," she said.

They continued down the road. A sharp wind gust blew snow off the trees.

Brody glanced at her. "You okay?"

"Yep. Let's just find Vic."

"You're dressed more appropriately than you were for the Rohan rescue." He moved in close to her. "Don't worry, though. I'll keep you from falling in the lake or another brook."

"I didn't fall into the brook. One foot went through the ice." She tucked her poles and snowshoes under one arm. "I know what you're doing. You're trying to keep my mind off the million bad reasons Vic didn't make it back to the house before Adrienne returned from helping Elly with the goats. He wouldn't worry about scaring you and Greg, but he wouldn't want to scare her."

"Or you."

"I got here a little early."

They walked a few more yards. "You still fell in that brook. You can admit it."

"How are you doing, Agent Hancock? You look cold." She grinned at him. "Your nose is red."

He grinned back at her, but Heather knew their moment of levity didn't allay their concern about the situation with Vic. They pressed on up the road. She kept up with Brody but noticed he stayed just ahead of her, as if to intercept any danger that might come their way.

When they arrived at the site of his old cabin, he pointed at prints in the snow, clearly leading into the woods toward the cove where the photograph of Adrienne and her mother had been taken.

"Vic's in boots," Brody said. "He must not have grabbed snowshoes before he left the house."

"The snow's still relatively deep. He'll wear out faster in boots."

Brody gave a curt nod. He pulled off a glove and got out his phone. "I'll update Greg," he said as he typed. "It's a hike down to the cove. If Vic's not dressed properly and not in his right mind, he could be in serious trouble."

Heather nodded. "Eric can get a rescue team started out here."

"Makes sense." Brody glanced at his screen after he sent his text. "Greg says two of your brothers have arrived."

"Eric and Christopher, probably."

"Three more to go."

Brody slid his phone back into his pocket. She could feel his intensity as they put on their snowshoes, quickly tightening the straps and adjusting the poles. They set off into the woods single file, Brody in the lead as they stayed to one side of the footprints, keeping them pristine. On a short, steep hill, she noticed a section of disturbed snow where Vic must have fallen, but the footprints continued through the trees, indicating he'd gotten upright again. He wasn't crawling, and she didn't see any sign of blood in the snow. She was tempted to rush but maintained a steady pace behind Brody.

They reached the cove and the scatter of boulders where Adrienne and her mother had sat with their feet in the water. Brody paused in the deep snow. Vic's footprints disappeared among the boulders and patches of mud and melting snow on the open lakeshore.

"Vic," Brody called. "Where are you?"

As if in response, a breeze blew through the trees, rattling bare limbs.

Heather stood on a small boulder, surveying the brush and trees on the edge of the cove. What a spot for a summer picnic, she thought. Had Sophia and Adrienne Portale walked out here on a whim? Had they stopped at Brody's cabin, or bypassed it and taken their break on the cove?

Who'd snapped their picture? Did it even matter?

Heather felt Brody touch her arm. He nodded to a cluster of boulders behind them. She saw a distinct footprint in the mud then another in the snow next to a knee-high boulder.

They heard a moan. "Help." Another moan. "Damn it."

Brody reacted instantly, leaping to the boulder. Heather jumped off her boulder and followed him past more boulders to a thick stand of oaks and hemlocks. They stopped at a chest-high boulder.

Vic lay sprawled on his back, motionless behind the boulder. Brody squatted next to him in the snow. "Vic," he said. "Talk to me."

"I hurt like hell."

"You've got a lump on your left temple. Were you unconscious?"

"No." Vic grimaced. "Unfortunately."

"Are you sure?" Heather asked.

He nodded and tried to sit up, but he yelped in pain, his face going gray. He was shivering, not wearing a hat or gloves, but he had on a warm jacket that would help delay the escalation of hypothermia.

"Anything broken?" Brody asked.

"My ego is in pieces."

"Vic."

He leaned away from Brody and vomited in the snow at the base of the boulder. He placed a hand on the gray rock, bracing himself, then sat up again. "That was unpleasant."

"No kidding," Brody said. He pointed at Vic's left hand, a bloody scrape extending from his wrist to his pinky finger. "You fell?"

"I tripped over a damn rock and landed here. I managed to protect my head, but I did get clipped. Most of the bruises and scrapes are on my left side. I wrenched my hip. Hurts like hell." He licked his lips, visibly chapped. "The pain turned my stomach."

"A rescue team is on the way," Heather said.

"A rescue team? I can walk out of here —"

"You're not walking out of here, Vic," Brody said, firm but not impatient. "I'm not carrying you, either. I could drop you and really break some bones."

"Ha. You'd like that, wouldn't you?"

"I have a first-aid kit," Heather said. "Do you want me to —"

"No. Thank you, Heather." He held up his left hand, looking at the scrape as if only now realizing it was there. He clutched Brody's upper arm and sat up straighter, groaning but not vomiting again. "I'm sorry for all the drama."

"You're the one who tore up the house?" Brody asked.

Vic nodded. "I stopped myself when I started throwing dishes. I put on a coat and left to get some air. I started walking. I intended to calm down and return to the house and get everything cleaned up before anyone arrived. Next thing I knew, I was here." He glanced around, squinting, obviously still in pain and somewhat disoriented. "Is it just you two? Or did Adrienne . . ." He didn't finish.

"She got back from Elly's right before I arrived," Heather said. "Then Brody and Greg arrived."

"Agent Rawlings." Vic grimaced. "I forgot about him."

"He's with Adrienne now," Brody said.

"I knew she went to Elly's, but I haven't seen her since last night." He licked his lips, visibly chapped. "I went up to my bedroom and drank an entire bottle of a very expensive wine she picked out for my cellar, and I got wild."

Brody's jaw was visibly tight. "Don't do this again, Vic."

He swallowed, shivering. "I couldn't stop thinking that my parents missed knowing Adrienne. Their only granddaughter. They're gone now, and they never had that chance . . ." He cleared his throat. "They were good people."

"I remember," Brody said. "Your father went fishing with my father a couple of times when you had them out here."

Vic muttered that he wanted to get moving, but Heather shook her head. "It's best to stay put until the rescue team gets here," she said.

He didn't argue. Brody stayed with him while Heather went back down to the shore, where she could get a decent signal and text Eric their exact location. The rescue team would already be en route based on Greg's instructions.

They hadn't wasted any time and arrived a few minutes later, with Heather's firefighter brothers, Chris and Justin, in the lead. She let them do their thing and sat on a knee-high boulder to take off her snowshoes. The snow was disturbed enough now by the comings and goings, and the road close enough, that she figured she'd manage in her boots.

Brody dropped back to her. He already had his snowshoes off. "Team's left with Vic."

She smiled up at him. "Good work, Agent Hancock."

"You, too."

"I imagine you've dealt with a few diplomats in trouble after a wild night."

"Oh, yes." He squinted out at the cove. "Not like this, though. Not on my home turf." He turned back to her. "At least we got to Ambassador Scarlatti before the damn fool froze to death."

But Heather knew how concerned Brody

was about his friend. She walked with him out to the road and on to the house, saying little. She wasn't surprised to find Adam and Brandon pacing on the front porch with Eric. As Brody had predicted, all of her brothers had responded when word reached them of the emergency on Echo Lake and her involvement. Greg Rawlings was chatting amiably with Eric. Heather assumed they were discussing the situation with Vic but then overheard Greg tell her eldest brother what a great guy Brody was, in addition to being a top-notch DSS agent.

Brody slung an arm over her shoulders. "With Greg here, your brothers are bound to warm up to me."

Brandon rolled his eyes but said nothing. Adam was grinning.

The rescue team returned with Vic, on his feet and arguing with Justin and Christopher, who were urging him to get checked out at the hospital.

Greg Rawlings cut through Vic's argument. "Into the ambulance, Ambassador. Now."

Vic acquiesced, letting the paramedics ease him onto a stretcher. He paused and looked out at the lake. "It all got to me. My life. What I've missed. What I've done. The mistakes." He smiled, tears shining in his eyes. "Look, though. There are signs of spring."

Greg frowned and turned to Christopher. "Make sure the doctors check his head. There are no signs of spring out here."

Christopher grinned but said nothing.

"I'm glad we don't have a missing ambassador on our hands," Eric said, then glanced at Brody. "Or a DSS agent who went off."

Brody shrugged. "I haven't smashed pumpkins in a long time."

Eric laughed and headed back to his car.

Once the ambulance was on its way, Greg clapped a thick arm over Heather's shoulder. "You're plucky as hell, Heather. No wonder Brody likes you."

TWENTY-TWO

Vic's entire body ached when he returned from the hospital and installed himself in his chair by the fire. He hadn't broken any bones or damaged any vital organs, and he didn't have a concussion. That was something, at least. He had multiple scrapes and bruises, and he'd strained his lower back, probably in his desperate sprawl to avoid slamming into the boulder. His left hip in particular was already ablaze with color. His left hand was in a bandage, but he'd dispense with that before bed.

"You're lucky," Christopher Sloan had told him.

A polite way to say he'd been a moron.

Never in his life had he lost it like he had last night and especially this morning, after he'd heard Adrienne and Rohan leave to help with Elly's goats. Once he'd started tearing up the place, he couldn't stop. He had a new understanding of blind rage. His was directed entirely at himself. He'd have stopped short of hurting anyone or setting the place on fire, and he doubted he'd have escalated if he hadn't been alone.

A rationalization, perhaps. Selfishness, thinking he'd only hurt himself.

Brody built a fire for him in the living room. Greg shook his head at Vic. "You ever throw a fit like that on the job?"

"Never."

The senior DSS agent grunted. "Good."

Vic cleared his throat. "You and Brody put your lives on the line for people like me. I'm not worthy of your sacrifice."

"Your worthiness isn't the point, Ambassador," Greg said, his eyes serious now.

"You're just doing your job. Yes, yes." Vic looked away from that steely gaze. "I want to be a better man. It isn't too late, is it?"

"Not in my book," Brody said, turning from the fire.

"Apologies," Vic said. "I didn't realize I'd spoken aloud."

Greg zipped up his jacket. "I'd have let you start by grabbing a broom and dustpan and cleaning up this place, but I figured you were too busted up to do much good. A couple of Sloan boys and I did the job for you while you were getting patched up." His expression softened. "What's done is done.

Move on."

Brody replaced the screen on the fire. "All you can do is your best."

Vic sat up, wincing in pain. "Spoken like two men who've busted up a bar or two." But his attempt at humor failed, and all he could do was sink back into his chair and shake his head. "I broke a beautiful vase I bought in Morocco."

"At least it wasn't the vase I gave you for your birthday when I was thirteen," Brody said. "Remember that, Vic? I made it myself in pottery class."

"A vase? Are you sure? It must be here somewhere . . ."

Brody grinned. "I never made you a vase, Vic. I did take a pottery class, though."

Greg was staring at his friend. "Pottery, Brody?"

"Yeah. I still have this little paper-clip holder I made. It's shaped like an ashtray. The teacher wouldn't let us make ashtrays. My mother signed me up for classes. She thought it would help me get in touch with my softer side."

"I need to get out of this town," Greg said, shaking his head.

He left through the front door. Brody started to follow him, but stopped on the entry threshold and looked back at Vic. "Get some rest. Call if you need anything."

"I noticed everyone knows about you and Heather."

"Are her brothers getting their tar and feathers?"

"I think they like you. Does that scare you?"

He grinned. "Only a little."

Vic thanked him and resisted the thousand self-deprecating comments that had congregated on the tip of his tongue. Brody didn't need to hear them, and Greg wouldn't stand for them. "That bastard will throw a brick through the window if he hears me whining," Vic muttered to himself as Brody headed out. But he could hear the anguish and regret in his voice, and he could feel the tears rising in his eyes.

He wasn't aware when Adrienne came into the room, Rohan tagging along behind her. "All you've seen in the world, Vic, and you're miserable because you cleared off a few shelves and broke a few dishes?"

"My father would have been horrified," he said. "My mother . . . not so much." But he could see she was struggling, too, with what he'd done. "Adrienne . . ."

"I'm sorry I've made you so unhappy." She sank onto the rug in front of the hearth. "If I could do it over again, I wouldn't tell you that you're my father. I'd just house-sit for you and get to know you. But when I tell myself that, it feels wrong."

"You're not a deceitful person."

"If you'd wanted a family, you'd have one."

"It's not that simple. Adrienne, I know I must not be the father you fantasized about —"

"You're better than I feared. My mother has had some unpleasant men in her life since her divorce. I had no reason to believe the men before her marriage were all that great, either. She's not easy herself."

Vic suspected Adrienne was trying to keep her tone relatively lighthearted, as if the events of recent days — particularly today — hadn't affected her as deeply as they so obviously had. As they would anyone, he thought, trying to ignore a sharp pain in his left hip.

"I should let you get some rest," Adrienne said.

"No, no. Stay. Please." He forced himself to smile through the pain. "I enjoy your company. I can't tell you how sorry I am that I upset you this morning."

"Don't be. I knew what had happened. Agent Rawlings called it a dark night of the soul. That's what it was, wasn't it?"

"You could say that."

"It was cathartic?"

Vic nodded, if not feeling slightly less like a fool, at least accepting that he'd been one. "If I have another dark night of the soul, I hope it's during summer. Lying in the snow, shivering." He shuddered. "Pure misery."

"There'd be red ants in summer. Ticks. Slugs. Mosquitoes."

"Well, aren't you a ray of sunshine?"

She laughed, and he laughed, too, although it hurt like hell. Rohan plopped down on the floor between him and Adrienne. She reached over and stroked his plump belly. "I checked my mother's photo albums last fall for any pictures that might lead me to you — to my biological father. I found that one picture of my mother and me on a lake. I asked her where it was, and she told me it was Echo Lake, on the outskirts of an out-of-the-way little town in Massachusetts called Knights Bridge. She said you had a house there. She and I were in Boston — she was at a conference and thought I should do the Freedom Trail — and then she decided to drive out here to say hi to you, her old friend from Paris. But you weren't here, and so we had a picnic by the lake and went back to Boston."

"Who took the picture?"

"It must have been Brody's father. He was out fishing. My mother never admitted that you and she had an affair, but I figured it out. I was so sure."

"And you were right," Vic said.

"It didn't mean that I knew you were my father. I only knew that when I found that picture of you as a young man. It was a mistake to manipulate you. I know that now, but I'm glad I got to know you."

"Me, too. None of this is your fault, Adrienne."

"You never had an affair with someone in Knights Bridge, did you, Vic?"

"Never. I don't kiss and tell but no, never. Categorically." He grinned. "Not that Knights Bridge lacks for tempting women, mind you. I wouldn't want to get into trouble for that. It's a tough place to keep a secret, anyway."

"Do you think you'll ever get married?"

"You *are* direct."

"Sorry. It's none of my business."

"Drugs and alcohol were never my problem. Stable relationships were. I deserve to be a lonely old man."

She scoffed at him. "With that attitude, that's what you'll be because you don't feel you deserve love — whether it's the love of friends or romantic love."

He smiled. "How did you get to be so wise?"

"Experience." She left it at that. "Don't just sit out here in your big house. There's so much you can do. Maybe you could help Noah Kendrick and Dylan McCaffrey with their entrepreneurial retreats. You could provide international perspective on business. You could lecture at one of the local colleges."

"I could help with Elly's goats. Maggie and Olivia's goat's milk products are taking off, and I could use a diversion. I can see my old bosses now, discovering I've gotten into goat's milk products. Elly also tells me her twin daughters have a theater venture going with the Hollywood fashion designer who used to live in town." Vic suddenly felt more his old, positive, can-do self, and yet different, too. More settled in his own skin. More at ease with himself. "Knights Bridge has a lot to offer for the next season of my life."

"And you have a lot to offer Knights Bridge."

"Thank you."

Adrienne snuggled up with Rohan and lay down in front of the fire. She seemed to have enjoyed offering him advice. She reminded him of his mother.

"Adrienne . . ." He hesitated, but he knew the time was right. "I would like to show you where your grandparents are buried in Schenectady. Where they raised me. They were good people." Vic smiled, picturing them. He felt warmer, the aches of the day more to do with his bruises and scrapes now than his emotional anguish. "You'd have liked them, Adrienne. They appreciated a good bottle of wine."

"I wish I'd known them. I know you wish that, too."

"Very much so."

"They must have been proud of you, Vic. An ambassador." Adrienne tucked her knees up. "You had lunch with my mother in New York." She rolled onto her side. "No sparks left, huh?"

"Adrienne . . ."

She grinned. "I thought that would break through your malaise. Or is it the pain pills? You *did* get pain pills?"

"I refused them."

"It's being around those two tough guys."

Vic sighed. "It's because I don't need them."

"If you say so."

He liked seeing the life back in her eyes. This was the Adrienne Portale who'd wowed the wine world and had shown up at his apartment in New York guessing — *knowing* — he was her father. Keeping that her secret as she sought information. Proof.

She put her hand out for Rohan to lick. "My mother is a force of nature, but she did what was best for her and believed that it was also best for me. I'm sorry for not being more open with you."

"You have nothing to apologize for."

"As you've told me before, Vic, at some point in life, you recognize and maybe even accept that your parents are only human, after all."

"Your mother isn't June Cleaver," Vic said half under his breath.

"Who's June Cleaver?" Adrienne laughed. "Kidding. She's the lady who vacuumed in a dress."

Vic struggled to his feet. He was stiff and sore, but he didn't collapse in agony. His dignity was in shreds, but that small victory helped. He got a log out of the wood box. "Knights Bridge is your home now as much as mine, Adrienne," he said, pulling back the fireplace screen. "I want you to know that."

"It's a great place." She sat up, her face flushed from the heat of the fire — and no doubt the emotions of the day, as well. "Does that mean I get to use the sauna?"

"Sauna, wine cellar, guest suite and any porch you want. It's going to be great." He watched as Rohan curled up in her lap. "He missed you."

"He missed *you,* Vic. I'm just giving him attention because he knows you're in pain. Like it or not, he's your dog. He's a Knights Bridge dog, though. He's not a New York dog."

"I didn't tell you? I'm giving up my New York apartment."

"Good for you. You're figuring out your life now that you're retired. I'm figuring out mine, too. I've been wandering, and I don't want to wander anymore. You've lived all over the world, but it was your job as a senior officer with the Foreign Service. Same with Brody and his work. His job is so intense."

"I really thought you two might hit it off."

"He is a stud, but I'm not ready for another relationship right now." She looked up at Vic. "There was never anything between you and Brody's mother, huh?"

"No. Never." He was so shocked at her question that he thought his heart skipped about twelve beats. "Good heavens, Adrienne."

She laughed, unrepentant. "What about Elly?"

"We're good friends. No question."

She pointed to his side table by his chair. "I notice you're reading up on goats."

"Goats and puppies. My goodness. My life has changed."

He placed the log on the fire and returned to his chair. He adjusted his position to ease the pain, but now he wished he hadn't been so sanctimonious about medication.

"You okay, Vic? Need some ice? Do you want me to call Brody —"

"I'm fine." He took a moment to let the surge of pain subside. "Now. Tell me about this wine-shop cad."

"I have no secrets left, do I?"

"None. You're in Knights Bridge now. You'll learn that it's damn tough to keep a secret here. His name is Thad, correct?"

"Yes," Adrienne said. "He was the wrong man at the wrong time in my life."

"Sometimes good can come out of that," Vic said softly.

His daughter smiled up at him. "Yes, it can." She gave him a conspiratorial look. "I enjoyed several excellent bottles of wine with him."

TWENTY-THREE

Greg was smoking a cigar in front of a roaring campfire he'd built after clearing a spot on the lakeshore below the guesthouse. "It's easier to do a campfire in summer, I'll give you that, but life doesn't get any better than this, Brody." He gazed out at the starlit lake. "I guess I could be here with a beautiful woman. That would be better."

Brody sat on a log Greg had unearthed somewhere. "No doubt."

"I've spent so much time in hot climates the past few years. I love this. It could be about seventy degrees warmer, though." He glanced at Brody. "It was fast and intense, but we did good work this past week. Mopping up. And today. Saving a retired ambassador from himself."

"Vic's getting his life in order."

Greg tossed his cigar into the snow. "Time I got mine straightened out."

"Ever a process with you," Brody said

with a smile.

But his friend was thoughtful, the ligl from the flames flickering on his face as h stared at the fire. "The job didn't destro my marriage. The job exposed what wa wrong with my marriage. It won't be tha way with you and Heather."

"You're jumping ahead of the facts, Greg."

"No, I'm not."

He spoke with the absolute certainty that was typical of him. Brody knew better than to argue. "What's next for you, then?"

"I'm going out to Minnesota to see the kids. Then I land in Washington for a few weeks to get ready for a new assignment. Probably won't be to a four-season resort." He picked up a stone and threw it into the snow on the lake. "When's this thing thaw?"

"Spring. Doesn't mean it's safe to ice-skate on it."

"I've never gone ice-skating. I never want to go ice-skating." Greg settled back on his log. "I'm glad it wasn't Vic on duty as ambassador two months ago. Don't let his mild manner fool you. He'd have had my head for screwing up."

"You did nothing wrong."

"Yeah, I did. I just didn't do a lot wrong. A lot wrong, and we'd both be dead."

That summed it up. "We can't know

everything ahead of time."

"These bastards didn't know the consulate we were securing was unoccupied. We got lucky when you think about it. We got them before they could stage another attack."

"The next would have been worse," Brody said.

"Yep. These were some major sons of bitches we stopped."

With the help of authorities in three separate countries, Brody thought. It had been a complicated mission, one, fortunately, with a good outcome.

He dug at a soft spot in the sand with the heel of his boot. "You're the best there is, Greg. Hands down."

"I learned I'm not a superhero a long time ago. You saved my ass that day, Brody."

"Damn right I did."

Greg grinned. "What about you? You taking the promotion to London? That's what this side trip to DC was about?"

"I'm still thinking about it."

"A year in London — maybe two years — and then you can see what else you're good for. Maybe me, too. I've had my finger on the self-destruct button for the last year at least. You're not going to be me, Brody."

"Hell, I hope not. I'd look terrible as a redhead."

"Damn straight. Good luck with plucky Heather. A lot she can do in London. Don't push her away because you don't think she'll be happy there. Don't underestimate her."

"Greg."

He paid no attention. "And, damn, Brody, don't corner her. She'll chew your leg off, and if she doesn't, her brothers will."

Brody sighed. "Take care of yourself. I'm going to need a best man."

"Preferably one who isn't six feet under. No worries there. I'm having my ashes scattered." The gallows humor evaporated. "I wouldn't miss your wedding, Brody, even if it's in this godforsaken speck of a town."

"When the time comes."

"It's already here. You and plucky Heather could do a destination wedding, you know. Nassau. Disney. Myrtle Beach. Laura and I got married in Jackson Hole. The marriage didn't last, but it was a hell of a wedding."

Vic was half-asleep in his chair when Brody entered the living room. He started to back out, but Vic stirred. "Where's Agent Rawlings?"

"Packing. He's leaving at first light."

"There's no saving his marriage, is there?"

Brody shook his head and sat on a chair

by the fire. He noticed Rohan was asleep at Vic's feet. He'd passed Adrienne in the kitchen, deep into researching Kendrick Winery, looking happier.

"I've never been in love," Vic said.

Brody almost shot to his feet. *Not* what he wanted to talk about. "I'll go now —"

"No, sit. Stay."

"You sound like you're talking to Rohan."

Vic gave a ragged grin. "Good. I need to learn. Heather's with her family. That's as it should be, with Greg here. She knows that."

"Vic . . ."

"I've done a great deal of thinking the past twenty-four hours. Too much thinking, perhaps." He picked up a wineglass, partially filled with a light red. "I've had passions, Brody, but I've never experienced the kind of love that is meant to last a lifetime. The kind of love you commit yourself to nurturing. The kind of love that seeps into your soul and becomes a part of who you are. I've dedicated myself to my work, but other people are just as dedicated and have that kind of love. You see it here in Knights Bridge. It's all around you."

"You *did* take the pain meds," Brody said.

"Bastard. I'm reflecting, contemplating the nature of romantic love." He waved a hand, wincing in obvious pain. "Don't worry. I won't break anything."

"There was never true love between you and Adrienne's mother?"

"That was passion. A flame that burned bright and then was gone. I knew from the start that Sophia and I weren't true love. There was never any doubt. That's not you and Heather. You're not fooling yourself about her, Brody."

He shook his head. "We're not talking about me, Vic."

"Oh, yes, but we are. We are, indeed."

Brody got to his feet. "I promised Greg I'd play a game of Risk with him before he heads out in the morning. He's never played Risk. Should be interesting. He hates the guest room there, by the way. He says it has squirrels."

"Red squirrels, probably," Vic said, matter-of-fact. He drank some of his wine, set the glass back on the table and stood, grimacing, going slightly gray. He rallied and straightened. "I'll be up early. Tell Agent Rawlings I'll take him to breakfast on his way out of town. You, too, Brody."

"You'll be up to it?"

"Absolutely." He grinned, the light catching a bruise near his left ear. "We can have a little bet as to how many Sloans we'll run into at the diner."

Brody made no comment. When he went back through the kitchen, Adrienne had shut her notebooks. "I'm going to walk Rohan," she said. "Vic won't be up to it for a bit. Thank you for everything today, Brody."

"No problem."

"It's not so bad being back in Knights Bridge, is it?"

He didn't want to have a deep conversation with her any more than he'd wanted one with Greg or with Vic. "Not so bad at all," he said, trying not to sound curt.

"It's home. It's just not necessarily where you belong." Adrienne smiled. "I'll see you tomorrow. Vic invited you and Greg to breakfast in town, didn't he?"

"We'll be here at six."

"I think Vic meant eight."

Brody pulled open the back door. "It's Greg Rawlings we're dealing with."

Adrienne laughed. "Six it is, then."

TWENTY-FOUR

Heather ran into Brody, Vic, Adrienne and Greg Rawlings on their way into Smith's as she was leaving with a breakfast sandwich. A night of tossing and turning had launched her out of bed earlier than usual, but just as well. She had work to do. She was meeting her father and brothers at the Sloan & Sons offices before heading up to Echo Lake. However tempting, lingering over pancakes and bacon with friends wasn't an option this morning.

Seeing Brody with Greg Rawlings had crystallized as nothing else could that Knights Bridge wasn't Brody's world.

Two hours later, she was back in Vic's cellar when Greg thumped down the stairs and joined her. "You're a woman who loves her work. You'd have to, given some of the places you crawl around."

"This isn't as bad as some. I thought you'd be off by now."

"So did I. I decided to burn off breakfast snowshoeing with Brody. He's a tyrant on snowshoes. It's that New England upbringing, but he says he never had snowshoes as a kid." Greg ducked under a low beam. "I want to see this place when it's finished."

"I'm sure Vic would love to have you back."

Greg grinned. "You're an optimist as well as plucky."

"You know *plucky* isn't my favorite word, right?"

"Cuts too close to the truth. Like when I'm called an unforgiving SOB."

Heather set her clipboard on the old workbench. "I don't imagine you're even remotely unforgiving."

"Maybe, but I never forget." His gaze turned serious. "I don't know if Vic or Brody told you, but my marriage recently ended. We both tried as hard as we could, but it didn't work out. We finally realized marriage shouldn't be that hard. You shouldn't wake up in the morning thinking I've got to fix this, this and this, and then for sure we'll be happy. It starts to feel like one of those New Year's resolutions you think you ought to want to happen but deep down, you don't."

"I understand. I'm sorry it's been a painful time for you both."

"Thanks. We do our best not to take it out on the kids." He grimaced, swiping at a cobweb to the right side of his head. "I don't usually go on like this, but I've had time on my hands the past couple months. All that thinking . . ." His grimace turned into an outright pained look. "It's good I'm going back to work full-time."

"Will you and Brody be assigned to the same place?"

He shook his head. "Not this time. Look, I'm not one to meddle, but — you know how I just said my wife and I tried hard? You and Brody don't have to try at all. You two are easy. You've got to figure out logistics — his work, your work, that sort of thing — but that's nothing compared to figuring out whether you're meant to be together."

"That's very sweet, Greg. Thank you."

He scratched the side of his mouth. "Sweet." Another grimace. "Even in the good days, my wife never thought I was sweet. Whatever. Adrienne says you're interested in interior design. Ever think about looking up design schools in London?"

"London? Why —"

"Idle question."

Nothing, Heather knew, was idle in Greg's world. "Is Brody heading to London next?"

"If he is, it would be a promotion." Greg gave a mock shudder. "I'm not big on small, closed-in spaces. Don't you get claustrophobic down here?"

"No, but wait until you see it after we're done. You won't even think about being underground. We're not converting it into a fully finished cellar, but it'll be clean, well lit, modern —"

"And it'll have a hundred bottles of good wine and a state-of-the-art sauna. Vic went on about them over breakfast. I think you should get lifetime rights to both for all you've put up with from him." Greg leaned toward her and kissed her on the cheek. "It's been a pleasure meeting you, Heather. Stay well." He stood straight. "You and Brody are easy. Keep that in mind, and don't make it hard."

Heather didn't know quite what to say. "I'll remember that. Safe travels, Greg."

He was halfway up the cellar stairs when she heard him repeat that she and Brody were easy together. She picked up her clipboard, not at all convinced that Greg Rawlings had sufficient perspective to recognize *easy* when he saw it. Given how difficult his life had been lately, anything short of bullets and divorce probably did seem easy.

When she reached the mudroom, she noticed Vic in the kitchen, dutifully trying to teach Rohan to sit. She didn't interrupt them.

She met Brody on the back steps with an armload of cordwood. "I hated hauling wood as a kid," he said.

"Do you like it now?"

"It feels normal." He paused and turned to her. "Suppose you put aside *The Scarlet Pimpernel* tonight and we go to dinner and a movie. Think you could do that?"

Heather smiled. "I think I could do that. I finished *The Scarlet Pimpernel.*"

"He got the girl, right?"

"In a way, he always had her."

She didn't breathe again until she was in her truck, starting the engine.

Easy.

Right.

She and Brody were easy as pie together.

The Sloan farmhouse kitchen was filled with the smells of roasting chicken and simmering mulled cider. Heather put two quarts of raspberries and a pint of heavy cream from a local dairy into the refrigerator and followed the sound of voices into the dining room. Her mother and paternal grandmother were discussing the next steps in a small quilt they were piecing on the table. In her late fifties, Cora Sloan had graying dark hair and lively blue eyes, with a spirit to match. She loved cooking, gardening, sewing, working at the Sloan & Sons offices and — most of all — spending time with her six grown children and two grandsons, all of whom lived within a few miles of the family homestead. She'd lost her own mother years ago and was close to her mother-in-law, Evelyn Sloan, an energetic, white-haired widow in her early eighties, well-known in Knights Bridge for the nursery school she'd run for decades.

Heather had never gone more than two weeks without seeing them.

Her mother looked up from a stack of bright fabric cut into small hexagons. "How was work?"

"Exciting. We're finally getting started clearing out Vic's attic and cellar."

"So I heard. That's a milestone.

"Where will Ambassador Scarlatti live during renovations?" her mother asked. "Not in the house, I hope. It's difficult to have someone underfoot with such a massive renovation."

"He'll be moving into the guesthouse once

we start tearing apart the house," Heather said. "He's decided to move to Knights Bridge full-time."

Her mother frowned. "When will Brody be leaving? I don't see him and Vic Scarlatti as roommates."

"I don't know how long Brody will be staying in town." Ignoring an incisive look from her grandmother, Heather instead pointed at the in-progress quilt. "That's a baby quilt, isn't it? Who's having a baby?"

"No one we know of," her grandmother said. "Yet."

Heather laughed. "We have had quite a number of new romances in town lately. Who knows, though, maybe Brandon and Maggie will have a third baby now that they're back together."

Her mother moved from her stack of hexagons and picked up a pair of scissors, inherited from her own mother, who'd died a few years ago. "The boys would like that." She lifted her gaze to Heather. "What about Brody Hancock? Do you know if he has a woman in his life?"

Heather fingered a twelve-inch square of solid yellow cotton. She enjoyed sewing, and was better at it than cooking. Normally, she would have offered to help with the quilt, but she knew she wouldn't, not tonight.

"Brody and I are actually going out tonight," she said, keeping her tone matter-of fact. "Dinner and a movie. I'm not sure where. It won't be in town, that much I know, since Knights Bridge doesn't have a theater."

"That sounds like a date," her grandmother said, her deep blue Sloan eyes as alert as ever.

"It does, doesn't it?" Heather didn't elaborate and decided to change the subject. "Overseeing Vic's renovations has convinced me that I really do want to pursue interior design. I'm looking seriously into my options."

Her grandmother perked up. "What a great idea. You've always had a good eye for color, Heather. I remember when you helped me pick out interior paint colors for my house last year. They're perfect."

"That's interior decorating, Gran. I love that, too, but I'm more drawn to interior design. It can involve interior decorating, but interior design focuses on the function and livability of the space itself."

"I see," her grandmother said. "Would an interior designer have made sure my kitchen wasn't too small for an island?"

Heather smiled. Gran's kitchen island had been bugging her since her son — Heather's father — had installed it three years ago, at her insistence. "That's one thing, yes."

"You'll have to go back to school," her mother said.

"I've been investigating schools on and off for a while. There are good schools all over the place." Heather took a breath, trying to appear casual despite how much her head was spinning with dreams and possibilities. "I'm even looking into London."

Her mother put down her scissors. "London? You've been talking to Samantha?"

Heather decided not to mention her conversation with Greg Rawlings that morning in Vic's cellar. His nonchalant certainty that she and Brody were meant for each other still had her rattled. Just because Greg was certain didn't mean he was right.

Her mother picked up her scissors again. She had the studied I'm-not-going-to-interfere look that Heather had seen multiple times — last fall when Samantha Bennett had burst into town, and before that when Brandon and Maggie had repaired their broken marriage. All six Sloan siblings had experienced their mother's self-control when it came to interfering in their romantic lives.

Cora Sloan smiled suddenly at her only daughter. "I've always wanted to see London," she said. "It's on Louise Frost's bucket list, too, although I hate that term. *Bucket list.* It makes me think about dying instead of living."

Evelyn tilted her head, eyeing Heather. "Why London?" she asked.

"Just a thought."

She shook her head. "It's more than a thought, Heather."

Heather shrugged. "Brody's DSS colleague mentioned London this morning. Greg Rawlings."

"I hear he was shot," her grandmother said, cutting in.

Heather ignored her mother's grimace. "That's right, Gran. I don't know any details, but Brody was with him."

"Are he and Brody being assigned to London now?" her mother asked.

"I know Greg isn't." Heather let it go at that and picked up a green calico square. "Didn't I have a baby dress in this fabric?"

Her mother smiled. "Toddler sundress. My mother made it for you. I keep everything."

Adam and Christopher came in through the front porch, two dogs trailing behind them. "Smells good in here," Chris said, kissing the two older women on the cheek. "What's with the quilt? You aren't having

416

another baby, are you, Mom?"

"Very funny," she said. "Dinner will be ready soon. We're eating in the kitchen."

Adam shrugged off his jacket. "Heather didn't cook, did she?"

"I brought dessert," she said. "It's great. You'll see. I can't stay."

"Why not?" Chris asked.

"She has a date with that handsome FBI agent who used to live in town," Gran said.

Heather zipped up her vest. "Brody's a Diplomatic Security Service agent, Gran."

"Same thing."

Eric made a face as he came into the dining room from the kitchen. "No, it isn't, Gran."

She scowled. "You'd argue with a fence post, Eric Sloan."

He shook his head. "I'm not arguing with you. I'm telling you."

Adam and Chris stood back, clearly enjoying the exchange. Their grandmother put her hands on her hips. "Is an FBI agent a federal agent?"

Eric sighed. "Yes, but that doesn't mean —"

"Is a Diplomatic Security agent a federal agent?"

"Gran."

"There," she said. "Same thing."

"They're not the same thing," Eric said, not backing down any more than she was.

Chris grinned at Heather. "You have the right idea getting out of here. Now these two will be arguing through dinner."

Eric, as the eldest, held a special place in their grandmother's heart, and she loved nothing better than to argue with him, regardless of who was right or wrong. He turned to Heather. "Gran's right, and you're going on a date with Brody?"

"It's just dinner and a movie." She was already on her way back through the kitchen. "I have to go. See you all later."

She passed Justin and Brandon in the driveway and saw their father coming up from the offices but managed to get into her truck without explaining her evening plans to them. As she came to the bottom of the driveway, she saw Samantha walking up from the Sloan family cabin on the pond across a sloping field. She had moved into the cabin in October to research New England pirates — and to be close to Justin.

When Heather arrived on Thistle Lane, she dashed inside and changed into a burgundy wool skirt, a charcoal-colored cashmere sweater she'd inherited from Maggie when her sister-in-law had decided it made her look "like a corpse" and boots.

She dug out earrings and her good watch. She put on makeup, although not a lot, and fluffed up her hair as she stood back from the bathroom mirror.

"Not bad, Heather Sloan," she said, smiling at her reflection.

She could have made a case for wearing jeans, but she didn't often have reason to dress up, especially in winter. And a date with Brody — why not put on a skirt?

She went out onto the porch as he drove up in his old BMW. He got out and came around the front of the car. She was aware of him watching her as she ran down the sanded steps, managing not to slip.

He opened the passenger door for her. She saw that he, too, had dressed for the occasion in a dark sport-coat, dark shirt and dark trousers. "A normal date," she said with a smile.

He returned her smile. "Feels good, doesn't it?"

He shut the door and in a moment slid in next to her in the warm car.

They made it to South Main Street before Christopher texted her, a group message to all six siblings.

A couple of quarts of raspberries and a pint of whipping cream aren't dessert.

Another text came almost simultaneously from Justin.

Dessert is pie.

Then Adam.

Cake.

And Brandon.

A DIY dessert, Heather?

She grinned and texted them back.

I washed the raspberries for you.

Brody glanced at her as he circled past the skating rink. "What's up?"

"My brothers are harassing me."

He smiled. "Nothing out of the ordinary, then."

She typed one last message to her siblings.

Going offline now.

But she didn't get her phone turned off before Eric texted her.

Don't do anything we wouldn't do, little sister.

She typed, I surely won't, and then switched off her phone as Brody took the winding road that led out of Knights Bridge to the main highway. "I'm taking a position in London," he said.

Heather nodded. "I heard. It's a promotion. Congratulations."

He kept his hands on the wheel and his gaze steady on the dark road. "Vic told you?"

She shook her head.

Brody sighed. "Greg."

"He thought I knew."

"No, he didn't. He meddled. No damn secrets in this town."

"He's not even from here."

"It's in the air. He breathed it in." Brody shook his head and laughed. "He's the best. You know that, right? He's impossible, but he's the best."

"There was never any question in my mind," Heather said.

"I'll be in DC for a few weeks of training and prep if I take the job. Greg will be in DC, too."

"You'll take it, Brody. You want to take it. I can tell by the tone of your voice."

He glanced at her, his eyes unreadable in the shadows. "You can, can you?"

"Am I wrong?"

"I'm not one of your brothers."

She smiled. "This is true. That doesn't mean I'm wrong, does it?"

"We'll see." He patted her knee. "No talk of work the rest of the night, okay? And no talk of your brothers, Vic Scarlatti, Greg Rawlings, wine . . ."

"Rohan?"

The spark in his eyes was visible even in the darkness. "We can always talk about your puppy rescue. Greg says you're plucky."

"Yes. He told me that, too."

"It's how he talks. You'll get used to it."

Heather warned herself not to read too much into Brody's words and the casual — even natural — assumption that she would be a part of his life after he left Knights Bridge. She sat back in her seat, looking out at the familiar landscape of her life on the edge of the Quabbin Reservoir. It had turned into a cold, clear evening. There was talk of more snow on the way. Would Brody leave before then?

She shook off the thought. Maybe what he needed tonight was a normal evening before he took the promotion to London and resumed his life as DSS Agent Hancock. He might be a federal agent all the time, but he was on home leave.

422

Maybe tonight he needed to think he wouldn't leave Knights Bridge, never to return.

Maybe that was what she needed, too. A normal evening with a man she was falling in love with and yet didn't really know. Fantasizing about London was fun, but this, she thought, was real.

"Greg says we're easy," she said.

"He's right. We are. It's everything else that's tough."

"Only if we look at it that way." But she settled again into her warm seat. "Now. On to important things. Do you think two quarts of washed fresh raspberries and a pint of cream qualify as dessert?"

Brody's soft laughter reassured her, and made her smile as they turned onto the main highway, a normal couple off on a normal date. At least for tonight.

TWENTY-FIVE

There was a line at the theater, and Brody suggested they skip the movie, never mind that he'd known the minute Heather had run up to his car that he wouldn't be able to sit through a movie. She hadn't hesitated, and they ended up back on Thistle Lane. They started out in the front room with glasses of wine and talk of interior design and his prep for London, picking up on the threads of their dinner conversation, but three or four sips and that was that. He had Heather in his arms and up the stairs to her bedroom.

He flung her discarded work clothes off the bed, and then he proceeded to get her out of her night-on-the-town outfit. It wasn't as much fun as removing her crazy Glinda dress, but the end result was just as good.

Better, even, he thought later, as he lay awake, unusually pensive, his arm around

Heather as she slept next to him. Mixed with the passion and urgency — the intoxicating taste and feel of her — was a surge of emotion he couldn't describe and didn't want to go near.

"Let me ask you this," Greg had said as he'd left Knights Bridge earlier that day. "What are you going to know six months from now that you don't know today?"

In the milky moonlight, Brody noticed Heather's dark lashes against her winter-pale skin. She opened her eyes, as if she'd known, even in her sleep, that he was awake, watching her. Her smile caught him off guard. Then her hand, sliding down his middle.

"I can't sleep, either," she whispered.

"You were just asleep."

"I was pretending."

"Getting your second wind?"

"More like my third or fourth wind," she said, easing on top of him, her hair hanging loosely in front of her as she looked down at him.

He wrapped his arms around her, lifted her and then drew her down onto him, thrusting deep into her. She was ready, more than ready. "I believe you about not being asleep," he said, the last words either of them uttered for a very long time.

■ ■ ■ ■

In the morning, Brody saw Heather off to breakfast at Smith's. He didn't join her. She needed time with her family and friends, and he needed solitude.

She seemed to understand.

He drove out to Echo Lake and found Vic outside with Rohan. "No leash," Vic said. "He'd pull on it, and I'd scream in pain. We don't want that."

Brody smiled. "No, we don't."

"It's back to winter this morning, isn't it? I'm glad it wasn't this cold when I had my little brush with hypothermia. Adrienne's sleeping in." He glanced back at the house. "We were up late drinking wine and telling stories. She wants to meet my cousins in Schenectady and their kids."

"That's good, Vic. I'm glad to hear it."

His old friend's eyes narrowed. "You didn't just come from breakfast in town, did you, Brody? You've been out all night?"

Rohan nudged Vic's leg, giving Brody his opening to change the subject. "I'm going to take a walk out to my land."

"You don't want company," Vic said, making it a statement. He bent down and patted Rohan. "You're a man of action, Agent

Hancock. That means you're at your best when you know your own mind and trust your instincts. It also means that sometimes you need to check those same instincts and pause to take a good, hard look at what's going on in your mind."

Brody tried to come up with a response but gave up. "I have no idea what you just said."

"Which makes my point."

"Right. I'll make coffee at the guesthouse and see you later."

Vic nodded. "Enjoy your walk."

"You're not looking as beat-up and haunted. That's good, but give a yell or text or call if you need me."

"And I'll be by the fire if you need me."

Brody didn't bother with coffee. He put on a hat and gloves along with his coat and walked out to his property — the place where he'd grown up. He stepped onto the ice at the edge of the lake. The snow was packed down now, with no new storms and the recent rise in daytime temperatures. No light, fluffy snow for the swirling wind to catch and blow around in the clear morning air. That would change. It was still February. A lot of winter left in Knights Bridge.

The truth was, he'd had a great childhood out here. He had become accustomed to telling himself it was Knights Bridge that had gotten to him, driven him to trouble-making, but it wasn't that simple. Nor was it his parents, easygoing, unambitious, not sure what to do with an action-oriented son who didn't want a life fishing and basking in the sun. They'd never tried to stop him from doing anything he wanted to do.

He and he alone had launched those troublemaking days. He'd been restless and uncertain about who he was and what his future held, and he'd taken it out on the people around him.

He could feel that same restlessness and uncertainty now.

He edged farther out onto the lake. If the ice gave way, he'd get wet, but the water wasn't deep here. He'd done this so often as a boy — pushing his luck, daring himself to see how far he could go. Several times, the ice had cracked under him, but he'd always gotten back to shore in time. And he'd never ventured too far out onto the lake, to where he'd have been in real danger if he'd gone through the ice.

In those days, it would have been Randy Frost who'd have had to rescue him, at least, and not any of the Sloan brothers.

The truth was, there would have been no one to rescue him, because there would have been no one to call for help. He'd never done this maneuver with his parents present. As lackadaisical as they could be, they would have told him to get the hell off the ice if there was any chance it wasn't frozen solid.

He smiled to himself, remembering. He'd been a natural at risk assessment and mitigation even then, and he'd had solid instincts based on knowledge and experience.

Of course, he hadn't known that. He'd thought he was a pain in the ass.

"And you were, Agent Hancock," he said to himself. "Damn, you sure were."

He scooped up a handful of snow, formed it into a ball and tossed it as far as he could out across the lake.

He didn't wait to see where his snowball landed. He turned around and walked back to shore. He was still restless, but he was no longer uncertain.

It wasn't uncertainty about how he felt that had brought him out here. He was in love with Heather Sloan. It was uncertainty about what to do about being in love with her.

Now he knew.

When he got back to the road, he had a text from Greg.

Minnesota is even colder than KB but the kids are happy here. See you in DC?

Brody didn't hesitate.

Yes.

Your hometown girl?

I'll let you know.

I already know but I'll let you find out on your own.

Typical Greg.

Brody went to the guesthouse, made coffee, showered, shaved and got dressed.

He had time. Some, at least. A few more date nights. Help Vic move into the guesthouse. Talk Heather into trying on the Cleopatra dress.

Make sure in his own mind that she was as certain as he was.

Brody smiled.

Sounded like a plan to him.

Ten days later, Brody got in his old BMW and drove into Knights Bridge, past the common and out to the Sloan farmhouse and the offices of Sloan & Sons.

Jack Sloan was alone in the office. "I'd like to speak with you, if you have a minute," Brody said.

"Yeah. Walk with me."

The father of six put on his jacket and led Brody outside, past bare shade trees and sleeping dogs, down the driveway and onto the back road.

"I walk three miles minimum every day," Jack said. "Only thing that stops me is freezing rain. I don't need one of my own kids pulling my ass out of a snowbank." He paused, looked at Brody. "That includes Heather."

"Are we walking three miles?"

The older man grinned. "No. Just making conversation. What do they call it? Small talk? I'm guessing you're not good at small talk, Brody."

"Probably right about that."

"You look like you want to call me *sir*. Don't. What's on your mind?"

"I'm in love with your daughter."

"Well, well. I've been getting reports to that effect. Are you asking my blessing?"

"Yes. I love Heather, and I want to marry her."

"You don't beat around the bush, do you? Isn't this all a little fast?"

"Yes, but it's right." Brody slowed his

pace. "I'll do whatever it takes."

"So will she. That's the word, anyway. She doesn't talk to me about anything but hammers and nails."

"Jack . . . sir . . . do I have your blessing?"

"This is old-fashioned as hell. Kind of fun, isn't it?"

"Not the word I'd use."

Jack laughed. "I bet the hell it's not."

"Does this mean I have your blessing to marry your daughter?"

"You do, Brody. You do." Jack shoved his hands into his pockets and looked at the view of the rolling uplands and Quabbin in the distance. "If you ask her and she says yes, her mother and I would be proud to welcome you to our family."

"Thank you."

They resumed walking along the quiet road. Jack grunted. "I'm glad you came back here as a DSS agent instead of an excon. What about your job? London's next, isn't it?"

"That's right, yes. I have several weeks of meetings and training in Washington first."

"Heather can go with you to London?"

Brody didn't hesitate. "If she wants to, yes."

"She wants to. She's already checking into interior design programs. Samantha knows

London. She has family there. My wife's always wanted to see England. Adam keeps talking about seeing the old stonework there. My mother is fascinated by the Tower of London. I'm trying not to take that personally." Jack grinned suddenly and clapped Brody on one shoulder. "We'll all come visit, Agent Hancock. You'll like that."

When Brody returned to Echo Lake, a large Dumpster had been delivered, and a crew was gathering to clean out Vic's attic. They'd finished cleaning out the cellar and the rest of the house as work on the renovations got underway. Heather's uncle, Pete, pointed vaguely to the lake. "Heather's taking a break while we get organized." He winked. "Good luck."

Either he had that look, Brody thought, or Heather's father had already been in touch with his brother. Maybe both.

He found Heather sitting on a log at the remains of Greg's campfire. She wasn't wearing a hat or gloves, and her vest and sweatshirt were both unzipped, as if it were a balmy spring afternoon instead of still February.

"The days are getting longer," she said. "Have you noticed the sun's higher in the sky? Spring's on the way."

Brody's throat tightened. Yet he was sure of himself. As sure as he'd ever been.

"Brody . . ." She stood, tilting her head back, her blue eyes narrowed. "Is everything all right?"

"I love you, Heather. I want to be with you forever. I want to grow old with you out here on Echo Lake." He stepped back, taking her hands into his. He'd been envisioning this moment for weeks, and now it was here. He smiled. "Heather Sloan, will you marry me?"

"Marry . . ." She laughed and leaped into his arms, throwing hers over his shoulders. "Yes, yes, yes. I love you. You know I do. Brody . . ." Tears formed in her eyes, even as she laughed. "Yes, I'll marry you."

He kissed her, lifting her off her feet.

"I would marry you today," she said. "Right now. We could elope."

"The only Sloan daughter and only Sloan sister?" Brody grinned. "I'd be hunted down by your posse of brothers."

"Probably. We are a can-do family."

"An understatement."

She slid out of his arms and stood in the spot Greg had cleared, muddy now with the warmish morning. "I've never been happier, Brody." Her eyes shone as she smiled.

"We're good together. We'll stay good together."

They heard someone yelling up toward the main house. "Sounds like Rohan trouble," Brody said. He nodded to Heather. "Shall we see what he's up to this time?"

Before they reached the house, the golden retriever galloped down the walkway, but he didn't jump on them. He was learning, Brody thought. He and Heather returned the puppy to his bed — and, now, crate — in the mudroom. Vic was there and explained that Rohan had stolen one of the crew's doughnuts and made off with it down to the lake. But no harm done. Knights Bridge was a town that loved its dogs.

Brody noticed Vic's color and mood were better since he'd torn up his house. "What have you two been up to," he asked, returning to the kitchen, "or don't I want to know?"

Heather beamed a smile at him. "Brody asked me to marry him, and I said yes."

"Well, congratulations to you both," Vic said, looking genuinely pleased. "As you might expect, this won't come as a surprise to anyone in Knights Bridge. I was at Smith's for breakfast this morning after you left, Heather, and they have a pool going on when Brody would pop the question."

Adrienne burst in from the dining room. "I win the pool! I *knew* it. You two — you probably started falling in love back when you were kids and didn't know it until now." She clapped her hands together, laughing as Rohan sat on Vic's feet. "Maybe Rohan can be your ring bearer."

Vic kissed Heather on the cheek. "You couldn't have fallen for a better man."

She glanced at Brody. "I agree."

"And, Brody . . ." Vic shook Brody's hand. "Knights Bridge's own Heather Sloan."

"Thanks for inviting me back here, Vic," Brody said. "I'd have let more time slip by if you hadn't."

"Turns out I was turning those molehills into mountains for a good reason, after all." Vic waved a hand. "That's my story, and I'm sticking to it."

Adrienne walked over to the counter and a line of wine bottles. She no longer looked embarrassed or uncomfortable. "I'm organizing a wine-tasting party tonight to celebrate the arrival of men with crowbars." She smiled. "Now we can celebrate your engagement, too. I've got a couple of bottles of a Kendrick sparkling wine chilling in the fridge. Heather . . . you won't be carting the fridge out of here yet, will you?"

"Not for a few days," she said.

Adrienne looked relieved, and pleased. "Excellent. Your entire crew is invited, and all your brothers and their girlfriends, and your nephews. Pass the word. There will be plenty." She glanced at Vic then turned back to Heather and Brody. "I've already invited Elly O'Dunn."

"She's bringing goat's milk?" Vic asked.

"Goat's milk cheese."

"I hear Noah and Phoebe are back in town," Heather said, studying her friend, who looked ready to burst. "Adrienne? Come on. Tell us your good news."

"I'm definitely going to be working for Kendrick Winery."

"That's great," Heather said. "Congratulations."

Adrienne gave Vic a tentative look, but he winked at her. "Bring on the bubbles."

"More to celebrate," Brody said.

He heard more vehicles arrive out on the driveway. Heather peeked out the window. "They're all here," she said.

"Who?" Vic asked.

"My brothers."

Brody put his arm around her. "Word's out. Let's go make it official."

"Not afraid?" she asked, mischief in her

Sloan blue eyes.

He grinned. "Not even a little."

TWENTY-SIX

Heather couldn't take her eyes off Brody that evening at Adrienne's wine tasting. She didn't care who saw her staring at him. Vic was in his element, making small talk, explaining details about his 1912 lake house and his plans for his new life. "Still in the works," he said, "but that's life, isn't it?"

Brody and Justin started a campfire, and next thing there was hot chocolate.

A couple of snowballs were lobbed from dark hemlocks. Heather suspected the work of Maggie and Phoebe, the two eldest O'Dunn sisters. She could tell Noah did, too. It surprised her how fast he moved, but then she remembered he was a master fencer as well as a high-tech genius.

Adrienne looked delighted as her classy wine tasting turned into an epic snowball fight on the shore of Echo Lake.

Heather made about a dozen snowballs and stacked them next to her on her log.

"My self-defense arsenal," she said as Brody sat next to her. "Christopher is the worst. You watch him. His aim is never off, and he almost never gets hit." But Brody, she saw, was watching her. "You're not paying attention to our snowball fight, are you?"

"I am. I see your nephews plotting against us. Mostly, though, I see us a few years from now, having hot chocolate under the stars with our kids and their five uncles, who would do anything for them." He slipped his arm around her. "As they would for their one and only sister and the woman I love."

"Brody . . ." She smiled at him. "I can also see us making love in the moonlight on a hot summer night."

"That, too."

Out of the corner of her eye, she saw Aidan and Tyler make their move, sneaking up behind her and Brody. She knew Brody saw them, too, but he pretended not to. They pelted him with snowballs, squealing in delight when he sprang on them, scooped them up and dumped them into a pile of snow.

"Aunt Heather, Aunt Heather, help us!"

She let them at her arsenal, and they got Brody again with her snowballs. Then they saw their father, a more tempting target. Heather gave them the rest of her snowballs, and they took off, giggling.

Brody sat next to her. "I should dump you in the snow."

She laughed, then laid her head against his shoulder. "This is a perfect spot, isn't it?"

"Heather . . ." He put his arm around her, and she felt him kiss the top of her head. "If you get homesick in London, just click your heels together three times. I'll get you back to Knights Bridge."

"I won't need ruby slippers or a magic wand?"

"No." He leaned in close to her. "But the Glinda dress might help."

AUTHOR NOTE

Now that you've read *Echo Lake,* it probably doesn't come as a surprise that I have a big family. Three sisters and three brothers. I'm the third eldest and second sister. Seven of us in nine years. We grew up on the western edge of the Quabbin Reservoir and its protected watershed . . . but that's more or less where my similarity to the Sloans ends! Although I do know the difference between pliers and a wrench.

If you're new to my Swift River Valley novels, *Echo Lake* is the fourth in the series. You'll find Olivia and Dylan's story in *Secrets of the Lost Summer* (1), Phoebe and Noah's story — and Brandon and Maggie's recommitment to each other — in *That Night on Thistle Lane* (2), and Justin and Samantha's story in *Cider Brook* (3). There's also *Christmas at Carriage Hill,* my first-ever Christmas e-novella, with Olivia and Dylan's Christmas Eve wedding as the back-drop.

I love writing these books. My mother grew up in the Florida Panhandle (Calhoun County) and my father was Dutch, but right before I was born, they packed up the car with my older brother and sister and all their belongings and moved to western Massachusetts. My mother still lives on our family homestead.

As I type this note to you, I'm working on my next Swift River Valley novel. For all the details, please pop over to my website and sign up for my e-newsletter. You can also write to me. I love hearing from readers!

Thank you, and happy reading,
Carla
www.CarlaNeggers.com

ABOUT THE AUTHOR

Carla Neggers is the *New York Times* bestselling author of more than 60 novels, novellas, and short stories. Her work has been translated into 24 languages and sold in more than 30 countries. She is a popular speaker around the country as well as a founding member of the New England Chapter of RWA, past president of Novelists, Inc., and past president of International Thriller Writers. She lives with her family in New England.

The employees of Thorndike Press hope you have enjoyed this Large Print book. All our Thorndike, Wheeler, and Kennebec Large Print titles are designed for easy reading, and all our books are made to last. Other Thorndike Press Large Print books are available at your library, through selected bookstores, or directly from us.

For information about titles, please call:
  (800) 223-1244

or visit our Web site at:
  http://gale.cengage.com/thorndike

To share your comments, please write:
  Publisher
  Thorndike Press
  10 Water St., Suite 310
  Waterville, ME 04901